ALL
THE DEAD
FATHERS

ALL
T̲H̲E̲ DEAD
FATHERS

David J. Walker

ST. MARTIN'S MINOTAUR ⚑ NEW YORK

www.minotaurbooks.com

Library of Congress Cataloging-in-Publication Data

Walker, David J., 1939–
    All the dead fathers / David J. Walker.—1st St. Martin's Minotaur ed.
      p. cm.
    ISBN 0-312-33454-0
    EAN 978-0312-33454-3
    1. Catholics—Crimes against—Fiction. 2. Clergy—Crimes against—Fiction. 3. Serial murders—Fiction. 4. Chicago (Ill.)—Fiction. 5. Child abuse—Fiction. 6. Revenge—Fiction. I. Title.

PS3573.A4253313A79 2005
813'.54—dc22

                                  2004051410

First Edition: April 2005

10 9 8 7 6 5 4 3 2 1

To Ellen, who loves radish sandwiches

ACKNOWLEDGMENTS

This is a work of fiction and the persons, places, and organizations appearing herein are either imaginary or depicted fictitiously. On the other hand, without the happening of certain real-life incidents, this imaginary and fictional world could hardly have been conceived.

And without the help of certain real-life people, the conception could hardly have become viable. These real-lifers include: Jay Daskal, M.D., for help with some medical issues; David Case, a police sergeant and a writer, for help with some firearms issues; Kelley Ragland, my editor, for pointing out so many things I hadn't noticed; and Danielle Egan-Miller, my agent, for providing both opportunity and direction.

Chi-ca-go *(shi-kaw-go)* n., a city in northeast Illinois, on the shore of Lake Michigan; the name is said to be derived from the Native American *chicah goo,* literally "stink root," or, perhaps more elegantly, "wild onion."

ALL
THE DEAD
FATHERS

1.

Debra Moore drove in behind the man and went on past him when he parked near the building where the restrooms were. Two-thirty in the morning, and no one else around. No one. God had given her this opening. It was time to get started.

She had followed him in here before, several times, and had studied the layout. There was a slight rise back toward where people walked their dogs, and once over that, on the downward slope, you couldn't be seen from the parking area. She pulled into the very last space and walked all the way back to the building—at least fifty yards—and waited.

Plenty of light here, and nothing about her would cause anyone concern. Besides, with men like this one, their special needs so often overrode their sense of caution. Not to mention that he'd been drinking.

She watched him come out the door. "Hi there, big fella," she said.

"What?" He was actually a rather small man, sixty-something, old enough to be her father . . . and depraved enough, she knew.

"I said, 'Hi.'" She smiled. "I . . . uh . . . I saw you back there."

That shook him. "I don't know what you're talking about." A man burdened with less guilt would simply have walked on by. "Back where?"

"At that store," she said. "Looking at the books and tapes and DVDs. It's nothing to be ashamed of. Still . . . I know what you were *really* wishing you'd find. I could tell, because that's my business."

"What, backseat blow jobs? Forget it." He turned toward his car.

"Wait." She touched the pervert's back, just lightly, and he turned around. "I'm not a hooker," she said. "I sell things. Helpful things."

"I gotta go."

"But I have what you want. What you *need*. Books, videos." She had his attention. "I handle the stuff you don't dare go near on the Internet." The hook was in now, she could tell. "They're in my van." She pointed. "Take a look, at least. Can't hurt."

She walked and he came with her. He seemed nervous, and she spoke soothingly about how she understood his needs. But then, way back, a car pulled in off the highway and the headlights shone on them from behind.

"I don't know," he said. "I better go." They both turned and watched the car pull into a space the other side of his.

"Just someone here for the washrooms," she said, stepping between him and the way back to his car. "It's all right, c'mon."

"No, I really have to go home." He was *whining* now. "I gotta—"

"Shut up!" She slid the gun from under her coat. A nine-millimeter SIG Sauer, silencer attached. Enough to frighten far more of a man than this maggot. "If you move, or say one word, I'll kill you."

His eyes bulged and his mouth fell open, and if he hadn't just emptied his bladder she knew he'd have peed down his leg.

"Turn around," she said, and he did. "Now . . . walk." They started walking and she heard car doors open and close behind them. She glanced back and saw two people, a man and a woman, heading toward the restrooms. She prodded the pervert with the gun and he walked faster. They were almost to her van when she looked back again, and saw the couple disappear into the building.

This wasn't the way she had planned it. The stripping and the slicing were to come first. But one must be both strong *and* flexible. "Stop walking," she said. "Stand very still and I won't hurt you. I promise."

He stood there, trembling, but otherwise as still as Lot's wife. Debra held the gun with both hands, the elongated barrel aimed midway between his shoulder blades. She crouched slightly and angled it up, almost touching the nape of his neck. "Please," he said. "I don't want—"

"I promise," she repeated, and carefully squeezed the trigger.

2.

The mutilated body of a man was found shortly after five A.M. by Mort, a Doberman pinscher who'd been dragging Alvina Martin by a leash along the edge of the southbound rest stop on I-90, just south of the Wisconsin border.

Dugan was in the kitchen eating breakfast and saw the news report.

"My husband used to say that the dog walks *me*," Alvina told the woman who stuck the mike in her face. "Anyway, like I told the troopers, all the sudden Mort goes into a crouch and starts one of them low growls, like it's somethin' up ahead there and he don't like it? And so I shorten up on the leash," she went on, "and go and look down into this here ditch, like a culvert? And when I seen it I said to myself, 'Oh, my God,' and ran back and hopped Mort in the truck and called it in. And after that I . . . you know . . . I threw up all over—"

"Authorities have identified the victim as one Thomas Kanowski," the TV reporter said, "but are releasing no further information. Meanwhile, police say this rest stop will be closed to traffic for several more hours while officers comb the scene of this horrific crime." The reporter gave the camera what Dugan figured was her best version of grim-and-solemn, and turned it "back to your local station."

Jim and Carol in the studio in Chicago did their own imitation of grim-and-solemn, and then Carol promised, "Up next, startling new claims from Viagra users." She gave a sly wink and they broke for commercials.

Dugan went back to his oatmeal and just then Kirsten stepped into the kitchen. She took the remote from the table and hit the mute button.

"Not interested in startling new claims?" he asked.

"No, but *you* might—" She shook her head. "Forget it. What was that business about a murder . . . on I 90?" She poured herself a mug of coffee and set it on the table.

"I might what?"

"That murder," she said, dropping half an English muffin in the toaster. "I didn't get the victim's name."

"Thomas Kanowski. I might—"

"Kanowski?" She seemed stunned. "Are you sure?"

"That's what they *said*. Thomas Kanowski. So what did you mean when you said I *might* something?"

"I know that name," she said. "I mean, it's possibly not the same—"

"Jesus, I might *what*, dammit?"

She popped the muffin prematurely out of the toaster and sat down across from him. "You might . . . I don't know . . . might listen to what I'm saying and not fixate on something I *didn't* say."

"But you started to say I *might* something . . . about Viagra. I mean have you noticed any—"

"Don't be silly. I don't remember *what* I started to say. God, is it just you macho lawyers? Or are all men so sensi—"

The phone rang and Dugan grabbed it. "Hello?"

"Hey, Doogie pal, how they hangin'?" The day wasn't starting well.

"Christ, Larry, it's only eight o'clock." Larry Candle, one of the three lawyers who worked for Dugan, was a pain in the ass sometimes—in fact, *always*—but he could work his round little butt off when he wanted to. The caller ID showed he was already in the office. "What's so important?"

"Nothing. I'm calling for— Hey, hold on." There was a pause and then Larry said, "I got the TV on here, and there's this doctor on, talking about Viagra. He says a lotta guys who use it discover they—"

"Yeah, that's interesting, Larry," Dugan said. "But I hope to God you didn't call me about some bullshit you saw on TV."

"Actually, it *is* about something on TV, but I'm calling for Kirsten. 'Cause I think this guy they found—"

"It's for *you*," Dugan said. He handed the phone to Kirsten and went to take a shower.

Half an hour later, Dugan and Kirsten were in a cab on their way downtown. It was a bright, warm September Monday and Dugan would have been happy to go anywhere other than his office. But he was the boss, after all, so he *had* to show up.

He'd given Kirsten the business section of the *Tribune*, but she just held it on her lap and stared out the window. Finally he couldn't out-silence her. "So . . . you gonna tell me what he wanted?" he asked.

"What?" She seemed startled to find another person in the same cab with her. "Oh, you mean Larry?"

"No, I mean Moe."

"He wanted to know if I'd heard the news about the body on the interstate, wondered if I recognized the name."

"And you did, right?"

6

"Yes, and Larry's wondering if it's the same Thomas Kanowski I know. I mean, not *know*. Just know *of*."

"Really? Who is he? Or was he?"

"There was an article in the *Sun-Times* a couple of months ago. I'm sure I showed it to you, or told you about it. It had a list of names of Chicago priests—some of them ex-priests, I guess—who had sexual misconduct charges against them."

"It was abuse, wasn't it? Not just charges. And involving children?"

"What the hell, Dugan? You're the lawyer here. The article said there was 'reasonable cause to believe' the charges were true. Not that all of them were *proven*, like in court or something. And minors, not necessarily children."

"Minors *are* children. Anyway, I didn't actually read the article. You told me about it, and you felt bad because your uncle Michael's name was there, and— Damn! Was one of the names on the list Thomas Kanowski?"

"Yeah." She shook her head. "I suppose even if it *is* the same man, there doesn't have to be a connection. I mean, the fact that someone killed him doesn't—"

"They said the body was . . . what? . . . 'mutilated' or something. But no, it didn't *have* to be because he's a pedophile."

"You don't know that he *was* a pedophile."

"Yeah, right. Just allegations, which there was 'reasonable cause to believe,' you said. The cardinal removed them all from their positions, didn't he?"

"But Kanowski wasn't necessarily a pedophile. He could have had sex with a minor, say a seventeen-year-old, not necessarily a young child."

"You mean like your uncle," he said. "Anyway, the man's dead. Or *someone* named Thomas Kanowski is dead. And *maybe* it's the same guy."

"If you were one of the priests on that list, wouldn't *you* be wondering? And maybe scared?"

"If I were on that list I'd have blown my brains out long ago. I wouldn't wanna live inside the skin of someone like—"

"Hey!" It was the cab driver, and the cab wasn't moving.

"Oh," Dugan said. "Here's my office. You going to yours?" When Kirsten nodded he gave the driver her address. "This nice lady will pay you," he said.

As he rode the elevator up to his office, it hit Dugan that Kirsten's being actually worried about her uncle Michael pissed him off a little. Jesus. Father Michael Nolan. Dugan hadn't spoken ten words to the guy since he represented him two years ago—but he wasn't about to waste any sympathy on him.

And why the hell Kirsten still cared at all about Michael Nolan he couldn't understand. She said she continued to get together with him from time to time, not because she still felt close to him but because she owed him that much. That made no sense to Dugan. The guy had obviously shredded any familial obligation she owed him. But she seemed to care more than she admitted, maybe more than she *knew*. And now?

Dugan didn't even want to think about where that might lead her now.

3.

Kirsten left the cab at Wabash and Washington and went up to her office on the tenth floor. The painted letters on the plate glass door said:

WILD ONION, LTD.
CONFIDENTIAL INQUIRIES
PERSONAL SECURITY SERVICES

She paused a moment, key in hand, feeling that odd, familiar mix of surprise and satisfaction those words always stirred up. She unlocked the door and went inside. She'd review her messages, check the calendar, return calls. Take care of her business.

It had never been part of her plan to run her own business. Her dad had been a Chicago cop until shortly before he died and, even though it wasn't happy for him at the end, that was all she'd ever wanted to be. After college she signed up for the police candidate's exam and started law school to kill the time while she waited. She scored high on the exam, endured the MMPI and the so-called POWER test, and the rest of the psychological and physical screening. Then one Friday she got a call to report to the Police Academy Monday if she wanted in on the next class. She and law school had never been compatible and she never set one foot back in the place after that. She didn't even attend Dugan's law school graduation. Which didn't bother him, since he didn't go, either.

She crouched to pick up the mail that had been shoved through the slot near the bottom of the door on Saturday, and took it with her through the tiny reception area, done in pastels and art deco, and into her office. Equally pastel and deco. The decor, which was not really Kirsten's style, was by Andrea Brumstein, a designer whose husband was a very successful diamond merchant. She had been Kirsten's first client.

Before meeting Andrea, Kirsten had been on the fast track in the police department. She became an investigator in the Violent Crimes Division, and was high on the list to make sergeant. Exactly where she wanted to be. Except as time went by she started to feel the job—the one she thought she loved—physically squeezing the heart out of her body. That's the only way she could describe it. So she quit.

By then her job skills were pretty limited. She joined a private security firm that bored her to death, then quit that and started Wild Onion, Ltd. That's when Andrea came along. Her case had to do, of course, with diamonds, among other things; and it had to be kept secret, of course, from Andrea's husband, among other people. Andrea was more than pleased with the result. She got Kirsten a great deal on this office, which had been carved out of her husband's retail showroom. She also paid twice the fee Kirsten asked for. "The secret, darling," Andrea confided, "is to imagine a really outrageous fee, then double it. You'll get *such* a better class of clientele."

As hard as she tried, Kirsten was never quite able to carry that off.

There were no e-mail or phone messages worth responding to, and her schedule showed no clients on the horizon. But there were no bills to pay, either. "I'm doing very well, thank you." She spoke those encouraging words out loud, to nobody but herself. That's who needed to hear them.

The only item on her calendar for the whole week was on Thursday: "Dinner, Michael." They'd become something of a burden over the last couple of years, those almost-monthly dinners, ever since the lawsuit and the revelation of what he'd done.

Way back when Kirsten was a toddler and he was an uncle she rarely saw, Father Michael Nolan had done something priests vowed not to do. Worse yet, he'd done it with a very mixed-up young girl, not yet eighteen years old, who'd been sinking in a sea of problems and had reached out to him. He'd been alcohol-dependent at the time, and in no shape to help anyone—and he sure didn't help that girl. Almost at once it was over and she was pregnant and he was sliding faster and deeper into his own downward spiral. A month later the girl was dead, and her family raged and hated him. And when money passed from the archdiocese to the girl's family in a confidential settlement, the payment eased none of their anger or ill will.

After the money, time passed, too. With therapy and rehab and AA, Michael Nolan finally managed to grab hold of the life that was slipping past him, and to hang on and drag himself into it. Growing up, Kirsten came to know him as her priest-uncle—her mother's only brother—who once had a drinking problem he'd overcome, but she never heard about the pregnant girl who killed

11

herself. He joined them on holidays and was pleasant to everyone, even though her mother and father barely spoke to him, and would never tell her why. He worked at various churches, all of them in the most poverty-stricken neighborhoods in the city. When he was finally named pastor of a parish he turned the rectory into a shelter for homeless families and lived in a storage room in the back of the church.

By then, too, Michael was far more to Kirsten than just her kindly uncle. He was the rescuer who'd gotten her through the lowest, loneliest, most frightening time of her life. An episode she'd kept bottled up inside her ever since, never revealing it to anyone—though God knows she'd tried to tell Dugan a hundred times. Meanwhile, and especially after her father died, Michael became like a second father to her. A week seldom went by when they didn't see each other or at least talk on the phone.

Then, two years ago, it all fell apart. The dead girl's family got a new lawyer and sued to set aside the decades-old settlement as "inadequate, fraudulent, obtained under duress, and coercive." The suit made terrible claims about what Michael had done so many years in the past. He was frightened and ashamed and was yanked out of his position as pastor. When Kirsten heard, she *knew* it couldn't be true, and she got Dugan to represent him. Then, when Michael *admitted* everything, she'd been shocked beyond belief, and hurt and terribly angry. And those feelings still lingered.

Michael, of course, hadn't had a dime to pay the girl's family. So it was the lawyers for the archdiocese—that's where the money was—who did all the legal work in the lawsuit. Since it was filed nearly thirty years after the suicide and the family had long ago received money to settle the matter, the suit was dismissed in short order. Dugan said that didn't bother him so much because that was, after all, the law. It also didn't bother him that he never had to deal with Michael again.

Kirsten, though, felt obliged not to abandon her uncle. She tried to hide the feelings she couldn't get over, and she watched him pretend he didn't know how much everything had changed.

And now? She reached for the phone and tapped out his number.

"Hello. Michael Nolan here." He couldn't call himself *Father* any more. That was one of the new orders he'd been given—since all the recent publicity about priests and sexual abuse—along with no more saying Mass and no more Roman collar. Not to mention no more job with the archdiocesan Office of Liturgy. They'd dump him entirely, if they could. "Hello?" he repeated.

"Oh . . . hi. It's me. Kirsten."

"Oh, how are you? You haven't forgotten Thursday, have you?"

"Of course not." Where once they'd gotten together almost every week to laugh and cry and share their everyday experiences, now maybe once a month they met and went through the motions. She had no expectation that one day things might be the way they used to be. Because no matter how she tried, she couldn't forgive him, not only for what he'd done, but also for hiding it from her . . . and for the lack of courage that showed.

"Kirsten?"

"Oh," she said, "sorry. The thing is . . . I have a conflict on Thursday night." Which wasn't true. "So how about today?" He'd been there for her. She had to be there for him. "Are you free?"

"Today? Well, Monday nights I usually—"

"I'm thinking lunch." She knew Monday nights were AA meetings. "Lambs Farm? Noon? My turn to buy."

"Sure. That's great. See you there." He sounded genuinely happy about the change, and she wondered if he'd heard about Thomas Kanowski.

With Lambs Farm maybe twenty-five miles north of the city, Kirsten would need about an hour to go home, get her car, and drive up there. So she had plenty of time. She stripped the rubber bands from the bundle of mail left from Saturday. It was usually 100 percent junk, but once in a while some *real* mail was lurking in there somewhere.

This was one of those times.

It was an ordinary postcard, the kind you buy already stamped. The postmark was Chicago and it was addressed to her "c/o Wild Onion, Ltd." with a mailing label, but a label that had obviously been cut from another piece of mail, probably a magazine or a catalog, and taped onto the card. On the message side, in penciled block letters, it said: HERE I COME.

4.

Three words. HERE I COME. Innocuous, really. So why did Kirsten find them so menacing? She thought of calling Dugan, then decided to wait. But until when? Until she knew *who* was coming? Until whoever it was arrived?

And the cops? No way. Even if they considered the postcard a threat worth spending police time and resources on—and they wouldn't—it would take months to get results back from a police lab. Instead, she went next door to Mark Well Diamond Company, Inc., where Mark Brumstein, Andrea's husband, gave her some clear plastic envelopes, the kind he used for sorting gems. They made good evidence bags, one each for the postcard and for every other piece of mail in the bundle. She could take them to Renfroe Laboratories. Any fingerprints Leroy Renfroe found on the card he could check against hers, which he had on file, and against the postal carrier's, which he might find on other pieces of mail. He could also look for any trace substances that might tell them something or could be used for DNA comparison if they ever got another specimen.

If there was anything helpful, Leroy Renfroe would find it. But she didn't go to Leroy's lab. She decided to wait. She was overreacting.

Or was she? Whoever sent that card had taken a piece of her own mail, maybe pulled it out one day through the slot, and cut off the label to tape to the card. The words were: HERE I COME. But the message was: "I've been here already." Like it or not—and she didn't—it spooked her.

She picked up her car and headed north for lunch with Michael. She'd gotten an anonymous note that on its face wasn't even a threat, and she'd learned that a man possibly connected with her uncle—connected in disgrace—had been brutally murdered. Did either she or Michael have real reason for concern? Maybe he and his fellow priests on that *Sun-Times* list did, but *she* certainly didn't. Or was it vice versa? And what perverse stroke of fortune caused both things to happen at the same time?

Yes, she was overreacting. And no, she couldn't keep her eyes off the rearview mirror.

She had picked the restaurant at Lambs Farm, a facility for adults with developmental disabilities, because it was quiet and unpretentious. More importantly, though, it was only about ten miles from the seminary in Mundelein, and at the seminary there was a retreat center called Villa St. George. That was where the archdiocese was warehousing Michael and the other accused priests—the ones who hadn't already walked away—while appeals to Rome and procedures to decide what to do with them ground forward. So Lambs Farm wasn't far from Michael, who had very little money for gas or anything else.

She took a table and ordered coffee and said her companion would have some, too, whenever he got there. Then she waited.

Punctuality had never been his strong suit. On the other hand, it didn't seem to bother him to wait for her, either, even if—as had happened several times—she didn't show up at all and hadn't been able to warn him. He had no cell phone and was hard to reach if he wasn't right there at Villa St. George.

When she saw him coming across the dining room she thought, as she often did, that even in what he called his "civvies" he looked exactly like you'd expect a priest to look. A silly thought, she knew. In his early sixties, he was maybe five-ten, slender, his skin more ruddy than tanned, and the few gray strands of hair he had left were combed over his head less from vanity, she thought, than from habit. He looked intelligent, kind, sensitive; not at all like someone who had abused a trusting young girl.

She stood up. "Michael," she said.

She didn't feel comfortable calling him either *Uncle* or *Father*, not since she'd found out what he had done. She knew too well what that poor girl had gone through. How could he have betrayed someone who trusted him? And not only the girl, but Kirsten, too, by not telling her what he had done and letting her worship and respect him as she had.

"Hi, Kirsten." He shook her hand. They never embraced any more, either. Maybe they were the same people they had always been, but two years ago everything changed.

They sat down and were joined at once by a waitress. Cheerful and heavyset and constantly squinting behind thick lenses, the young woman had difficulty with her consonants and was certainly a Lambs Farm resident. Michael frowned and hesitated over the menu, then finally ordered chicken and dumplings.

"I don't know what's to think about," Kirsten said. "You always order the same thing here."

"I thought this time I might try the chicken pot pie," he answered. "But it's probably the same, only less."

17

Once she'd have joked about how she always knew what he meant even when he didn't really say it. Today she ordered the seafood salad.

The meal began like their times together always did these days, the conversation starting slowly and never really getting anywhere. Michael read voraciously and he saw lots of movies, mostly on video. So at least there were a few things to talk about. Things outside of themselves.

She used to tell him everything, including about the cases she worked as a cop, even the violent, heartbreaking things—and how they affected her. And later about her hopes and dreams about running her own detective agency. He loved all that, and he'd tell her about whatever parish he was working at, and his hopes and dreams for the people. And even though Dugan had rarely joined them, she used to talk about all the weird, funny things he did. Now, since the lawsuit, Dugan's name was hardly ever mentioned. Michael had urged her once to bring him along, and she told him the truth. "He won't come. He can't get by what . . . you know . . . what happened. He's . . . pretty angry."

"And you?" he had asked.

"It was a long time ago," she said. "Let's not talk about it."

It would have been nice to be able to say: *Even though I hate what you did, Michael, I forgive you.* But she couldn't. Oh, she still felt a great debt to him for being there when she'd needed it. And from what people in the churches he worked at said about him— before he'd been removed from parish work—she knew he'd helped lots of others, too. But forgive him? How could she?

Today, though, she could at least see whether the Kanowski murder was worrying him, and offer reassurance if it was. But neither of them mentioned it, and they struggled through lunch as usual. Finally, when they were on dessert, or *he* was, anyway—apple pie—she leaned forward a bit and asked, "Did you . . . um . . . happen to see the morning news? I mean about . . ." She didn't want to say it.

He looked back at her with an expression she first thought was sadness but then understood to be fear. "Thank you," he said.

"What? Did I do something?"

"Thank you for meeting me today." He lowered his head and poked at his pie and then laid the fork on the plate. But he didn't look up. "I thought I didn't get scared any more, not *really* scared. But now . . ."

"I don't understand." She did, but what else was there to say?

There were tears in his eyes now. "I got over being afraid of what people might say, or think. Even got over being afraid of dying . . . or that's what I thought." He shook his head. "Thomas Kanowski. I knew *about* him, but never knew him personally very well. He . . . his problem was with a boy. Eleven years old." He paused, and Kirsten shuddered to think of that poor little boy. "He denied it all the way, but I guess they proved it with . . . I don't know . . . DNA or something."

"He . . . went to prison?" she asked.

"Oh yes. He's been out about a year, but nobody I know has seen or heard from him since way before that. Then a couple of months ago his name appeared on that list in the paper, along with me and the others. And now . . . well . . . the way he was killed. It was brutal, they said on TV."

She folded her napkin, then unfolded it again. "You don't even know for sure whether it's the same Thomas Kanowski. And if it is, you don't know that his death had anything to do with—"

"It's him, all right. They told us this morning. And why else would he have been hacked to death? I mean, there I was, driving over here to meet you today in broad daylight, and I'm looking

19

around to see if someone's following me. Tonight, when I go to AA, I'll come out in the dark. Go to my car. How do I know . . ." He slipped the tips of his fingers up behind his glasses, and wiped the tears from his eyes.

"Are you . . . going to finish your pie?" Again she didn't know what else to say. She hadn't expected tears.

"I have to get back," he said. "There's a meeting we all have to attend. But it's really so stupid, this fear." He smiled a little, and she could see it was an effort. "Why am I so scared? People are tortured and die terrible, painful deaths all the time. Iraq, Somalia, El Salvador. Many of them heroic deaths. They suffer and it's over. But me, I'm scared."

She couldn't remember ever seeing an old man cry like he had . . . out of fear. He wasn't crying now, but he looked very old, indeed. And there was nothing at all she could do. What he needed was someone to comfort him, tell him everything would be okay. He needed someone to hug him. But how could she?

Kirsten followed Michael as he drove out of the Lambs Farm parking lot. She had told him to call her if he needed to talk to someone, and they'd agreed to meet for lunch again next week. They went under I-94 and he continued west while she turned onto the entrance ramp to take the interstate back to the city.

By now it was being reported on the news that the victim was indeed a former Chicago priest who'd been convicted of child molestation. Since his release from prison he'd been living with a relative near Rockford. The authorities were being stingy with details about what happened. There was no reference to any motive or even to a cause of death.

Although Michael spoke of the man being hacked to death, he'd been watching the TV during breakfast in the company of some other priests who were as uninformed, and as scared, as he was. All she had heard was that the body had been mutilated. Now, even that much was omitted.

She considered the possibility of her finding someone from the Illinois State Police—or would it be the local county sheriff?—to give her information about the case. Her chances were somewhere south of zero, she thought, and then suddenly remembered that there *was* no case, not for her.

She had no client, only an uncle who was afraid the killer would come after him, too. But no one knew that to be true. The only proof that someone was out to kill any other priests on the list would be more killings of priests on the list. There was no case, nothing for her to do.

Meanwhile, she couldn't keep her mind off that damn postcard. HERE I COME might simply be someone's idea of a harmless joke, although she couldn't imagine who that someone might be. On the other hand, she'd made her share of enemies, and the card and its mailing label address showed how close to her someone could get, how vulnerable she was. If the card wasn't a joke, it was meant to sow the seed of fear in her heart.

How well that worked was entirely up to her.

5.

On the day after she dealt with the pervert Father Kanowski, Debra Moore stood in her bathroom and studied her two images: her new self reflected in the mirror, her old self looking out from a snapshot tacked to the wall. The photo, taken when she hadn't been expecting it, was a good likeness of how she used to look. Strikingly pretty, yes, but also looking angry in the photo, and Debra realized that when she wasn't thinking about it her face fell into a frown.

Her new self and her old self. Anyone who didn't know better would easily be fooled. It wasn't just the plastic surgery, but also the auburn hair, the blue contacts, the weight loss. And when she smiled . . . well, that made a big difference. So she practiced smiling.

Debra Moore was the name she'd chosen when she created her new identity and came back to the United States. With money not a problem, she'd settled here at the farm north of Detroit and used her time well, working out on the weight machines, growing stronger in mind and body. She bought a full-sized van, a used Ford Econoline, to haul things around in, and began making regular trips to Chicago. The woman lived there, and Debra gradually spent more and more time watching her. Whatever else she did, though, Debra was always, always, counting down the days until Carlo's return.

Then one day, as though out of nowhere, came the turning point, the sign. She might easily have missed it, that list of eighteen priests in the newspaper. By then she'd been going to Chicago three or four times a month, staying several days at a time, but otherwise she never saw a Chicago newspaper . . . which was how she knew it was a sign. From God. God made someone leave that particular *Sun-Times* at that particular Burger King in Saginaw, 300 miles away from Chicago. God knew Debra would pick it up and read, and God knew she would feel once again the rage against such men as those eighteen evil fathers, a rage that boiled up inside and set her trembling.

Always before when that happened—and with all the recent publicity the episodes came more often—she would eventually calm down and tell herself not to be distracted, to concentrate on one desire, one goal, at a time. But this was different. This time when her mind cleared she was staring down at an actual list of names. And at one name standing out from all the rest: Michael Nolan. *That name, on this list?* It was a clear sign. God was not only calling her, but had brought together her two deepest, seemingly separate, goals: to punish that bitch who went about ruining people's dreams, and to purge the world of those loathsome beasts who used their position to prey on the helpless.

Her trips to Chicago had focused almost entirely on watching the woman, that whore who broke into people's lives and destroyed their dreams for money. Debra had followed her patiently, studying her habits, and on several occasions had seen

23

her meet a priest for dinner. An older man. A former teacher? She thought it worth looking into, and learned the priest's name, Michael Nolan, and learned he was the bitch's uncle.

Then, only days later, she found herself paging through the *Sun-Times*, hardly interested . . . and there was the sign. A list of eighteen priests guilty of sexually abusing children was disturbing enough. But one of the names was Michael Nolan. A priest guilty of the worst betrayal of all, unfit to inhabit this world. She'd scarcely been able to breathe. In God's name she would make Father Nolan pay—make all of them pay, and purge the world of them.

And the bitch? Surely she was well aware of the evil this uncle of hers had done. Treating a beast like him as a human being was reason enough for her to suffer, without all the rest of it. So, even as Debra commenced dealing with the evil fathers, she sent a message to the woman, as well . . . to set her wondering.

Now, as Debra stood in the bathroom and practiced her smile, her mind was far from idle. Although her work had just begun, she already faced some major decisions.

She had begun with Father Kanowski for no reason other than that he was unprotected and available. Afterward she'd driven home, stopping once to dismantle the pistol and drop the barrel off a bridge over the Paw Paw River. Her bloody clothing she incinerated when she got back to the farm. Everything had gone perfectly, a result of careful planning and diligent study of that disgusting man's habits, along with her being smart enough to adapt to changing circumstances.

Now, though, one thing was clear: She had been overly optimistic in thinking she could purge the world of all eighteen priests on the list and still be ready for Carlo. She knew now how time-consuming each purging would be. In addition, her risk would increase as the number of victims rose and the range of targets narrowed.

If it weren't for Carlo, of course, neither time nor risk would matter. But Carlo could not survive without her, and he would be returning soon. She had to be ready for him, and she had decided to present the bitch to him as a homecoming gift. Yet she could not simply ignore God's sign. Clearly, it was His will that all these beasts pay the price. But how many of them were specifically her responsibility? And when she knew the number, which ones was she to choose?

She went to her desk. She had already made an index card for each priest: last name, first name, then adding bits of information—the nature of his crimes, where he lived, his habits—as she learned them. Now she spread the eighteen cards before her on the desk. Divine Wisdom would help her decide.

She placed Thomas Kanowski at the upper edge of the desk, farthest away from her, then studied the remaining cards. Sliding them around on the smooth surface. Staring at them. Rearranging them. And suddenly, as though someone had twisted a lens into focus, the picture became clear.

She selected six additional cards, with alternate choices for three of them, and placed them one under the other. The number itself was obvious. God willed that she should purge the world of seven of these beasts herself. Seven, the biblical number of fullness and perfection. But what she saw laid out in front of her was not only how many, but which ones, and in what order. Seven evil fathers, ending with Michael Nolan, and leading her, step by step, to the woman . . . another one for whom mere purging was not enough.

6.

It was the following week, Tuesday. Dugan walked into the kitchen and found Kirsten already up and sitting at the table in jeans and a rather flimsy yellow top that was a favorite of his. She was staring down into her coffee mug.

"Want some more?" he asked.

"What?" She was in a different galaxy somewhere.

"Coffee," he said. "Your mug's empty."

"Oh, sure." She held the mug out and he filled it.

"Did I ever tell you," he said, "that you have the world's nicest—"

"Smile," she said, "yes." Then she *did* smile and tilted her head so he could kiss her on the cheek.

"Well . . . that, too," he said, accepting the invitation. "The smile's good." He tapped his finger on his watch. "I'm late. I take it you're not headed downtown today?"

"What? Oh, I guess not."

He stared at her. "You seem a little . . . distracted," he said, and then it suddenly occurred to him what it must be, and he got a little nervous himself. He poured a mug of coffee and sat down. "It's been a little more than a month, hasn't it? You got any . . . uh . . . news?"

She smiled again, as though coming back to Earth. "Yes, but . . . not what we were hoping for."

"Oh. Well . . ." He didn't know whether he was more disappointed or relieved, but he said, "You think it's time to . . . I don't know . . . talk to someone?"

"Damn," she said, "don't be so negative. It's way too soon for doctors and all that bull—"

"Okay, okay," he said, raising his hands in surrender. "Take it easy. I was thinking that's what *you* might want. I'm happy to just keep trying. That's . . . you know . . . got its own rewards."

"Anyway," she said, "that's not what I've been thinking about. What's bothering me is I have to meet Michael for lunch today."

"Jesus, didn't you just do that a few days ago?"

"It was a week ago yesterday. We agreed we'd get together again today. And here it is already. It's just . . . it's hard to know what to talk about."

"You could talk about how nice it is that there've been no more of his pervert buddies found—" He let that go. "You've been working long hours on that disability case. Why don't you just call Michael and cancel?"

"I can't. I promised."

"Yeah, well, Michael's one guy knows all *about* breaking promises. He should—"

"Dugan."

"Yeah, right." He stood up. "I better go."

"I can't just abandon Michael. Not after what— Not after all these years."

"Yeah? Well . . . fine." Just talking about her uncle irritated him. Whatever good things he'd done for her in the past, they would never outweigh the wrong he did to that girl who killed herself. Not in Dugan's mind. "I gotta go." He left her in the kitchen and headed for the front door.

Their condo was the third floor of a three-flat, and on the way downstairs he was seriously hoping there'd be no more of those damn priests killed. He didn't want Kirsten worrying about it or thinking she should do something. Michael's problems were his own damn fault. She knew that. She hated what he'd done as much as anyone did, and she should just cut herself loose from him, once and for all.

With her mug in one hand, Kirsten was rummaging around the kitchen counter for the TV remote. When the phone rang, she jumped and splashed coffee on the counter as she reached for it.

"Hello?" she said.

No one said anything. Which happened all the time with these damn automated telemarketing systems. But this was pretty early in the day, and she'd put their number on the "Do Not Call" list. The caller ID was blocked. She hung up, wondering whether or not she had actually heard someone breathing on the line.

She made herself some toast and was buttering it when the phone rang again. She grabbed it. "Hello!" she said, not wanting to sound friendly.

"Oh. Kirsten? It's me, Michael."

"Did you just call," she said, "a few minutes ago?"

"How'd you know? Your line was busy."

"So . . . what's up?" she asked.

He told her he'd just learned the night before that he and the other priests who lived at Villa St. George had to be downtown that day, at what he called "the Pastoral Center," for a lunch meeting with the cardinal.

"Oh," she said. "Well, we'll get together some other—"

"But I could meet you somewhere down in that area? Somewhere convenient to you. At . . . say . . . eleven? Just for coffee or something?"

"That'd be fine," she said. Less painful than an entire meal, anyway.

It was supposed to be a warm day, so she suggested they meet at a tiny park on Superior Street, not far from the Pastoral Center.

She took a cab and when she got to the park—really no more than a tiny patch of green grass surrounded by tall buildings—Michael was already there, sitting on one of the few benches. He looked tired and somehow smaller than usual. He wore tan slacks and a brown tweed sport coat that was too big for him and looked like it came from a rummage sale. Maybe that's why he seemed small, she thought. He and the other accused priests apparently weren't allowed to wear their clerical outfits even for a meeting with their boss.

He stood up to greet her, and he thanked her for the coffee she'd brought. They sat side by side and sipped from their cardboard cups. "Mmm," he said, "that's good." His was a café mocha with whipped cream. Hers was blend-of-the-day, black.

"So," she said, "how is everything?"

"Everything's okay. Thank God there've been no more murders. Everyone's calming down . . . a little." When she didn't respond, he said, "Thanks for seeing me again. I know it's not easy."

"Don't be silly. It was a ten-minute cab ride."

"That's not what I meant," he said. "I just . . . well . . . I miss talking to you."

"It's only been a week. And before that it was . . . what? . . . a month?"

"I mean I miss the way it was. I miss *you*. I think you know what I mean. All these years, you've been the only family I had. And I don't know what to do about . . . about what's happened between us."

"There's nothing anyone *can* do about it, Michael. Short of going back thirty years and not . . . and doing things differently. Or maybe if you'd at least have *told* me, not left me to learn it from—" She shook her head. "Anyway, what's the meeting about?"

"I'm not certain, but I think the cardinal just wants to tell us he hasn't forgotten about us. Actually, I know he'd *like* to. He and all the bishops are taking a pretty hard hit on all this."

"Yeah? Well, why shouldn't they? My God, they find out Father So-and-so is groping little boys—or worse? And their answer is to hush it up and send him somewhere else? Not even *warn* anyone about him? There's your 'hard-hit' bishops."

"Too often they did that, yes. It was stupid, and wrong." He sipped from his cup. "But a lot of them tried different things. Sometimes they sent the man for treatment and were assured he was okay. And then he turned out not to be. Most of the bishops, I think, did what they thought was best."

"Best? For who? Themselves? Their screwed-up, homophobic, pseudocelibate old-boy system? 'Okay, guys, let's all hang together, and pretend the pedophiles aren't—'" She stood up, then sat back down again. Michael was part of the problem, sure, but she knew he wasn't a pedophile. "Let's talk about something else, okay?"

"That's up to you," he said, "but don't ever put me in that group." He was clearly angry himself now, sitting up a little taller inside the tweed jacket.

"I didn't put you with any group."

"But you came pretty close. Pedophiles are . . . Even *them* we shouldn't hate. They're seriously damaged people, and they so often do serious damage to others. But I'm not one of them."

"I *know* that," she said. "Let's change the subject."

"I'm trying to get what's between us out in the—" He stopped. "I know how you must feel. But I just—"

"Dammit, Michael!" she said. "You *don't* know how I feel." Even *she* couldn't sort out all her feelings, at least the ones beyond anger, which was easy. "Forget it." She stood up again. "I have to go." She turned away, then turned back. "Listen, I don't feel like talking, but I'm not gonna abandon you, okay? Call me if . . . if something comes up."

He nodded without looking up at her, and she walked away.

At the edge of the little park she looked back, and he was already headed in the opposite direction. She knew he hadn't finished his mocha, but he dropped the cup in a trash container as he passed it. He had his own anger and pride. And his guilt and all the rest of it. He'd done a terrible thing, but she knew he wasn't really a terrible person. Still, he should have told her about his past, right from the start, way back when he'd come down to Florida for her. He shouldn't have pretended to be perfect. He shouldn't . . . It went on and on. It always did.

She didn't know who she was madder at—herself or Michael.

Kirsten took a cab home. There were cars parked along both sides of the street. There always were, day and night. At night, with lots of bars and restaurants not far away, there were always people on the sidewalks, too, and cars going back and forth, and it could get pretty noisy. But during the day there was seldom anyone in sight.

Their building had a wrought-iron fence, with a gate that no one ever bothered to lock, and a tiny yard. There was a cement stoop, and then the front door. The door was thick plate glass and led into a small foyer, and it was always locked.

She was already at the gate when she first saw the red paint on the door. Grafitti happened around here once in a while, but it always appeared overnight, and this hadn't been there when she'd left an hour earlier. She'd get someone to remove it before Dugan saw it.

It wasn't the usual stylized gang grafitti. Just a thick dot, or a blob, with a circle around it; and around that, a larger circle, and then a still larger circle. And long fingers of red paint—like blood—dripping down on the glass from the circles.

7.

It was about noon on another Monday, exactly two weeks after the murder of Thomas Kanowski, that the body of the second priest on the list was found. He'd been dead for some days, maybe as long as a week, when his body was discovered in the middle of nowhere in central Minnesota. His name was Stanley Immel.

Kirsten learned of it when her uncle called at ten o'clock that night with the news. He was obviously shaken. He'd known Father Immel well. The two had talked often over the last few years about their cases, and about how both of them thought they'd gotten their lives back together until the recent national uproar about priests and sex abuse. They'd both been removed from their positions and told that if they wanted to keep their insurance coverage and get a small monthly stipend they had to live at Villa St. George.

"But Stanley refused to sit here and vegetate with the rest of us," Michael said. "He left to start a new life, on his own. Stanley Immel had more courage than I."

Right, Kirsten thought. *And Stanley Immel is dead.*

The next morning, Tuesday, broke dreary and cold. Rain started pouring down about ten o'clock and gave every indication it would last forever. Michael had said on the phone that he needed a few hours away from Villa St. George, and he'd decided to take the train downtown today and visit one of the museums. She said she'd meet him at the station at noon. He hadn't asked her to do that, but she could tell he was glad to hear it.

She'd been hoping his fear was as unfounded as she'd told him it was, hoping there wouldn't be a second priest killed, that there wasn't some crazy out there planning to go down the *Sun-Times* list and cross out one name after the other. Because if there was, even though Michael would never ask her, how could she *not* try to help? When she'd been in trouble and reached out to him, he hadn't hesitated for a minute. Yes, that was some fifteen years ago, and no, it wasn't a debt easily repaid.

First, though, she had a report to write. For a week she'd been working fourteen-hour days, doing surveillance for a lawyer wanting proof that the man his client ran over with a truck wasn't really disabled. Her report wouldn't be complicated. The subject hadn't been out of his house except to go to physical therapy.

She met Michael at the station and they took a cab to Michigan Avenue. The gloomy weather was no help at all. They went to the Art Institute, had a cafeteria lunch in the Court Café, then wandered the galleries. For two hours they struggled to focus on the works they were viewing, from the French Impressionists to the African Collection, to some amazing mobiles by a Belgian artist she'd never heard of . . . although Michael had. But finally, as though by unspoken agreement, they ended up back at the cafeteria for coffee and the conversation turned to what was actually on both their minds: the murder of Stanley Immel.

Once he got started, the words poured out of Michael's mouth. What he knew about Immel's sex abuse case he had learned from the man himself. At fifty-one, Immel had been the pastor of a parish when he was found to have engaged in incidents of improper sexual touches with two sisters, aged ten and eight. At the time, they had been foster children under the care of Father Immel's sister, Louise, and her husband. The couple had no children of their own, and this was their first experience with foster care.

Unknown to Louise and her husband, Michael said, the girls had been in four other foster homes in three years and had been removed from every one of them when they complained of sexual abuse by their caregivers. The ten-year-old, Maggie, a small, pretty girl with a wide smile and large dark eyes, was quite precocious and talkative. Her little sister, on the other hand, hardly ever said a word, other than to agree with whatever Maggie said. The frequency of their claims of abuse was not deemed by the social workers to affect their credibility.

The incidents with Father Immel were said to have occurred on two nights during a week when he was visiting his sister's family at a summer cottage they owned near Brainerd, Minnesota. He'd offered to babysit, to give Louise and her husband some well-earned respite from the two girls.

On the second occasion, the couple had gone out to a movie, and Father Immel sat on the sofa with the girls and read to them, which they seemed to like. But when he told them it was bedtime all hell broke loose. Maggie went out of control and threatened to run away. He was scared and finally locked the girls in their room.

The moment Louise and her husband got back, Maggie started screaming uncontrollably. She accused the priest of molesting her and her sister on both nights. "According to Stan," Michael said, "Maggie kept saying, 'He picked us up and made us sit on his penis and wiggle around.' He said she used those exact words and never varied from them. Like she had memorized them."

Torn between her faith in her brother and her belief that little children could never lie about such things, Louise took the girls home to Chicago the following morning. She reported the matter to the social worker, who reported it to the archdiocese. Father Immel was called in and interviewed by a priest from the cardinal's sex abuse task force, and a lawyer.

"Did he bring his own lawyer with him?" Kirsten asked.

"Of course not," Michael said. "To him it was just a conversation, to explain what really happened."

What Father Immel explained was that Maggie had become enraged and threatened to "get him good" when he insisted the kids had to go to bed. In addition, however, while he denied any sexual contact or sexual interest in the girls, he did admit under questioning that there were some "embraces and caresses" that occurred as he cuddled the two girls and read to them, and that these were "probably imprudent." He agreed that he "should have known better" and "should have avoided that."

When criminal charges were filed Father Immel *did* get a lawyer. Later, the state's attorney dropped the charges and the priest entered the archdiocesan sex abuse program. He was removed from his parish and went through the required course of evaluation and treatment. He was eventually certified as "not a danger" to children. Still, when he was returned to priestly work, it was at the Catholic Center at the University of Illinois, the Chicago Circle Campus, where he wouldn't come into contact with young children.

"Stan worked as chaplain there for almost four years without incident," Michael said. "Then, suddenly these new policies were put in place and, like me, he was removed at once from his position."

"And later, like you, his name got into the paper," Kirsten said.

"Right."

"It sounds like he suggested to you," she said, "that what got him in trouble was his not being more careful answering questions, and that they interpreted his answers in a way to make him look guilty, when he wasn't."

"Exactly," Michael said. "Those girls lied. They'd done it before and—"

"But you know, don't you, that *he* might have been the one lying? That maybe he *did* abuse those girls?"

"I . . . well . . . I don't think so. Not at all. The psychologists said he was okay, and there was never any other incident."

"No other incident that *you* know of." His eyes widened and he was about to object, but she raised her palm to stop him. "Look, I'm not saying he did it. I'm only saying . . ." She let it go. "Anyway, he wasn't appealing to Rome about his removal from the priesthood, like you are?"

"No. Stanley was angry that they would send him back to square one after he'd already done everything they asked him to do. Basically, he told the cardinal the hell with it, and walked away. I heard he bought a rundown summer cottage near his sister's place in Minnesota for next to nothing and was trying to fix it so he could live there year-round."

The rundown cottage was on tiny Two Skunk Lake, and that was where Stanley Immel's body was discovered. Kirsten had already read a very sketchy report from a Brainerd newspaper's Web site.

51

The report didn't identify the victim as a priest or an ex-priest but did say that according to the coroner, he'd been dead about a week when he was found by a woman who delivered propane gas in the area. "I wondered where he was, because he always comes out when I drive up, and the dog's usually barking and all," she was quoted as saying. "So I peeked in the kitchen window. Gosh, it was a mess in there. Blood all over everything."

The paper said the Crow Wing County Sheriff's office had classified the incident as a homicide. There were no suspects.

8.

Jesus, are you totally out of your mind?" Dugan got up and walked to his office window and looked out, as though to study the rain streaming down, or the gray building hardly visible across the street.

Kirsten was sitting in one of his client's chairs and wasn't surprised at his reaction. She'd left her raincoat with Michael in the reception area and gone alone into Dugan's office and closed the door. "No," she said, "I wouldn't say *totally*." She crossed her legs and wondered how much these new wool pants—soaked through up to the knees—would shrink. "Anyway, I'm *thinking* about it. Michael's, you know, in serious trouble."

"Uh-huh, and why is that?" Dugan turned to face her. "Oh, I remember. Because he's a so-called man of God, and when a mixed-up teenager comes to him for help . . . his solution is to fuck her. And . . . gosh . . . now he's in *trouble*."

"I didn't say he didn't do something bad. It was the worst thing he could have done."

"You *say* it's bad, but you sugarcoat—"

"I'm not sugarcoating anything. I'm saying it's possible—not

39

certain, but *possible*—that someone intends to kill him in a brutal way for something terrible he did thirty years ago. He was a priest, yes. But he was a drunk, too, with his stupid friends covering for him when they should have gotten him into a recovery program. And you? You never did anything in your past you were ashamed of?"

"I never got into the pants of a sixteen-year-old client."

"She was seventeen, almost eighteen. It happened just once."

"Right. If you believe what *he* says."

"That's what her *family* said. He never denied anything they said."

"So what? So it's okay because he fucked her 'just once'?"

"Of course not, but—" Why the hell was she defending Michael's indefensible conduct, anyway? That wasn't the point. "You know what, Dugan?" She stood up. "You're starting to really piss me off."

"I'm just trying to keep you from wasting a lot of time and money. For no good reason. Why don't you save your pissed-offness for that uncle of yours who couldn't keep his goddamn pants zipped up?"

She was about to leave before she said something she'd regret, when she suddenly realized the problem was hers, not Dugan's. She'd come to him to talk it over, when she knew damn well what his opinion would be. Now she needed to turn this conversation around. "Okay," she said, "you've raised a good objection. Let's both relax and think this through." She sat down, and gave him her best I-love-you-more-than-anything-in-the-world smile. It was 100 percent genuine, too, but it still took a while to work.

He stared at her. "Is this the part where you try to talk me into something?" he finally said, but he sat down and she could see him softening.

"Who in the world ever talked *you* into *anything?* Uh-uh, I'm

40

just running an idea past you, and you think it's a *bad* idea because it could get quite expensive."

"That's not my main object—"

"No, but you brought it up and it's an important consideration. I know Wild Onion's net each year has barely been half what I made as a cop, but this year—mostly because of the Willoughby divorce—I should double last year's income."

"I don't care what your income is. Jesus, I don't care if you work at all. Maybe when you get preg—"

"Let's not go there, okay? Not until there's something to talk about."

"Yeah, well, you'd go nuts if you didn't work. I understand that."

"Right," she said. "And you also understand I'd go just as nuts if my business had to be supported by you as though it were my hobby. So I have to make enough so I could support myself even if you and your law practice weren't around."

"Don't talk that way. I *am* around. And I will be."

"Of course. But that's how I have to think about it. For my *own* sake."

"Okay . . . so?"

"So, if I decide to help Michael and the others, maybe they'll be able to pay a fee. Or at least expenses."

"Michael's in no position to pay anything near what it would cost."

"But he'll pay *something*. And probably most of the others will join in. I mean, they're all scared. And reasonable or not, I'd be scared, too, in their position. Some of them must have some money, from their families or whatever. So . . ." She shrugged and spread her hands out, palms up.

"So you're gonna do it, whatever I think."

"I said I'm *considering* doing something to help."

"And so you got me twisted into talking about money," he said, "instead of about the kind of creeps those guys are."

"You give me *way* too much credit."

"Yeah, right." He picked up a pen and tapped one end of it on his left palm.

She stood up and went around the desk and rested a hand on his shoulder, but he just sat there tapping his pen and playing tough guy. She put her other hand on the back of his neck and leaned and kissed him on the left ear . . . and felt the shiver that went through his body. She knew it would. Both ears were hot-wired, but the left one? Dynamite. "Gotta go," she said. "Michael's out there waiting. Um . . . I don't suppose you wanted to say hello to—"

"Anything I have to say to that guy, you don't wanna—"

"Great. So, anyway, thanks for helping me sort this out." She headed for the door.

"I give up," he said. "He's your uncle, damn him, and you're gonna get mixed up in this whether you get paid or not, aren't you?"

She turned at the door. "Not relevant, counselor, because I *will* get paid." At least she hoped so.

"So now it's '*will* get paid'? I thought you were only *considering* getting involved."

"I was," she said. "But talking to you has helped me decide. That's one of the things I love about—"

"So you're gonna run around from state to state and investigate two murders?"

"Two we know of so *far*," she said. "But catching killers is what *cops* get paid for. Me, I'll concentrate on protection."

"Protection for a bunch of damn—" He didn't finish. "So how many are left? Sixteen? You're gonna bodyguard sixteen people?"

"Just the ten who are living at Villa St. George," she said. "But even so, I'll need . . . some help."

His eyes widened. "You don't think you're gonna get *me* involved with those—"

"Of course not," she said. "You're much too busy squeezing dollars out of innocent, helpless insurance adjusters. I'll get . . . oh . . . someone."

Understanding spread slowly across his face. "You're gonna get Cuffs Radovich, aren't you?"

"If he's available."

"Jesus." Dugan shrugged. "Well . . . creeps like those guys, I guess they *deserve* a babysitter like Cuffs."

9.

ey, Doogie pal. *¿Qué pasa?*"

Dugan, startled, looked up from his desk. Kirsten had left two hours ago and he was deep into a client's tax returns. "Jesus, Larry. Try knocking, huh?" He'd long ago given up trying to get Larry Candle to can the "Doogie" crap.

"What's to knock on? Door's wide open, partner."

"We're not partners." He'd never give up on that. "You *work* for me."

"Figure of speech, pal. Figure of speech."

Larry was incorrigible. He was also short and round, with a head the shape of a bowling ball and covered with lots of curly black hair—certainly permed, probably dyed. He had a bottle of beer in each hand.

"It's not six o'clock yet, Larry. We made a—"

"Think fast!" Larry yelled, and tossed one of the bottles across the office. Dugan caught it with two hands before it hit him in the face.

Larry balanced himself on the edge of one of the client's

chairs—probably so he could see what was on Dugan's desk—and twisted the top off his beer. A Berghoff Dark. Larry loved microbrews, and he had taken over the beer buying from Mollie, Dugan's office manager, whom Larry liked to call "the Enforcer." Mollie always bought Miller's or Bud, whichever was on sale.

"I'd watch out for that," Larry said, pointing at Dugan's beer.

Dugan swiveled away from his desk, held the bottle away from him, and twisted the cap just enough to let a little beer fizz out and drizzle down over his hand and into the wastebasket. He swiveled back and lifted the bottle and drank. You couldn't fault Larry's taste in beer, anyway. "I'm, uh, kinda busy here, Larry. What's up?"

"Whatcha got there? Myron Tarkington's tax returns?"

"Uh-huh."

"I can see the defendant's lawyer now. 'Well, Mr. Tarkington, you testified that you lost seventy thousand dollars because you couldn't run your car repair business for a year. So tell the jury, are you lying *now?* Or have you been lying to the *government,* since you've never reported more than thirty-five thou in your life?'"

"Don't worry," Dugan said. "This'll never get to trial." Dugan handled only injury cases, lots of them, and his goal was to settle and *never* go to trial. But he also never lowballed a client. If he couldn't get a fair offer from an insurance company he referred the case to another law firm to take it to trial, and they split the fee. Saved Dugan a lot of headaches. And if a court appearance was required *before* he could send the case out, he had Larry handle it. Larry loved arguing with lawyers and judges, and he never got headaches. He gave them.

"Not to change the subject," Larry said, "I saw Kirsten here a while ago."

"Uh-huh."

"But she got away before I could talk to her."

"Uh-huh." Larry irritated the hell out of Kirsten, so she avoided him.

"She gonna try to help those priests?" Larry asked.

"What're you talking about?"

"Hey, don't forget. I'm the one called her on the phone that morning after the first guy got it. Y'know, on I-90? Kanooski, Kanowski, whatever. Anyway, then there's this one in Minnesota. Guy messed with some little girls, they say. Now he's dead. And I'm thinking Kirsten might get involved, you know, because her uncle was on the same list in the paper along with those two, and—"

"How do you know all this stuff, Larry?"

"Hell, I pay attention, read the papers, ask around. Do that for twenty-five years and you get to know things . . . and people. I told Kirsten I knew someone who could give her some facts on that I-90 murder, but she blew me off."

"Who do you know?"

"Just the detective in charge of the goddamn case, that's all. Winnebago County Sheriff's Office. Ex-client of mine. Years ago I got him off on a police brutality rap when he was with the Cicero Police Department. He owes me, y'know? 'Cause to get him off I hadda—"

"Wait." Dugan raised his hand. "Don't tell me."

"Anyway, his name's Danny Wardell. He's a sergeant now, I think. She can use my name. He owes me."

"I'll, uh, I'll see if she's interested."

"She sure as hell wants this guy caught before he gets down the list as far as her uncle."

"No one even knows if those two killings are related. It could be a coincidence."

"Could be, I guess. But it's a hell of a coincidence, Doogie pal."

46

Larry drained what was left of his beer. "Because this afternoon? It was on the news. They found priest number three. As dead as the first two."

Five minutes later Dugan had managed to get Larry out of his office. He wished Larry hadn't told him anything at all. He didn't want any part of helping Kirsten get more deeply involved in a series of homicides, or in helping a bunch of creeps who . . . Damn! He punched out her cell phone number.

"Hello?"

"It's me," he said. "You in the car?"

"Yes. Taking Michael home. What's up?"

"You have the radio on?"

"I did," she said, "but Jesus, it's all Iraq, Iraq, Iraq. I put in a CD. Why?"

"Larry Candle heard on the news that a third priest got murdered. Or ex-priest, I guess. The guy was on the list."

"You mean they *said* that?"

"No, but Larry's got a copy of it."

"Why would—"

"Says he likes to stay on top of things. Anyway, it happened sometime early this morning. In the victim's apartment, somewhere on the northwest side. Name's Emmett Regan. That's all I know."

"Shit."

"Yeah," he said. "Right."

"Okay, then. I guess I . . ." There was a pause, and then she said, "Larry told me two weeks ago he knew someone with information about . . . you know . . ." She obviously didn't want to talk with her uncle there in the car with her.

"About the first murder, yeah. He told me that today, too. A detective with the Winnebago County Sheriff. A sergeant. Name's Danny Wardell. Larry says you can use his name."

"I give the guy Larry's name, he'll throw me out the door."

"I don't know. Larry says Wardell owes him." Dugan wondered why he was encouraging her, for God's sake. "Anyway, why would you need to talk to some police investigator? You'll just be providing security, right?"

"Uh . . . yeah. Right."

"Plus, you don't want to get so wrapped up in this that you forget that other problem. You know, that 'Here I come' note?"

"I'm thinking that was bogus," she said. "I've put it completely out of my mind. You should, too."

"Yeah? Good. Okay."

He hung up, then realized he'd forgotten to ask what time she'd be home that night. But he didn't call back. Wouldn't want her to think he was worried, right? Or that he wanted to clip her wings, or anything.

10.

Kirsten slipped the phone into her purse. Michael was too polite to ask what Dugan had said, and she didn't tell him. Any hope that the murders of two men on the list might be merely coincidental was gone now, and she wasn't ready to deal with his reaction. He'd hear soon enough, and maybe he'd get a night's sleep first. Plus she'd had a long day herself, and it looked now like it wasn't over.

Heading north from the city on the tollway, they got off at the exit near Lambs Farm and drove to a Wendy's, where they both ate salads. Then Michael directed her to Villa St. George, tucked away on the campus of the University of St. Mary of the Lake. Driving through the gate and down a long, empty road, she thought how odd it was that he'd been living here for going on two years now, and she'd never once been here, not to pick him up, not to visit him. "It's a big place," she said, "this university."

"A thousand acres, mostly untouched woods and lake," Michael said. "None of us priests, though, calls it a 'university.' We all just call it 'the seminary.' That's the only major school on campus.

49

They put it here back in the nineteen twenties, because they wanted it smack in the middle of nowhere."

Now, though, the seminary was an island of calm in a sea of suburban sprawl, about an hour's commute from the city. It was very dark out, but she asked Michael to give her a driving tour of the grounds, and he seemed delighted. Other than what he called "the main chapel," a flood-lit redbrick church that looked like it had been lifted from the green of a Vermont village, she didn't get much of a view of the various buildings he pointed out. But they all seemed large, brick, and colonial-style, with white pillars lined up everywhere. They drove across several bridges and even through one small tunnel. The whole place looked pretty deserted, though they did see a few other cars coming and going.

One encouraging thing was the obvious presence of a private security force. She saw two different patrol cars in the half hour it took to follow Michael's guided tour, navigate the dark winding road around the lake, and finally arrive at the narrow lane that led into the retreat house, Villa St. George. By then she'd also seen two motionless deer, a fat, waddling raccoon, a half-dozen joggers in reflective vests—all male—and a blur that streaked past her headlights and might have been a fox.

She thought the private police force might explain why, of the three men from the list who'd been murdered, none had resided here. Unlike Michael and the others living here, those three had chosen—if indeed each of them had the choice—to walk away and make no appeal to Rome about being stripped of their priest-hood.

They broke out of the trees and approached the retreat house, which was also colonial-style, surrounded by lawn and shrubbery. "Well," she said, "if you're gonna be put in dry dock somewhere, you could do worse."

"Oh, it's a beautiful setting all right," he said. "Great for prayer and study. But none of us wants to be here, you know? Not day after endless day. So it's hard not to turn a paradise into a prison. And now, these killings. It's terrifying."

Earlier that day, during lunch at the Art Institute, Michael had told her how he and the other priests were afraid the authorities wouldn't put serious effort put into apprehending a killer whose only targets were men a lot of people thought deserved whatever they got.

"We're not even sure there *is* such a killer," she had said then. "But I told you all along, I won't abandon you. One of the things I do is provide security services for people. And I could do that for you. I could—"

"Oh no," he objected. "I wasn't implying you should do that."

"I could put you up in a safe place."

"But I'm supposed to live at Villa St. George, and—"

"I know, but they'll make an exception under the circumstances."

"Even if they did, Kirsten, what about the others? I mean, it's gotten so they look to me . . . for encouragement." He seemed embarrassed. "Anyway, I'm not going anywhere."

"Fine, then I can provide extra security right there."

"No, there's the expense. I can't ask you to do that."

"You don't have to ask. You were there for me when I needed it, and I owe you." And this might be her chance to finally get that debt off her back.

"You don't owe me anything," he said. "What I did for you was . . . well . . . it was a long time ago. And I didn't *do* that much. Anyway, listen to me." He leaned across the table and sounded almost angry—or like someone *trying* to sound angry, anyway. "I want you to stay out of this."

"Sorry," she said. "But what *you* want has nothing to do with it."

She meant that, and she could tell that he knew it. They finished lunch in silence and hadn't spoken again of her involving herself.

They'd gotten very good at not speaking about things.

Now she pulled to a stop near the building entrance. Michael opened the car door, then closed it again and turned to her. "I really don't want you to get caught up in—"

"Like I told you at lunch," she said, "it's not about what you want."

"But—"

"Wait." She took a deep breath. "Dugan told me there's been a third killing . . . from the list."

"My God, what—"

"I don't know anything more and I don't want to discuss it now. I'm going to do what I can."

"Well then, at least . . ." He was having difficulty talking. "At least you should be paid. I'll talk to the others about . . . I guess . . . putting our money together."

She sat in the car and watched him disappear into the building. His earlier statement, that he hadn't *done* much for her, just wasn't true. She was the only one who knew. She'd never told a single person about what happened to her in Florida. It was so . . . stupid . . . and embarrassing. She always knew she should at least tell Dugan but could never get herself to do it. She'd kept it a secret so long, and it just never seemed to be the right time.

It had been only a few weeks after she'd graduated from high school. She'd been struggling with her parents for years and, finally, after a huge fight with her mother, she took the Greyhound to Fort Lauderdale—literally ran away from home—with a girlfriend. She was eighteen, after all, and they refused to treat her like an adult. She took her graduation money and the two girls planned to party awhile, then get an apartment and get jobs. What could be simpler?

What actually happened was that the friend got homesick and went back, while Kirsten—suddenly free of a lifetime of rules—threw herself into a whirling blur of beaches and volleyball and all-night parties. She got drunk way too often and got way too little sleep. Then one night, in a bar, she met the most wonderful guy. He was older, like thirty or something, but he was single and had his own business—a real estate office. His father's business, really, but his father was retiring soon and he would be taking it over. He seemed so wise and sophisticated—not immature and irresponsible like the guys her age. This man actually listened to her, tried to understand what she was *about*.

Sexually he was way ahead of her—who wasn't?—but he was patient and considerate, and with him life wasn't just about drinking and having sex. It was about tenderness, and humor, and interesting, fun things to do . . . *plus* drinking and having sex. He cared about her as a person, too. She ran out of money and he got her a job in the real estate office, and advanced the security deposit and a month's rent on a tiny condo one of his clients owned as a rental unit. Only later did she realize that she should have talked to the receptionist who was let go to make room for her.

When she got pregnant she was surprised, and terrified. Worst of all, he was enraged. It frightened her to listen to him. He said she'd lied to him about her precautions. But she hadn't. It was just . . . well . . . they hadn't always been thinking clearly. He was beside himself, like a person she didn't even know. Didn't she realize that he couldn't afford to be saddled with a baby? He said there was only one choice for her. He'd pay for an abortion and he'd talk to his dad about letting her keep the job . . . until she got on her feet.

She cried for two days straight and then called home, but they had their own crises to deal with. Her mother was severely depressed and angry at Kirsten and at the world. Her dad, a Chicago cop, had just shot and killed a woman and was entering into a terrible struggle that would eventually make him leave the department. So she told them things were going great with her, and she'd be coming home for a visit any time now.

She stopped drinking, but still she was sick all the time. She missed a lot of work and they had to get someone "more reliable." She went through two horrible months of pregnancy while she made up her mind, and then she had the abortion. This was followed by some complications that she didn't quite understand, but which kept her too tired and sick to look for another job. After the abortion she never saw the guy again and didn't want to.

She couldn't pay her rent and, finally, after one more long, sleepless night on a sofa in the apartment of some people she barely knew, shaking and cramping up and terrified, she called the only person she could think of—her priest uncle, a man who had once had a drinking problem, and had beaten it.

Michael flew down the very same day, got her to a doctor, paid for a decent hotel room for her. She cried nonstop and eventually told him everything. He listened, and kept telling her that her life was going to work out just fine, and that we all do things we wish we hadn't. At the time, she had no idea just how well he knew that. She *did* know how much he disapproved of what she'd done, especially the abortion, but he never said she was stupid, or selfish, or sinful. He never asked her to go to church, or even to pray. He said God loved her, and she should just try to hold onto that idea, and that would be enough for now. Eventually he took her back to Chicago and never told her parents or anyone else what she had done—or even that he'd gone down there and brought her home.

All her family knew was that she came back. She had a really nice tan, her friends said, and seemed a little more . . . well . . . grown up or something.

11.

As she drove away from Villa St. George Kirsten dug out her cell phone and called the Winnebago County Sheriff's Office in Rockford. "Sergeant Daniel Wardell, please."

While she waited she realized Dugan was right. If she was only providing security, there was no real necessity to talk to the cops investigating the murders. But she was in it now, and she couldn't help wanting to know more about the killings . . . and the killer. It might help her protect Michael. Besides, Wardell probably wasn't in, and if he was, he probably wouldn't—

"Wardell here."

She introduced herself and he seemed willing to talk to her. She said she thought maybe the state police would have taken over the case by now.

"No way," he said. "Those guys would drag a body across the road to get it *out* of their jurisdiction. This one's mine."

She was fifty miles away, but the body count was growing and she didn't want to waste time. So she pressed him and he said he'd meet her at ten o'clock, at a Dunkin Donuts near the sheriff's office.

At five after ten, Kirsten walked into Dunkin Donuts just as two cops in uniform were leaving. A slope-shouldered, heavyset man in a rumpled gray suit sat in one of the place's two booths, nursing a cup of coffee. She was sure the lone patron was Wardell, but neither of them acknowledged the other. She ordered coffee and corn muffins at the counter, feeling his eyes on her the whole time, and then took the cup and the bag with her to the booth. He didn't stand as she slid onto the seat across from him, just nodded and lifted his hand in a sort of vague salute. He was fiftyish, with intelligent eyes and a confident, world-weary demeanor. She'd worked with lots of cops, and she could pick out the good ones. Wardell was one of them. She showed him her ID and thanked him for seeing her.

He said he promised Larry Candle he'd talk to her if she asked, because he appreciated what Larry had done for him. "Twenty years ago," he said, "I was a Cicero cop and my career was in the toilet. He saved me."

She shook her head. "I haven't heard that many favorable stories about Larry. What happened?" She asked because Wardell seemed to want to tell her about it, and it was a way to get the conversation started.

"I'll make it the short version," he said. "It's three A.M. one night and I'm solo and I pull over this drunk who's driving half on the sidewalk. The guy's belligerent and tries to pop me one. He missed, but I was young and stupid and I totally lost it. Beat the shit outta the mope. Turned out later he was mob-connected, but I didn't know that. So I rough up my uniform and rub dirt on my face and call for backup, and we take him to the E.R. to get him patched up first, and then to the station and charge him with resisting arrest and battery of a police officer. The usual. The next day, though, he's got witnesses. Two guys, also low-level Outfit, saying they were in a car behind me. Total bullshit, but they claimed they saw it all. I was going down for sure, but one of my buddies was a cousin or something of Larry Candle. The guy was mostly an ambulance chaser but he had got my buddy out of a jam. So I went to see him. I'd have swore he stepped out of a cartoon, but he got the job done for me, too."

"Really," Kirsten said. "Larry doesn't strike me as having . . . I don't know . . . a keen legal mind."

"Yeah, well, he fucking saved *my* ass, pardon the expression. The mayor of Cicero at the time—not the woman who went to jail—but one of the ones before her, he was supposedly mobbed up, too. And Larry claimed he knew somebody who knew the mayor. All I know is, pretty soon the police brutality charge got dropped, the charges against the mope got dropped, and everyone was happy. Except that Larry . . . ah . . . *suggested* I better leave the Cicero department. So here I am. Best move I ever made."

"Damn," Kirsten said, "just when I think I have Larry Candle figured out—like he's an obnoxious, little loudmouth shyster—I discover some new something he's done that I hadn't—"

"Uh-huh." He looked at his watch. "I don't have a lotta time, y'know?"

He told her that after Larry Candle's call he'd checked her out through some contacts he had . . . Chicago cops. He didn't say what responses he got, but they must have been at least halfway favorable, because he agreed to share "a few of the facts" with her "off the record," things not given to the media about the killing of Thomas Kanowski on I-90.

She had the clear impression that as they spoke he was trying to make up his mind how far he could trust her.

He said his supervisors were stressing the lack of similarity between his case and the murder of the ex-priest Stanley Immel in Minnesota. "Still," he said, "some people—including *you*, or you wouldn't be here talking to me—think the two killings are connected, and that they're just the beginning." He paused. "Some people also think the priests on that list are animals and deserve whatever they fucking get." He leaned toward her, staring. "Guess you don't feel that way, huh?"

"My feelings, and yours," she said, "aren't on the table." She leaned forward then, too, and kept her eyes fixed on his. "Some cops—including *you*, or you wouldn't be here talking to me—do their jobs the best they can, Sergeant Wardell, regardless of their feelings."

She waited, and finally he nodded, just slightly. "The name's Danny," he said, and leaned back in his seat.

She did, too.

12.

The Minnesota killing," Kirsten said, "Stanley Immel. That was a stabbing, right?"

"Don't have all the written reports yet," Danny Wardell answered, "but 'carving' sounds more like it. Victim stripped naked and tied to a kitchen chair, then sliced repeatedly with a large knife. Skin hanging off in strips. Bled to death." He paused. "Oh, the guy had a small dog, some kind of mutt. Dog got it, too, but not the same treatment. Just laid out on the kitchen table and smothered under a sofa cushion. The thing is, although it beats the shit outta me how they can tell, they say the dog was done before the *man*."

"God," Kirsten said, "he made the victim watch his dog die first." She put down the corn muffin she'd been buttering and took a deep breath. "But anyway, Kanowski's murder was brutal, too. So that's a similarity."

"Murder's *always* brutal, but these two were very different. Kanowski died of a bullet through the brain. Entering at the back of the neck, angling up and exiting out the top of his forehead." He demonstrated with his hands. "Except by that time he had no forehead, because it was blown away. No slug found. Weapon probably an automatic, maybe nine millimeter, possibly silenced. I say that because he was probably shot not far from where he parked his car at the rest stop, and even if there were no other cars there at that time of night, it would have been risky to fire a gun. The trail isn't entirely clear, but it seems the body was dragged about thirty yards to an area not visible from the parking area, then laid out on its back and cut up with some kind of knife."

"The mutilation was post mortem?" she asked.

"Doc says no question."

"Was there any . . . you know . . . pattern to the cutting?"

"Pattern?" Wardell shook his head. "Whoever it was opened the victim's jacket and shirt to expose his skin, pulled his pants and underwear down to his knees, and went to work. Throat, chest, stomach, lower abdomen, down to and including his genitals. No pattern. Not the sort of careful strips it sounds like there were in Minnesota. Just a mess of blood and organ tissue all over."

"With the victim already dead," she said, "so he couldn't suffer any more, anyway. And maybe the killer's in a hurry because it's a public place and just slashes away, maybe to make a statement, and then takes off."

"Maybe, but they're not the same."

"Even so," Kirsten said, "there's the stripping of both victims, and an expression of a certain . . . hostility, toward both."

Wardell shrugged. "I'd say so."

"If the killer was waiting at the rest stop he must have known Kanowski would stop. Maybe they were meeting there."

"Maybe," Wardell said. "Or maybe the killer followed him there from somewhere. Or maybe they were two ships bumping in the night."

"He lived near Rockford, right? With . . . what, an aunt?" The sergeant lifted his cup and nodded, and Kirsten went on. "He was

61

on the southbound side of the interstate, just inside Illinois and coming out of Wisconsin. So, possibly on his way home. Any idea where he'd been?"

"You know I can't share the fucking fruits of my investigation." Wardell sipped at his coffee. "But it's no secret Kanowski worked maintenance at a factory in Rockford, or that he clocked out at midnight the night he was killed."

"So he wasn't coming home from a fishing trip."

"The body was found about five, and time of death was two to four hours prior." Wardell stared at her. "If you go north on I-90, there's a crummy late-night bar called Bunko's and two twenty-four-hour adult book stores along the road. About twenty miles. On the Wisconsin side."

"And if I had a picture and I went to these establishments and showed it around?"

"You might get nowhere," Wardell said. "Or you might get lucky and find out he was at all three places that night. But no sign of anyone paying any attention to him. Like . . . stalking him or something." Wardell crumpled a napkin into a ball and stuffed it in his empty cup. "I'm about out of sharing mode."

"Okay." She paused. "But . . . Emmett Regan? Not yours, but you heard about it?"

Wardell's eyes widened a bit, as though surprised she already knew of the murder of the third man from the *Sun-Times* list. "Heard about it, yeah. Body found in his apartment early today. That's all I know so far."

"Anything else I should know? I mean, before you're *fully* out of 'sharing mode'?"

"Just this," he said. "Another similarity between Minnesota and here—and Chicago, too, so far—is there's not one fucking sliver of evidence tending to lead anywhere. This bad guy is—or all of them *are*—either very lucky or very smart."

62

"It's one guy," she said.

Wardell checked his watch. "My wife's gonna be pissed as hell, and I believe I've repaid whatever I owed Larry Candle . . . and then some." He put his palms flat down on the table, hefted himself to his feet, and looked down at her. "You come highly recommended," he said, "and not just by Larry Candle."

He took a piece of paper from his shirt pocket, unfolded it, and put it on the table. It was a photocopy of a picture of a man, head and shoulders. It had that wild, disheveled look of a police mug shot, and had obviously been copied from a newspaper. "That's your victim," Wardell said. "If you show this, don't use my name. But I expect to hear about anything you turn up. Facts, impressions, anything at all."

"Count on it," she said.

He nodded, turned away, then turned back. "One more thing. If you're thinking of tracing Kanowski's steps over again? It's too late tonight, so don't even think about it. Especially Bunko's— people get hurt there. I myself wouldn't go near the place past midnight, not without backup." He smiled. "And I'm . . . you know . . . less *interesting*-looking than you are."

13.

When Wardell was gone Kirsten sat a few moments, staring down at the picture of Thomas Kanowski. Police don't like to share information with non-police . . . even ex-police. But Wardell had shared with her. A lot. Sure, Larry Candle made the intro, and some cops spoke well of her, but that didn't explain it. The explanation was that Wardell was working a homicide with no leads, and he wanted to solve it. He was reaching out, doing whatever he could that might bring in *something*. Whatever he'd heard about her was important, though, because it made him believe he could trust her, and that she might even be of help.

And maybe she could, but how? The various police departments surely suspected by now that they were faced with a serial killer. They could call in an FBI profiler—if they could find one not working twenty-five hours a day on terrorism. They could assign forensic experts to analyze and compare the tiniest bits of evidence taken from the three scenes and the three victims. They could share information with each other and with a phone book full of federal, state, and county agencies and offices and databases—by computer, at the speed of light.

They could do all that, assuming anybody *cared* enough. And even if they did, she'd be outside the loop—and no way Wardell or any other cop would get her inside.

So?

So, just as she'd told Dugan, to help Michael her focus shouldn't be on identifying and apprehending the killer. Her job was protection. On the other hand, she'd be most effective if she could figure out which priest on that newspaper list was the next target. The eighteen had already been whittled down to fifteen. Was there a pattern?

There certainly was a pattern in the sense that so far none of the victims had lived at Villa St. George. She had a copy of the list, but she hadn't asked Michael which ones lived there and whether he knew where the others lived.

What about a pattern regarding the type of abuse? The charge against Thomas Kanowski—denied, but proven in court—involved an eleven-year-old boy, almost certainly prepuberty and thus classic pedophilia. The charges against Stanley Immel—denied and not proven, although certainly possible—involved two young girls, probably both prepuberty and therefore pedophilia also. So what about Emmett Regan? Was it boys or girls? Pre- or post-? All of the above?

Meanwhile, though, she was very close to the Kanowski crime scene and she had a photo to show. And what investigators do best is investigate, not read tea leaves. She slipped her bag over her shoulder and went out to her car. She had "a crummy late-night bar called Bunko's and two twenty-four-hour adult book stores" to visit.

Stepping out into the cool, damp night air, she felt around in her bag for her cell phone to call Dugan. But no, it was late. He might be asleep already. She dug out her car keys instead and hit the button to unlock the door, then stopped and stared. The Celica was parked right under a light in the lot. But something seemed—

Damn! The right rear tire. Flat. How could it go flat just sitting there? Had some idiot asshole punk let the air out? She squatted down beside the wheel. The valve looked fine. And then she saw the hole, right in the wall of the deflated tire, near the metal rim. A puncture, like an ice pick would make.

Her breath froze in her throat, and a bone-deep chill and a clammy sweat broke over her body simultaneously. She stood up and whirled around, looking in every direction, hand wrapped around the Colt .380 in her purse. The two clerks were clearly visible inside the doughnut shop, talking and giggling. A car passed by on the street, then another one going the other way. Otherwise, nothing.

She pulled her raincoat close around her. Idiot asshole punk? Possibly. But the muscles tightening around her heart questioned that, said maybe it was someone who *knew* her. Maybe someone who had promised her HERE I COME. Someone who had called her and said nothing, then painted a blood-red target on her door.

She didn't know how long she'd been standing there when a couple of sheriff's officers pulled up in a squad car. Kirsten managed to stop them in their dash for coffee long enough for them to tell her about an all-night truck stop out near I-90. Not that she couldn't change her own damn tire, but it was drizzling now and she wasn't about to. She went inside and called.

By the time a tow truck finally arrived the rain was pouring down. She finished her coffee and a second glazed doughnut— God only knew how many grams of fat—and watched out the window as a black man, in a yellow hat and slicker, changed her tire. He came inside, smiled, and said she could either pay him on the spot and go on her way, or follow him to the truck stop and buy a new tire.

"I'll buy a new one."

His smile widened. "That's the smart thing. You don't wanna be driving around without a spare. And you can't fix the bad one, either. You run over a nail and I'll put in a plug that'll outlast the rest of the tire. But a hole in the sidewall? No way."

She figured anyone who could change a tire in five minutes in a hard cold rain and not lose his smile knew what he was talking about. She followed him, bought a new tire, and had them check the spare. She took the punctured one with her, too. This time, overreaction or not, she *would* go to Renfroe Laboratories . . . with the tire and the postcard both.

By the time she filled her tank with gas and paid for everything, it was midnight and still raining, although now it was back to a drizzle again. She was dog-tired and emotionally drained, and hyped up on coffee. She was also ninety miles from home. She sat in the car and used the cell phone to call Dugan. It rang about five times and he finally picked up.

"Is that you?" he said.

"Your favorite wife," she chirped. She could tell she'd woken him up, and she didn't want him to lose more sleep than he had to. "Just called to say I'm way out in Rockford and I don't feel like driving home in the rain, so I'm gonna find a motel and crash, and drive back in the morning. Everything's fine. No problem. Don't worry. See you tomor—"

"Kirsten."

"What?" She didn't like his tone.

"You're not telling me the truth."

"No, really. I'm in Rockford." Chirping again. "I had a flat tire and it's late and—"

"Not about that. I mean about 'everything's fine' and 'no problem' and the rest of that bubbly bullshit. What happened?"

"Jesus," she said, "aren't I entitled to have a secret? Maybe I've taken a lover."

"Uh-huh," he said. "I hope he hasn't forgotten his Viagra. Now tell me, what's going on?"

"Okay, I give," she said. "I had a scare, but it may have been all in my mind. Anyway, it's over and no one's hurt or anything. I'll tell you about it, but tomorrow, all right? Honest. Right now I'm beat, and I'm gonna crash."

"Good. I believe you."

"And you're not gonna worry, right? Because—"

"G'night, Kirsten. See you tomorrow."

"Love you, too." But he'd already hung up.

Kirsten meant what she'd said about calling it a day. She left the truck stop and drove around until she was certain there was no one following her and then went to a Holiday Inn. But when she got there she didn't even go inside.

Besides, she knew the *real* reason she didn't feel like driving twenty miles north and showing Thomas Kanowski's picture around wasn't because she was tired. It was because she was nervous. No, make that afraid. Not of the clientele she might run into at a dingy bar and a couple of porno stores in the middle of the night, but afraid of something . . . some *person* . . . entirely unrelated.

Unless her punctured tire was random vandalism—which she didn't believe for a minute—someone must have been tailing her all day: from home to the train station, the Art Institute, Dugan's office, the seminary, and all the way to Rockford. And she'd never spotted him. What bothered her even more than her carelessness, though, was that now she *had* been careful, and *knew* there was no one behind her . . . and still she wanted to hide away in a safe place. Which is why she had to go forward, tonight.

Because she would not allow herself to be shut down by fear. Not tonight. Not ever.

14.

It was past midnight when Debra pulled into a motel south of Rockford. She paid cash and went to her room. By later that day, Wednesday, they might finally connect the three deaths and roll out the term "serial killer." But there was *such* a difference between her and some psychotic, compulsive killer, one driven by secret voices or bizarre sexual urges.

Debra heard no voices, and even if she did feel a deep, delicious stirring with each kill—all that blood, the torn flesh, who *wouldn't* feel something?—hers was no compulsion. Hers was a free decision, made under Divine urging, to take action against evil, to even the scales for the terrible, secret suffering those priests had caused. And for Debra there was something else. Every dead priest led her closer to the bitch.

Debra knew she had God-given gifts that not many people had. Among them, she was able to distinguish between the significant and the incidental, and so knew where to keep her focus. For example, she had recently been distracted by thoughts of revenge against the one who'd so horribly slashed open her neck and face that long-ago night, but she put such thoughts aside. That one had been but an ignorant girl, acting out of mindless fear . . . and the damage she'd done had been repaired. Debra would maintain her priorities: dealing with the bad priests and the woman.

Besides, God had shown again how he brought good out of evil, even out of the terrible wounds the ignorant girl had inflicted on Debra, and the disfiguring scars that followed. Deprived of medical attention, bleeding and in pain beyond measure, Debra had fled, and God had given her strength and wisdom. She made it to the compound in Sicily, where her great-uncle Umberto took her in. Umberto, her grandfather's youngest brother. Even in his old age he was ruthless and maintained his hold on his family. Still, he was no match for Debra.

Although secretly naming him *la capra* because he was a skinny, grotesque goat of a man, she'd quickly adapted to his perverse sexual desires. Umberto enjoyed her moans and gasps, no matter how artificial, reveling in her attention. She became his princess, and he made his servants cater to her. One of them, his driver, who also piloted his small plane, came to taking Debra on long drives in the country—"love drives," they called them, filled with fierce pleasures of which there was no need to fabricate—and he even taught her how to fly the plane.

Meanwhile *la capra*, filled with loathing for the greedy family that was anxiously waiting for him to die, was wildly generous to his newfound protégé, lavishing upon her large sums of money, all of which she wisely moved at once out of the country. And above all else, he helped her create her new self.

Most of the plastic surgeons studied her snapshot and promised to restore her to her former beauty. Debra, however, wanted more. She interviewed surgeon after surgeon until she found the one whose computerized predictions most pleased her. He was flown down regularly to the little hospital near Umberto's compound, bringing with him his staff and his specialized equipment.

There had been so many painful procedures. First to remove the scarring from her neck and her face, and then to give her the new look she desired. She became the new Debra, unrecognizable to her foes, and able to carry on. After that was accomplished, and before Umberto's paranoia could embrace her as well, she fled Sicily and came back home.

Yes, she'd been gifted, but being gifted was not enough. Debra knew that. One had to work hard, too. And she did. Her careful surveillance of Emmett Regan on Monday—before she'd helped him pay for his sins—had unexpectedly brought an answer to the problem of how to get close to the priest to come after Regan. She hoped she hadn't squandered her opportunity by not acting at once. But again, action without careful planning was dangerous, so she'd spent Tuesday working out the possibilities.

Even as she strategized, she kept up her surveillance of the bitch, and this brought its own rewards. The woman took her pervert priest uncle to visit her husband, and a new idea sprang up in Debra's mind, one that beared nurturing. *God was good.* And then the trip to Rockford to meet with the sheriff . . . that verified the woman's intent to seek to interfere, to insert herself into Debra's world. *God was very good.*

The punctured tire would keep the woman on edge, and tomorrow . . . priest number four. Already. Things were moving quickly.

Now, though, she needed sleep.

———

But she couldn't sleep. *It wasn't fair.*

Wide awake, Debra stared up at the ceiling in the dark. It was unfair that she had to lie there and relive an awful deed she had never intended. Unfair that she had to hear again the muffled whines and gasps, feel again the hopeless struggle for life, the writhing and jerking under her powerful hands. The sudden stillness.

It wasn't fair. She hadn't *wanted* to kill him, even when he lunged at her. That was his nature, his instinct. It was easy now to think of more humane solutions, but all she could think of then was that someone would hear and come to investigate before she could finish her work with the miserable Father Immel. But the priest's cute little dog—braver than the pervert himself—just wouldn't stop barking. She'd had to do a bad thing.

She consoled herself that out of every bad thing, even sadness and guilt, God drew something good. Always. She had run away in fear and abandoned her brother, Carlo, and God was using her flight to make her available to love Carlo back into wholeness. As a child she had been violated, over and over, and God was using her rage to make her into Lizzie Borden multiplied, taking the axe not to one, but to seven abusive fathers. Treating each of them according to His holy will.

"You must treat each priest according to God's holy will." That's what Sister Clare had said, that day way back in sixth grade when the other kids were complaining about the new priest, Father Lasorda, who was mean and sarcastic and smelled like ladies' soap. But Debra, the only one who knew just how evil this priest really was, said nothing. She knew Sister Clare would never believe such a terrible thing. *No one* would believe her. Not her classmates, because her family was so rich and so powerful, and she was so pretty and so smart, and they were all terribly jealous and hated her. Not her mother, because . . . well . . . she just wouldn't. And her father? He knew already, and he let it happen. So Debra had sat at her desk, wanting to scream out the truth but not able to.

"I understand, dear children," Sister Clare said when the children complained. "But remember, every priest bears the mark of the most holy priesthood, placed by God upon his soul. This is why you must treat each priest—including Father Lasorda—according to God's holy will."

A difficult teaching then for Debra, a child always waiting, always wondering whether this night she must lie again, speechless, breathless, under those whisper-soft strokes—tantalizing, terrifying strokes—from the man her parents embraced and called "Father." But a teaching that made perfect sense to her now. "Treat each priest according to God's holy will."

Perfect sense. And so she finally slept.

15.

Kirsten went to both stores, one after the other. If either night manager—first at Triple X Book & Video and then at Cupid's Den—thought it strange that she showed up after one A.M, he didn't say so, but both said they were too busy to talk to her. She put on her best cop face and, though her ID was private, they both gave in when she said she was assisting Sergeant Wardell. If that got back to Wardell and he objected, she'd just have to deal with it.

Both managers had other clerks assisting them, and had only a few customers poking around. She showed them Kanowski's photo and said it was a routine follow-up, and both insisted that Wardell's people had already followed up once, and that no, nothing more had occurred to them. Neither had known Kanowski's name, but each recognized him and said he'd been in the night he was killed, and they'd seen no one paying any attention to him. Even though she didn't ask, each manager said he couldn't reveal to anyone—not even police officers—what any customer bought. But both were quick to add that Kanowski never asked for kiddie porn, which of course they didn't stock. Never had, never would.

By the time she left Cupid's Den she was angry at the managers for pandering to weaknesses, angry at Dugan for not even *trying* to understand her uncle, angry at herself for not being able to share her deepest sorrow with Dugan, and angry at a goddamn world where people sliced the skin off fellow human beings. She was getting nowhere, proving nothing.

She was tired and frustrated and, she had to admit, still anxious about some silent, unseen presence watching her, even now, when she knew that wasn't possible. That's what a stalker can do to a person.

Bunko's was on the access road along the west side of I-90, easily half a mile from its neighbors on either side and backed up to what looked in the dark to Kirsten like farmland. A squat, concrete-block building with bay doors that were no longer in use, it must once have been a gas station or an auto repair shop. There were easily two dozen vehicles—about half of them pickups or SUVs—pulled up tight around the tavern like cowboys around a campfire. There was one dim streetlight on the road, and the only other illumination came from beer signs shining out through barred windows and a very tall highway sign about a half block away, visible from both directions. It said BUNKO's in huge red-neon letters, and below that, half as large, TAVERN, NEXT EXIT.

The rain had stopped and she parked far apart from the other cars and picked her way among the puddles on the wet, uneven gravel. At the door she took a deep breath and stepped inside. Forty or fifty people were crammed into a smoky, smelly barroom that was too hot and too humid, with stools and chairs enough for only about half of them. They were 90 percent male, most of them shouting and banging on tables. A few wailed along with some country and western guy who mourned from a jukebox that there weren't no jobs no more for us folks who are "all-American, born and bred." The bar ran along the left side of the room and she headed that way, her eyes filling with tears from the smoke— and maybe, too, from her own weariness, anger, and frustration.

The highway sign must have delivered some customers to Bunko's probably earlier in the evening, but right now the place had the feel of a neighborhood bar—and not a great neighbor- hood to hang out in. Some of these men probably worked hard when the auto plants were going full tilt and construction was booming. Right now, though, they were mostly drunk and seemed well accustomed to it, and not likely to be up and showered and on their way to work in the morning. Despite the ceaseless whoops of laughter, there was restless hostility in the air and the catchphrase of the moment had to do with "kickin' some god- damn Arab ass."

She was thinking how she'd been in dozens of loud, dingy places like this, mostly on police business, when she spotted two young women—girls, really, eighteen or nineteen and looking way out of their element in tight jeans and short jackets—come out through an open doorway under a sign that said REST- ROOMS. They hurried straight toward Kirsten, and she realized she was blocking the exit. As she stepped aside, a large man with an ugly grin grabbed one girl's arms and said something to her. She pulled away and spat something back at him, and the two girls went on past Kirsten and out the door. They looked scared.

The man started forward, clearly meaning to go after them, but Kirsten stepped back to the door and blocked his way. "Sorry," she said, "but they don't want to be bothered with you."

"What?" He stopped and took a step back and stared at her. He had small eyes and a greasy baseball cap turned backward, and he smelled like sweat and alcohol. She didn't move, and when he started forward again she raised her left hand, palm toward him.

He stopped. "Look here, bitch, you—"

But another big man—one of his buddies, she thought—pulled him aside and back into the crowd. The entire incident didn't take fifteen seconds, and that was the end of it.

She looked for some opportunity to get close to the bar without having to squeeze too tightly against some other body. No one spoke to her or even looked straight at her, but she sensed that most of them were aware of her. *Some broad. Not from around here.* Finally a skinny guy jerked away from his spot at the bar, one hand clasped over his mouth, and bolted toward the doorway to the restrooms, and she stepped into his spot. There were two men and a woman dealing drinks. All three were thirtysomething, and all husky and solid enough to stop most fights. All three ignored her.

Maybe she didn't look like a customer. Maybe she looked like a cop. She waved her ID at the guy who seemed to be in charge and finally got him to come over and say, "We just quit serving. We close at two."

"Good," she said. She showed him Kanowski's picture and gave him the "assisting Sergeant Wardell" line.

"I talked to them guys twice already. What I know, they know."

"Yes, but sometimes people later remember—"

"Not me."

She put two tens on the bar, laid her right hand on one, and slid the other over to his side.

He stared at the bill, but didn't pick it up. "That was a slow night," he said. "This guy . . ." He tapped a finger on the photo. "I didn't know his name, just he came in once or twice a week and sat alone. Drank too much." Which Kirsten thought was exactly the point of this dive, but didn't say so. "Anyway, yeah, he was here that night. I don't know when he left, but it mighta been when we closed."

"And you didn't see anyone with him? Or anyone watching him or—"

"Uh-uh. Wasn't hardly anyone here that night I didn't recognize. I gave the sheriff all the names I knew." He looked at his watch, and then at the ten under Kirsten's right hand. "I gotta get going."

"Not quite," she said. "Who else was here?"

"What?"

"You said there was *hardly* anyone you didn't recognize. So who didn't you recognize?"

"I don't . . . well . . . there were some college kids that I carded. Had a few beers and shots and left."

"Anyone else?"

"No. Oh, there was this woman said she was on her way up to Madison. Came in for coffee—which people do when they're on the road and it's late. Didn't stay long. Ten minutes, maybe."

"Was she here when Kanowski was here?"

"I don't know. Yeah, she musta been. But she didn't sit with him or anything. Just some woman. I couldn't even describe her. Glasses, under forty. Smiled a lot. I don't know." He paused. "That's all I remember. Okay?"

"Yeah, thanks." She lifted her hand and he put both tens in his shirt pocket and walked off.

She turned away from the bar and discovered that the other two bartenders, male and female, were emptying the place out— like sheepdogs herding the restless, noisy crowd toward the door. Trading curse for curse, insult for insult, smiling all the while, never touching anyone. And not giving an inch, but moving the whole flock out the door.

16.

Kirsten left Bunko's feeling like a stranger in a group of raucous, unruly friends. She'd had enough for one day, and she couldn't think of anything of real substance she'd accomplished. She wanted to go back to the Holiday Inn, and be left alone.

With the tall highway sign turned off the parking lot was darker, but there was still the dim streetlight out on the road, and headlights were going on as engines roared to life. Cars and pickups lurched backward, skidded, then spun around and splashed through potholes toward the road. They sprayed up gravel and fishtailed, then squealed as their tires hit wet pavement and caught hold.

Her Celica was where she'd left it, some twenty yards out. But no longer isolated. A Chevy pickup—perched high on oversized tires—was drawn up right in front of it, nose to nose. The truck's tailgate was dropped, and three guys were sitting on it, feet swinging, facing her across the wet gravel. They chugged from their cans and laughed at each other's comments, things she couldn't hear. But she could see they were waiting for her. The one in the middle was the punk she'd kept from following those two girls, and one of the others was the guy who'd pulled him aside.

She was one . . . and a woman. They were three . . . and men. Their collective judgment—to the extent they had any at all—was clouded by alcohol and who knew what else. Pretty soon this place would be deserted and they'd have her to themselves. Maybe just to degrade and humiliate her, verbally. But possibly something far beyond that. Whatever they *wanted,* that was the point. Or at least, she thought, that was the belief they shared.

Facing them, she felt a surprising sense of ease. This was no silent shadow, creeping in close to leave sly, disturbing messages and then melt away. Nor was this an unknown killer stalking men she wasn't sure she could help . . . or wanted to. No, this threat was simple, up-front, in-your-face. Of course it wasn't fair to take advantage of a drunk, or even three of them. But this had been a long, frustrating day, and here was a situation she could actually do something about—if she had to. She stood and stared at them.

Most of the cars were gone by now, but one of them stopped momentarily, its headlights catching both her and the punks on the tailgate. All three were large, maybe high school football players five or ten years ago. They'd put on a lot of soft fat since then, though, and gotten that much uglier—inside and out—and more convinced that somebody owed them something, for reasons they couldn't quite put their finger on.

The stopped car sped away and left her alone with them. They were still clowning around, screwing their baseball caps this way and that on their heads, until finally the one in the middle called to her. "Check this out, bitch!" Grabbing his crotch. "I know you want it."

This called forth whoops of laughter from his buddies. She

started walking again—slowly, but without hesitation—and as she drew closer they all fell suddenly silent.

She stopped ten feet from them. "Get in your truck," she said, her voice strong and even, "and drive away."

They looked at each other and then laughed again, but she knew she was making them nervous. She waited. Finally the crotch grabber tossed his beer can away and eased his butt off the tailgate. "Fuck you, cunt," he said, as though remembering who was *the man* here. "We got plans for you."

That gave a shot of courage to the other two and they jumped down, and one of them, the one to her right as she faced them, made a show of slowly unbuckling his belt. "Yeah," he said, "we're gonna have a party."

"That's a shame," she said. She took a step right at them and not one of them could resist the impulse to back up, though there was nowhere to go but against the edge of the tailgate. "Poor babies."

She took another step, this time as though to go on past to her car. The man with the loosened belt moved in and grabbed at her her . . . but he was way too slow. In one sweeping motion she pulled the Colt .380 from her shoulder bag and raked the barrel across the side of his head. He howled, and with her forearm she shoved him hard against the crotch grabber. They both stumbled and went to their knees. The third man turned to go.

"Freeze!" she said.

He stopped and turned back to see the .380 pointed at his face. "Hey, c'mon," he said, "we were just—"

"Flat out on the ground. All of you. On your faces. Now!" They all did what she said without a word, except for some weeping and moaning from the man she'd hit. "Don't move, not even a twitch." She went to the truck and with the butt of the gun smashed out the taillights on both sides.

She heard the door to Bunko's swing open, and turned and saw the bartender she'd spoken to. He didn't say a word, and she didn't either. She doubted he was a big fan of these mopes, and a call to the cops about a fight on the premises wouldn't be a plus for a dive like this. She checked the Celica to make sure it had no flat tires, then went back and stood over the drunks. They hadn't moved.

"I have your plate number," she said. "I can identify all of you. You shouldn't have touched me. That's sexual assault."

"Hey, nobody touched you, bitch." The crotch grabber again, still anxious to be *the man*.

"Know what?" she said, and crouched beside him. "You moved." She lifted her hand and slammed the butt of the gun down deep into his flank, below his ribs, into the kidney. When he got his breath back and settled down, she said, "You're the dumbest, so you get the prize. Sit up and take off your shoes and your jeans."

"What?"

She tapped him on the head with the gun barrel. "Shoes and jeans." He sat in the gravel and took them off. "And your shorts." He did that, too, and rolled his shoes and shorts up inside his jeans when she told him to. She took them and made him lie facedown again. "Evidence," she yelled across the lot to the bartenders. All three were looking out the door now. "Did you call the cops?"

"Cops?" the guy she'd spoken to called back. "Why? Is there some problem?"

"Not really. But if some creep with no pants comes looking for help," she called, "you give him Detective Wardell's number. He'll have my report, about how one of them stripped down and tried to . . . well . . . maybe you saw it."

"Maybe we didn't see anything."

"Maybe not."

Knowing they weren't about to call anyone, she turned and fired a shot into the sidewall of one of the pickup's oversized rear tires, then got into her car and drove away. She could feel the guy's wallet in his rolled-up jeans, and she tossed the whole bundle out into the weeds along the entrance ramp to I-90.

She might feel differently about it in the light of day, after a good long sleep. But right now? It seemed the most useful thing she'd accomplished in two weeks, and she felt pretty damn pleased with herself.

17.

Dugan took the call from Kirsten just before noon, then went out and told Mollie, his office manager, that he was taking the afternoon off.

"Uh-huh." Mollie looked up from a desk loaded with papers, mostly bills to pay, and shook her head. "But you'll regret it."

"Taking a few hours off on an occasional Wednesday afternoon isn't such a bad idea," he said. "Some people take actual vacations."

"I've heard rumors of that myself. Anyway, I didn't say it was a bad idea. I said you'll regret it."

"Why?"

"Because you always *do*. You took an afternoon off . . . what? . . . two months ago? And Dan Miller called in a great case. A radiologist rear-ended by a utility truck, as I recall. The victim's family called from the E.R. and you weren't in, and by the time you called them back the next morning five lawyers had been to the hospital sweet-talking them, and you lost the case. So you regretted taking the afternoon off. Plus, Miller missed out on his package."

Dugan's father had built up a stable of cops he used to pay—he called the payments "packages"—for referring clients to him, usually accident victims. Some, like Dan Miller, still referred clients after Dugan took over the firm when his father died, and Dugan still gave them their packages. That was against the ethical rules, unfortunately, although he had difficulty seeing it as much different from advertising, which was allowed. Nobody *had* to call Dugan, just because some cop suggested—

"Hel-lo-oh!" Mollie was waving her hand, trying to get his attention. "I said Miller hasn't sent us a case since then."

"I know. And maybe that's not so bad."

"Really?" Mollie's eyebrows lifted. "With all these bills to pay I should think you'd want every case you can get."

"I do, but I also don't want to lose my license over—"

"Well, well, well," Mollie interrupted, looking past Dugan and clearly wanting to cut him off, "look who's here."

Dugan turned. It was Larry Candle, with the usual grin plastered across his pudgy face. "Hey, Doogie pal."

"What've you been up to, Larry?"

"*Up* to? Just a morning of practicing law, my friend. Sat around the courtroom four hours, and when the clerk finally called the Crockett case I convinced Judge Raven to give us thirty more days to file a response to the defendant's bullshit motion. Now you can send the case out to some firm where the lawyers *like* to do research."

"Jesus, Larry, you could have spent just *one* hour looking up a couple of cases and filed the response today."

"Not my area of expertise. I do court work and settle cases. You acquire the clients and—"

"And settle cases," Dugan said.

"And I work all day," Mollie said, "while Larry goes to court and gossips, and you take half the day off." Mollie loved to complain, but she also loved the fact that Dugan paid her more than even some lawyers made—because she was *worth* it to him.

Her phone rang, and she picked it up and waved them on their way. Larry followed Dugan into his office. "What's up?" he asked. "Taking the afternoon off?" Dugan sat at his desk and picked up the phone, but Larry stayed in the doorway. "That means Kirsten's up to something, right?"

"I don't know, Larry. Does it?"

"She's looking into those priest murders, right?"

"I don't know. Is she?" He waved the telephone receiver at Larry.

"You want me to get my ass outta here, right?"

"I'd like that," Dugan said, "very much."

Dugan knew better than to question Kirsten's instincts because they were right so damn often, but he still had a hard time agreeing that the hole in her tire and the HERE I COME postcard from two weeks ago were related. She started talking about that the minute he was inside the apartment.

"Wait, wait, wait," he said. "First things first. You're stressed out. You need a nap. Let's go." He pulled her toward the hall to the bedroom.

"I don't need a nap, for God's sake." She yanked her arm away. "What I need is—" She stopped. "Oh. You must mean a *nap* nap."

"Yeah, I suppose you could call it that. Anyway, that's what *I* need. I've needed a . . . *nap* nap . . . ever since yesterday afternoon when you were nibbling on my *ear* ear."

"Poor thing." They started down the hall, she pulling *him* this time. "We better turn off the *phone* pho—"

"Please," he said, and pressed his fingertips against her lips. "No more. Don't we have some chablis in the kitchen?"

"It's fume blanc," she said. "But hurry."

"So you think this guy was behind you all day." It was two o'clock and Dugan sat at the kitchen table, savoring his corned beef and wondering, as always, whether anyone in the world but Kirsten ate radish sandwiches. "This, of course, after two weeks of doing nothing. But anyway, you think he follows you all the way to Rockford, just to poke a hole in a tire outside a Dunkin Donuts where police officers show up every five minutes."

"I'm saying it feels that way to me," she said. "I don't really know that he's been 'doing nothing' the whole time, and if I'm right he didn't just poke a hole in a tire. What he did was announce that he's watching me, and that not only can he walk right up to—or even inside—my office and steal a piece of my mail, but he has the balls to puncture my tire while I'm sitting just a few feet away, in a public place, talking to a police officer."

"But a detective, right? Wasn't this guy—Wardell, is it?—wasn't he in civilian clothes? So nobody would know he was—"

"His car was a clearly marked sheriff's patrol car, parked thirty feet from mine."

"So the bottom line is . . ." He paused, knowing she didn't want to hear it. "Whoever this guy is, he scares you."

"Not at all," she said. "He *concerns* me." Then she explained how she'd been threatened by three punks outside a bar after she talked to Wardell, and that she'd handled it—she didn't say how—and that that hadn't scared her, either.

"Congratulations," he said, "but I'd swear you told me you were gonna 'find a motel and crash' after you had the new tire put on."

"That's what I intended to do, but I couldn't sleep. Anyway, the point is, even though I can handle these things, it doesn't make sense to ignore a . . . a stalker."

"If there really *is* a—"

"I can't *prove* it, dammit. I just *feel* it."

"Okay, okay." He poured them each another mug of coffee and sat down again. "You know, I was just telling Mollie how long it's been since you and I took a vacation. We could go to . . . I don't know . . . how's Spain sound? Three weeks?"

"No way. First of all, you're already leaving this weekend for that trial seminar thing in—where is it?—Asheville? Second, if we went, we'd come back and—assuming there *is* a stalker—he'd still be here. Besides, this *other* wacko, this priest killer, he's not gonna go on vacation. By then he might have struck a fourth time—or a fifth. And sooner or later, you know, he'll be going after Michael."

"Okay, no vacation," he said, taking a pass on what he *wanted* to say about her damn uncle. "But I forgot about that trial workshop. I have to be there Friday night for orientation. Meanwhile, though, this is today, and Mollie graciously gave me the whole afternoon off. Maybe another *nap* nap?"

"I'm going to regret ever using that expression, I know," she said. "But anyway, I have work to do. Did you see the morning news? Or the paper? Was there anything about the Regan murder?"

"To take them in order," he said, "yes, yes, and not much." He consulted an imaginary notebook he'd taken from his shirt pocket. "Here's what I got, Boss. Victim found dead yesterday morning in his apartment, second floor of a two-flat. By a woman who comes in to clean every two weeks." He licked his thumb and turned an invisible page. "Talk of slashing and lots of blood. Word's out that the victim's a priest from that list. Neighbors pissed as hell at the building owners—who live on the first floor and are out of town—for renting to a pervert and putting the kids on the block in jeopardy. Victim often seen going in and out, but kept to himself. Police not speculating as to motive or suspects." He grinned and closed the invisible notebook. "How'm I doing so far, Mr. Wolfe?"

"Admirable work, Archie," she said. "But it appears that you've omitted something."

"Really?"

"Yeah. What about all the goddamn clues?"

18.

Kirsten drove and headed north to the seminary. She liked having Dugan along. She always did. She enjoyed his wondering out loud whether she'd ever get a *real* job, and she enjoyed reminding him she'd listed him with the state as an employee of Wild Onion, Ltd., and telling him she *might* one day make him a partner. But Dugan never seriously questioned her decision to follow her own path, and she never seriously entertained the idea of a partner, or anyone she'd have to answer to.

They had reached the seminary campus, and the drive to Villa St. George, when Dugan asked, "Is this an officially sanctioned meeting?"

"What are you talking about?"

"I mean . . . do the authorities even *know* about you? Don't these priests have to ask permission or something to go out and hire someone like you?"

"Not as far as I know," she said. "Anyway, Michael didn't say anything about anyone's permission. He just said he'd meet me and take me to his room to meet the others."

"How many others?" Dugan asked.

"He's got four or five signed on," she said. "Of the eighteen listed in the paper, ten of them live here. The other eight—well, five now, with three already dead—are living on their own somewhere."

"And all eighteen of them have, at one time or another, sexually abused children. Jesus."

"Not quite true. All of them are *alleged* to have engaged in some sort of sexual misconduct with *minors,* and someone has decided the allegations are credible. Actual proof is another—" She gave up. "We've been through all this before."

"Yeah, right."

"You didn't have to come along, you know."

"I came along to be with *you,*" he said, "not to make friends with your clients."

"Who said anything about making friends? Anyway, you can wait in the car. Or go for a walk." It was a beautiful fall evening. Cool and crisp.

"Are you kidding? Nothing but trees in every direction, and the sun going down any minute. God knows what's creeping around out here in these woods."

"I know," she said. "That's what Michael and the others are afraid of, too."

"Yeah, well, that's different. They brought it on themselves." He was making her regret bringing him along, after all. "I mean, they deserve—"

"They deserve what? To be tortured and murdered?"

"Anyway," he said, "I'm coming in."

They followed Michael down a corridor on the ground floor of the building to his room, and Kirsten was surprised to find so many people there. Eight men—nine, including Michael—all in sport shirts and black pants, standing around chatting with each other. As they became aware of her presence, they turned her way and conversation gradually died out. Most of the men held glasses in their hands. It was six o'clock, cocktail hour.

It was hardly Bunko's, but the room did smell of perspiration and alcohol; too many frightened men in too small a space. Luckily, there wasn't much furniture: a chest of drawers—the top now a makeshift bar with bottles and glasses, and a foam plastic cooler—a desk and two chairs, and, in an alcove to her left, a narrow bed. No TV, no audio system.

Beyond the alcove were two doors: one closed, probably a closet; and one open just enough to show a tile floor—a bathroom. Floral drapes were wide open on two windows in the wall opposite her. They were huge old double-hung windows, with their sills just a couple of feet above the floor, looking out on evergreen bushes, then lawn, then woods. The view was to the west, and the evening sun sent plenty of gold-tinted light into the room.

A stack of metal folding chairs leaned against one wall, and a chalkboard was set up on the desktop. The eighteen names from the newspaper list were printed on the board in two columns headed VSG and OUT. The VSG column had ten names, Michael's among them; the OUT column had eight. Both lists were in alphabetical order, with the names of the three murder victims—Immel, Kanowski, and Regan—crossed out.

Michael introduced her as his niece, the private investigator he'd told them about, and made a half-hearted joke about nepotism. He suggested they all sit down and the men milled around, replenishing drinks and setting up chairs. Finally, after they were all seated, Kirsten asked Dugan, who'd been leaning against the doorjamb, to open a window. He went across, unlocked one window, and tried to raise it, but he couldn't get it open more than a few inches.

"I could never get the bottom parts of either window open at all," Michael said. "But try the top half. It's a little easier."

Dugan ignored him and Kirsten smiled as he struggled with the window, knowing he'd tear every muscle in his back and shoulders before he'd take advice from any of these guys. He got it open another inch or two before he gave up, then he went and sat on the edge of the desk beside the chalkboard.

"Oh," Michael said, "I forgot to introduce Dugan. He's Kirsten's—"

"He's one of my operatives," Kirsten said.

Michael nodded and sat down with the others, but she stayed standing—near the door so she could see out the windows—and they all adjusted their chairs to face her. The room was hushed now, and she felt a strange awkwardness in the air. Maybe because these priests, men who lived apart from women, found themselves suddenly this close to one, asking for help. Or maybe because they were outcasts who aroused nothing but disgust and hatred in just about everyone, and wondered why they should trust this woman to be any different.

Four of them seemed Michael's age, sixty-something; the others in their fifties or late forties. Mostly gray-haired or balding. There was one light-skinned African-American and the rest were obviously of European ancestry. They were a bespectacled, bookish-looking group and, except for Michael and two others, they were overweight—one of them quite obese.

She gave them a rundown of her background and qualifications, and then gestured toward the chalkboard. "I take it," she said, "that the people listed under VSG all live here."

"Yes," Michael said. "Five of the ten of us have decided for sure we want to hire you, and we'll pay. One of that five is in the hospital in Waukegan with a kidney stone, but he wants to be a part of it. Three are undecided, and two aren't interested. But—"

"Not interested in *paying*, I guess," Dugan cut in, "but they're here with the rest of you."

"Some of us don't have any money!" That came from the heaviest of the men, his voice high and shrill. "And we don't even know yet what you're promising." That brought a sudden chorus of discussion and disagreement, mostly about how much it would cost.

"Hold it!" Kirsten glared at Dugan, who she wished would keep his damn mouth shut, and then at the priests. "I'm not here to sell myself, for God's sake. My uncle says you all know my rate, and tells me he has commitments enough to meet the cost." Which wasn't really true. "So I'm on the case already, until I decide differently. It's not my problem how much comes from any individual, or whether everybody pays. Someone wants a free ride, or thinks I'm not worth it, that's up to him. So forget all the cost bull— All the cost stuff. Okay?"

"The thing is, we don't really know you." It was the fat guy with the shrill voice again. "You might make things worse and . . . well . . ." He paused, then said, "But you know what? We don't have a lot of choices here. There's a madman out there with our names on his mind. I mean . . . we have to trust *someone*. So, I guess, count me in."

"Fine," Kirsten said. "First, we're assuming the three murders so far are connected, since all the victims were on the same list you're on. Second, we're assuming the killer isn't finished." No one said a thing, and she went on. "So far, he's only gone after men that don't live here at Villa St. George. That *could* be because he knows the seminary has a security force."

"But only one man on patrol between midnight and eight A.M.," somebody said, "and as far as I—"

"It *could* be the presence of security," Kirsten went on, "or it *could* be that there's some pattern, some system dictating the order the killer's following, and that you've just been lucky so far."

"Plus, we all go *off* the grounds on occasion," Michael said, "some more than others. So we're all vulnerable until they identify and catch whoever it is."

"The police are working on that," she said. "But just as important, until he's caught, is for each of you to take whatever measures you can to avoid being the next victim."

She went on to tell them there was safety in numbers, not to leave the building alone if possible, to be careful when they left the seminary grounds altogether, and to be especially cautious at night, wherever they were. "To the extent possible, you ought to stay right in this building at night. I understand your rooms are all on ground level, along this side of the building."

They agreed and pointed out that they had an eleven o'clock curfew they were supposed to keep, and it struck her that even though they weren't locked in, it *was* a little like being in jail. They said other groups used the facility during the day for retreats and conferences, so people came and went, and that made everyone feel safer. But nights were a different story. Even though some of the retreatants stayed overnight, they were housed in a separate wing of the building.

"Our corridor can be kept locked from the inside," Michael explained, "but there are several entrances, and people are sometimes careless. Plus, we're on the first floor and there are windows like these in all our rooms." He gestured toward the window Dugan had struggled with.

"I understand, and I make no guarantees," Kirsten said. "But I'll tell you this, if I were you I'd feel very safe from sunset to sunrise inside this building."

"I'm sorry, Kirsten," Michael said, "but none of *us* feels that way."

"It's true, though. Starting, actually, last night." That got their attention, but she ignored their comments. She made a point of looking out the window. "I'd say it's about sundown now, wouldn't you, Michael?"

Along with all the others, Michael twisted around toward the windows. "Yes," he said, "just about." The sun had dropped below the trees, and it was getting pretty dark outside—and in the room, too.

Kirsten flipped up the wall switch beside her and a bright overhead fixture lit up, and all heads turned back to her. "I've arranged for additional security for this building at night. Did anyone notice anything last night?" They all said no, and she said, "Good. My man prefers it that way. But he was there."

"If there *was* someone out there," Michael said, "wouldn't he be more effective in keeping someone away if he's open and obvious?"

"Except," Kirsten said, "there are *two* things I want to do here. One is to keep you safe. The other is to *catch* this maniac if he shows up. My people will stay hidden."

"But how do we know anyone's really out there?" someone asked. "You could just be—"

"Turn and look," she said, and switched off the light again.

They all turned and of course saw nothing at first, until, rising up outside the slightly open window, the head of a man slowly appeared. As he stood up it was obvious he was a very large man. He put one black-gloved hand under the edge of the window to lift it higher and, like Dugan, ran into resistance.

"That's as far as it'll go," Dugan called.

The man let out a sharp sound—Kirsten was sure it was "fuck," but as though barked by a huge dog— and with both hands he raised the window all the way up. Then he stuck one huge, black-booted foot in over the sill, and came into the room with a smooth quickness that surprised even Kirsten.

19.

It was just about sundown when Debra parked on the street a couple of blocks away from the building and walked back. It had been a long day, and there was more to come. At least there was if God was with her.

She went inside, through the lobby, and on toward the elevators. She walked as one with a purpose in mind, not stopping at the desk for a pass. There were people everywhere, but no one challenged her or paid much attention to her at all. She wore a business suit and carried a leather attaché case under her arm, and she had a smile for anyone whose eye she couldn't avoid.

This was her third visit. The first had been on Monday, two days ago, when she'd been following the pervert Regan and he had led her here. Then earlier today she'd come back for another look and to locate the stairwells and the exits. Riding up on the elevator, she kept her smile in place. She could feel her heart beating. So many people around. This was the sort of risk she hadn't taken until now. But if she was to complete her work, and in the order Divine Wisdom itself had revealed, she might not get a better opportunity for a long time—time she couldn't afford.

The elevator stopped, and she got off and headed down the corridor. Not so crowded here, of course, though people were still coming and going. She knew well that courage and foolishness were not the same thing, but if there was any realistic opening she would seize it. She hoped to take him with her—something she hadn't considered with Father Kanowski—and carry out the job where she could do it properly. And if she could do that, she would leave behind a sign that she had taken him, so that the order she was following in these purgings would be ascertainable. That was crucial.

His name was in the slot on the door. She pushed it open and went inside. There was no one there. Disappointing, but God's will—not hers—be done. She turned and went out into the corridor again, and started back toward—

"Excuse me, ma'am." It was a woman. "Can I help you?"

Debra desperately wanted to keep going, to pretend she hadn't heard. But that had its own risks. She stopped and, fixing her smile wider than ever, turned around.

Five minutes later, riding down on the crowded elevator, Debra was tempted to exit at the lobby and head straight for her car. The woman had seen her! Looked right into her face. Still . . . she was an old woman, and obviously not very bright. She had no idea who Debra was and couldn't possibly identify her unless she'd already been caught . . . and then she would have failed anyway. She'd taken a huge chance by telling the old woman who she was looking for, but God rewarded bold courage.

Everyone else got out at the lobby and Debra rode down to "LL1." She found the snack bar where the old woman said she would: past the main dining area, around a corner, and halfway down to the next corner. It was a small room, with a wall of plate glass separating it from the corridor. There were several round tables, and vending machines for soda, coffee, snacks, and sandwiches. And there he was, her reward for not losing her nerve.

He was the only person in the room, seated at a table near the door, drinking Diet Coke from a plastic bottle and looking down at a newspaper. About her height, she thought; a thin, delicate-looking man. When he reached for the bottle she noticed he had unusually long, slender fingers. An artist's fingers, or a musician's.

She stood in the doorway and looked up and down the hallway. No one else was around. "Hi there, big fella." When he looked up he was staring right at the pistol pointed at his face, shielded from view through the window by the attaché case. "Do exactly as I tell you," she said, "and I won't hurt you. I promise."

20.

With the light back on and the priests settled down and facing her again, Kirsten introduced the man who'd come through the window. "My man in charge of security," she said, "Milo Radovich. But you can call him Cuffs." She turned to him. "Right, Cuffs?" She waited, but his only answer was a scowl, so she addressed him again. "Some of these gentlemen here were questioning whether you were actually on duty last night."

Cuffs Radovich was a rectangle, the shape of the window he'd come through, and seemed only slightly smaller. His black raincoat hung open over a black turtleneck and black pants. His black fedora was narrow-brimmed and looked too small for him. His face was dark and deeply lined, and a thick gray mustache drooped down along both sides of his mouth. He studied the priests in front of him like they were creatures in a zoo.

Finally he shifted his attention to Kirsten. "I'm not *your* man—or anyone *else's* man." His voice was deep and harsh. "And I don't give a fuck *what* these 'gentlemen' question. As long as I get paid, I'll keep their sorry asses in one piece."

An hour later Kirsten pulled out through the seminary gate and they headed for home. "Cuffs is always such a treat, isn't he?" she said. "I love the raincoat. And that fedora!"

"The only treat about Cuffs," Dugan said, "is watching people meet him for the first time. Are the seminary's security people happy about him hiding in the bushes?"

"It won't always be him. He's got another job going, too, so he's hiring guys to be there when he can't. Anyway, he worked it out with the chief of security. I guess he's an ex-cop Cuffs knows from somewhere."

"Uh-huh." Dugan shifted around in his seat, and she knew he was hoping to get some sleep.

"By the way," she said, "I really enjoyed that little act you put on." She laughed. "I mean, pretending to struggle with the window like that? So those priests would think Cuffs was super strong? Nice touch."

"Very funny," he said. "Why didn't you *tell* me he was already on the job?"

"Because you aren't interested in the case. You only came along to be with *me*. If Michael and those other men are tortured and murdered . . . hey . . . they brought it on themselves, right?"

"I didn't say that."

"I think you did, but let's not get into it."

"Right." He squirmed around some more, but was too large a man to get really comfortable in the Celica. Finally he said, "Those guys . . . the priests . . . they can really knock down the alcohol."

"Yeah . . . well . . . so can you when you put your mind to it."

"And most of them are overweight."

"Yeah . . . well . . ." She let that one go.

"I know, I know," he said. "I need to get to the gym."

"I didn't say that."

"I think you did, but let's not— Anyway, I was watching those priests, and I talked to some of them. After the meeting, you know?"

"Uh-huh."

"A couple of them are really oddballs," he said. "But some of the others, I don't know. They're scared shitless, but they seemed pretty . . . normal."

"Watch out, Dugan. Pretty soon you'll be thinking these are actual human beings."

"Just barely," he said. "You can't separate them from what they did. Disgusting, repugnant. And don't tell me the charges haven't been—"

"Michael gave me a list of the charges against each one," she said, "and what each one has admitted or denied. But the way I think about it? In my own mind? It's that every last one of them did exactly what he's accused of."

"Really. So why keep reminding me that not all the charges have been proven?"

"Because that's the truth. Just like it's true that way too many people are found 'guilty' of things they didn't do. But let's face it: a few of those guys might be innocent, but probably *most* of them are guilty. I know Michael is. And since I don't *know* about the others, I've decided to assume that they're *all* guilty and not try to kid myself about any of them."

"So why spend all this time and money on them? They'll never be able to pay what it's worth, you know." He finally managed to adjust the seat into a reclining position, and lay back. "I don't get it."

"I have my reasons," she said. "One, they'll pay *something,* hopefully at least enough to cover what I have to pay Cuffs and his crew. Two, I'm not in favor of maniacs running around torturing and murdering people, guilty or not." He emitted a sort of groan, and she went on. "And three, I owe this to Michael. And maybe . . ." She paused. There would never be a perfect time to tell him, and she might as well get it over with. "Maybe it's about time I finally told you why. It's . . . sort of a long story."

She paused again, holding her breath, but got no response at all. Dugan had fallen asleep. She let out her breath in a sigh . . . more of relief than exasperation.

When they got home they had one phone message. It was past ten o'clock and Dugan said to let it wait until morning. Kirsten would have preferred that, too. Instead, she listened to it.

"Kirsten, it's me . . . Michael. I couldn't find your cell phone number." He sounded out of breath. "Remember I said one of the guys was . . . was in the hospital? With a kidney stone? Carl Stieboldt. Well, the hospital just called. He's gone. Disappeared."

21.

Kirsten didn't return Michael's call. He had no cell phone, and the only phone she could reach him on was out in the corridor and would have woken up everyone.

The message had gone on to say that Stieboldt passed his kidney stone that afternoon and he was to be discharged tomorrow. "Except," Michael said, "they called. Asked if someone from here picked him up. I said no, and they said they don't know where he is, that he must have walked out. But he'd *never* do that. Not Carl."

Michael hadn't said the name of the hospital, but earlier he'd mentioned it was in Waukegan, a small city on the lake about forty miles north of Chicago, so she checked the phone book and found only two hospitals: Memorial and Queen of Mercy. She called Queen of Mercy because it had to be Catholic, and asked for Carl Stieboldt's room.

"Do you know the room number, ma'am?"

"No," she said.

"No problem. I'll check." There was a pause, and then, "I'm sorry, but I can't put a call through to the patient's room."

Since she wasn't told that they *had* no such patient, she hung up without objection. It was getting late, but she'd slept that day until nearly noon. So—over Dugan's objection—she packed a small bag and was back on the road in less than an hour.

At about midnight Kirsten stepped into the emergency room at Queen of Mercy Medical Center and was stopped at once by a security guard. She told him she was there to see a patient, Carl Stieboldt, and identified herself as Stieboldt's "representative"—which sounded more official than "friend." The guard was polite and said it was too late for visitors. She was equally polite and said she wasn't leaving. Finally she demanded to speak to whoever was in charge.

"Right now!" she said, when the guard still hesitated. "Or I'll file a complaint." With whom, or about what, she had no idea.

"Wait here." The guard stepped a few paces away, then turned aside and spoke softly into his two-way.

He turned back and invited her to sit on a nearby chair. She declined the invitation and the two of them stood there, Kirsten tapping her foot on the tile floor to show how she wasn't taking any shit from anyone when it came to her client's safety and welfare.

She had a growing sense, though, that it was a little too late for concern about Carl Stieboldt.

The interview room was small and brightly lit, and Kirsten sat at a tiny table across from Andrew Dexter, a nervous, likable young man in an inexpensive suit, whose name tag said ADMINISTRATOR ON DUTY. The room had only two chairs, so Doreena Brown, SUPERVISOR, SECURITY, a stout black woman of about forty, stood leaning against the wall, arms folded across her more-than-ample chest.

Kirsten showed her private detective ID and explained that she'd been retained to provide security services to Carl Stieboldt. She said she had assumed he would be safe within the confines of the hospital, then added that she certainly wasn't accusing the hospital of any misconduct. "At least," she said, "not at this time."

Dexter's eyes widened a bit. "I came on at eleven," he said, "and was informed that the patient was not in the house—the hospital, that is. He left without checking out. And AMA, 'against medical advice.'" He opened a file folder on the table before him and consulted its contents before speaking again. "The patient had passed a kidney stone, and Doctor Adamji wanted to examine him again in the morning before he went home."

"But he disappeared," Kirsten said.

"He's not in the house. When the patient didn't return to his room, and didn't appear to be on the premises, the administrator on duty at the time called . . ." Dexter consulted his papers again. "She called a Father Michael Nolan, whom the patient had listed as his next of kin. Father Nolan wasn't aware that the patient had left the hospital."

"He has a name, you know."

"Um . . . right." Dexter looked confused. "Father Nolan."

"No, I mean Carl Stieboldt. You keep calling him 'the patient,' as though he had no name."

"It's simply a way of speaking."

"I know it is." Like cops always speak of *the victim* or *the offender*, because names make things too personal. "I want to see his room."

Dexter pursed his lips. "Father Nolan said you might be contacting the hospital, and I was told that if you called tonight, I was to tell you to contact Howard Arnett in the morning. Mr. Arnett is—"

"But I didn't call," Kirsten said. "Instead, here I am, now." She paused. "Mr. Dexter, I guess you know Carl Stieboldt's a priest?"

"Of course."

"Are you aware that there might be a big problem here, about his disappearing?"

"A problem? I *do* know that the police were contacted about the matter. But I'm not sure why. It doesn't seem . . ." He turned back to his folder. "The police advised that an adult could come and go as he liked, and there was no reason for their involvement. Which sounds right to me. I mean, there's no indication of foul—"

"But you *do* have a folder about it."

"That's procedure for an AMA."

"Does your report say what Stieboldt was wearing?" Kirsten asked. "I mean when he was walking around."

"Really, I don't think I—"

"Humor me. What harm can it do?"

Dexter consulted his papers. "At seven-thirty the patient was dressed and up walking." He looked at her. "Patients—especially when they're feeling better—often don't like walking around in hospital gowns."

"I want to see his room."

"I'm afraid I'll have to draw the line there."

"Listen to me!" Kirsten stood up. "This man disappeared from *your* premises, while under *your* care. His listed 'next of kin' doesn't know where he is and tells you I'm his representative. It's my job to find him. The police don't want any part of it, so we're not interfering with them. You can come with me. Or Ms. Brown here can come. What's the problem?"

Dexter stood up, too. "Ms. Brown," he said, "would you step outside with me a minute?"

It was more like five minutes, and maybe they called someone or maybe they just talked it over, but when they came back Dexter said, "Ms. Brown will accompany you. The room hasn't been cleaned yet. You're not to disturb anything."

It was a private room, and other than Stieboldt's name on a sign on the wall above the bed there was nothing in sight that was personal to him. The two books on the bedside table—both paperback westerns—had HOSPITAL LIBRARY stamped on the title pages.

Kirsten opened the door of a small closet, then turned to the security guard. "Strange, isn't it, Ms. Brown? Wallking off without his jacket and shoes?"

"Happens all the time," the woman said. "Family brings them fresh clothes to wear home and they forget what they came in with. Plus, it's such a warm night. Probably wouldn't have missed the jacket."

The tan windbreaker, the only thing hanging on the rod, was marked size "S," and the shoes, well-scuffed black oxfords with the beginnings of a hole in one sole, were size eight. "Not a large man," Kirsten said.

"I really wouldn't know."

"What 'family' is there to bring him some 'clothes to wear home'?"

"I don't know that, either."

"The only 'family' he lists," Kirsten said, "is another priest, who says he didn't pick him up. Did he have any other visitors?"

"Listen, why don't—"

"No, *you* listen. Please." Kirsten was careful to keep her voice calm, conciliatory. "The hospital obviously has concern about his

110

disappearance, and I'm not saying you guys didn't do all you could. You called the police, who saw no reason to get involved. The thing is, no one knows where this man is, and morning might be too late."

"Too late for what?"

"I don't know, but it would sure put my mind at rest to know someone picked him up and he's all right."

"I have no authority. I can't—" She shook her head, but at least she seemed sympathetic.

"I don't want to get you in any trouble," Kirsten said. "I just need to know . . . I mean . . . what is it, one A.M. or something? Would there be anyone still at the nurses' desk who was here when Stieboldt was walking around?"

"Only if someone's working two shifts in a row. Which is possible. We're short-staffed. Everybody is."

Doreena Brown turned up a nursing aide named Clara Johns who worked seven-to-seven. She was a friendly woman who had to be over sixty, Kirsten thought, but was obviously full of energy.

"That father?" Clara Johns said. "A nice enough man. I hear people saying he had a problem once, y'know, with young boys. But I don't know nothin' about that. I guess everybody got *some* kinda problem."

"That's fine, Ms. Johns, but what I'm wondering about is possible visitors."

"Visitors? No way. Not at night, not when I'm here. He was only in the hospital a few days. Got that pain quieted down with meds, and then yesterday he pass that stone and I *know* he feeling better after that. Me, I wouldn't stay up in no hospital, neither, once I got to feeling better."

"So, last night," Kirsten said, "no visitors? Nobody came to see him?"

"Like I say, he never—" She shrugged. "Except . . . it *was* this woman by his room asking about him, but she wasn't a visitor. She from the insurance company."

"A woman?" Kirsten's heart picked up speed. "Did she talk to him? What was her name?"

"I don't know if she even *found* him. I told her he must be out walking around somewhere. Maybe downstairs by the candy machines, 'cause he had asked me where they were. If she said her name, I didn't get it."

"What did she look like?"

"Look like? I guess . . . like a woman from an insurance company. Tall white lady. Kinda big, but not fat. Big smile on her face the whole time. But definitely on business. Italian-looking, except reddishlike hair."

"How old?"

"Oh, I'm no good at ages. Maybe your age, maybe older. Hard to say. Not old, though; not like me." She laughed.

"She talk to anyone else?"

"Not as I know of. She just say thank you and turn and walk away. Last I seen of her."

"Did you tell anyone about her? I mean, like someone from the hospital administration?"

"Tell anyone? I mean, no one asked—"

"Clara Johns." The soft, disembodied call came from a speaker hidden in the ceiling. *"Clara Johns. To the nursing station."*

"You go ahead," Kirsten said. "And thanks."

The woman left in a hurry, and Kirsten turned to Doreena Brown. "You better make a report. I mean, you don't have to say *you* found Clara for me, if you don't want to. Just say I talked to her on my way out and that's what she said."

"Right. And . . . you better go now."

Kirsten had no real right to be in the hospital, and didn't want to press her luck. Besides, poking around in the candy machine area when it had been five or six hours since Stieboldt was there—if he ever *was* there—would have been useless.

Doreena Brown told her the shortest way to the hospital parking garage. She had to negotiate a maze of corridors and two elevators. Her mind was whirling. She didn't know Father Carl Stieboldt at all, but she didn't believe for a minute that he'd simply walked out of the hospital on his own, without explanation. Shoes or no shoes. Michael had *said* he wouldn't. She kept imagining a custodian with a mop yanking open a closet to find a naked, bloody man folded into the slop sink.

And who was that damn woman? Supposedly from the insurance company. Wasn't the Archdiocese of Chicago self-insured? Still, though, someone had to administer the program, investigate and verify claims. But going to a patient's room? In the evening?

She stepped out of the second elevator and went through a glass door into the garage. Her footsteps on the concrete seemed suddenly too loud—as though the floor were hollow. She stopped walking and listened. Traffic noises in the distance; a constant hum from what must be the hospital's ventilation system. It was three in the morning and there wasn't a living soul around. She was quite sure no one had followed her up here from home, but still she had to force herself to walk again . . . and not to run.

The Celica was down at the end of a row of parked vehicles, hidden from view behind that Ford Explorer. What if . . . ? But there was no flat tire. She got behind the wheel and slid the key into the ignition, then hesitated. What if . . . ? But the engine turned over and took hold and she wasn't swallowed up in a roaring fireball. She drove west to the interstate. There was a Motel 6 there and she got a room and called to tell Dugan where she was. Then she went to bed.

Nothing bad happened. Not to her, anyway. Not so far.

22.

By eight-thirty A.M. Kirsten was back at Villa St. George. She found Michael sitting alone on a bench overlooking the lawn, reading the morning *Tribune*. He said there'd been no word from Carl Stieboldt.

"Why'd he put you down as next of kin?" she asked.

"He's got no family except some cousins who live out of state. I'm the one who drove him to the hospital, and the woman there said he should name someone nearby they could call."

"You're a close friend?"

"We both love music. He plays the violin and I play *at* the piano. I may know him better than most, but he has no close friends that I know of. Well, maybe one. But not anymore. That is, he and Emmett were—"

"Emmett Regan? The one who—"

"Yes. They're both . . . you know . . . gay. I believe they . . . they saw each other fairly often."

"Really? Is that consistent with Stieboldt's remaining a priest?"

"I don't know that they were sexually involved any longer. Actually, I don't *know* that they ever *were*. I just—"

"Anyway," she said, "the hospital's suggesting that a friend or relative might have come and picked him up last night."

"Not possible. Even if Carl would ever leave against medical advice—which he wouldn't—I can't imagine who there'd be to pick him up. It obviously wasn't Emmett. He was . . . his body was found sometime Tuesday. You mentioned it to me, but didn't say who it was. It's here in the paper." He showed her the article, which included Regan's photo, and let her tear it out and keep it. "I suppose Carl *could* have called a cab," he said, "but that—"

"They suggested someone came, brought him a pair of shoes."

"Shoes?"

"When you took him in, did you bring along extra shoes or clothes?"

"Nothing. Let's see . . . this is Thursday. It was Sunday evening. Carl was in terrible pain, and he hadn't told anyone until he couldn't stand it anymore. I managed to reach my own doctor and he said it sounded like a kidney stone and to take him to the hospital right away. Carl was doubled over and crying from the pain, and I just grabbed him by the arm and dragged him to the car. We didn't go back to his room for anything. At the hospital they said they could get things like a razor and slippers for him."

"So he was there Monday, Tuesday, and yesterday. And sometime yesterday afternoon he passed the stone."

"You said something about shoes," Michael said.

"He was dressed and up walking around after supper before he disappeared. I suppose he could have been wearing hospital slippers. I checked his room and his shoes were still there, and a jacket, too."

"My God, what do you think happened to—"

"What I think is that you should call the Waukegan police and insist that they treat Carl Stieboldt as a missing person, try to get

116

them involved. Plus, you should notify the archdiocese. Maybe the cardinal can pressure the cops."

"I hate to say it," Michael said, "but my guess is the cardinal would be delighted—I mean, not to have something *terrible* happen to Carl—but to have him disappear. And to have one less of . . . of *us* . . . to deal with. Everyone wishes we'd just crawl back into the woodwork."

"Yeah, well . . ." She stood up. "I better be on my way."

"Wait." He stood, too, and started to reach out toward her, but then withdrew his hand. "I didn't mean *you*. That is, I'm sorry I got you into this."

"Look, Michael, you didn't *get* me into anything. Like I told you, I'm here because . . . well, because you were there for me when I needed someone. I owe you for that."

"I know. I wish . . . The thing is, when I helped you it was because I wanted to. And it didn't create any debt on your part. I appreciate what you're doing, but I wish . . ." He didn't finish.

"You wish I was helping you, not out of debt, but because I care about what happens to you. Well, I *do* care. I mean, maybe it's not like it was . . . before I found out." She shook her head. "It might be different if you'd told me yourself, I don't know."

"I should have, but—"

"Let's let it go, okay? It's over, and there are more important things to do than sit around talking about things we can't change."

She turned and left quickly, so he wouldn't see the tears in her eyes.

She drove back to Queen of Mercy Medical Center and at ten o'clock met with Howard Arnett in his office. He was a sharp-featured, bespectacled man and—given that he was the hospital's in-house counsel—surprisingly agreeable. He knew she had spoken the night before with Clara Johns, and he didn't complain about that. He told her he had already checked with the day shift and turned up one person, a nurse, who recalled Stieboldt having a visitor. "It was a man," he said, "and he was here on Monday. But she never saw him before and doesn't know his name. The shift changes at three, and I'll have someone speak with them, also. We don't keep a record of visitors, so it's a matter of someone noticing someone, and then remembering."

Kirsten asked about the woman Clara Johns said had been looking for Stieboldt, and Arnett thought it unlikely she was from the company that handled insurance claims for the archdiocese. "I've already got a call in to them," he said, "but I can almost guarantee the answer."

"You'll call me when you hear, though, right?" Kirsten asked. "And leave a message one way or the other?"

"Absolutely." He stared down at his desk, and at the business card she'd given him, as though trying to make up his mind, then looked up and said, "I know who Father Stieboldt is. That is, I've seen the news reports and I know—or I *think* I know—what the concern is here."

"Oh?"

"He's one of the priests on the list of sex offenders. And two of them have been murdered." It was actually *three* now, but she let that go. "The hospital notified the police once about him being missing, and I don't intend to call them again or to tell them their business. But I want you to know that we'll cooperate with them, and with *you*, to the extent that we—"

"Right," Kirsten said. "In the meantime, if I were you I'd have the hospital searched."

Arnett smiled. "Security is conducting a search as we speak. I'll call you on that, too."

"One way or the other."

"Of course." Arnett stood up. "I believe that's all."

"Not quite. I need to talk to the nurse, the one who saw the visitor."

"She's nurse manager of a double unit, and she's very busy. She doesn't know his name."

"It'll just take a minute. You can come along if you like. I want her to look at something." Kirsten pulled the folded newspaper clipping from her purse. "It may be a picture of Carl Stieboldt's visitor."

The nurse manager's name was Irene Delgado, and from the newspaper photo she recognized Emmett Regan. "It was, oh, about four in the afternoon," she said. "I'm supposed to be off at three, you know? But on Monday I stayed late because . . . well . . . that's a long story. Anyway, that's how I remember it was Monday. He came up looking for Father Stieboldt's room and I showed him. I don't know what time he left."

"Was there anyone with him?" Kirsten asked.

"Not that I noticed," she said. "But there were lots of people coming and going, you know. Staff and visitors alike." She stared at Kirsten. "Why? Is there something wrong?"

"Just routine," Kirsten said, as if she were a cop, and as if the answer made sense.

23.

Kirsten left the hospital and drove back to Chicago. She left the punctured tire, along with the postcard and the mail that came with it, at Renfroe Laboratories, and then went to her office. She was two steps into the little waiting room when she stopped, dead still. She looked around but didn't touch anything. She moved to the inner office door, opened it and again looked around without touching anything. Back out in the hall she called Dugan on her cell phone.

"It's no use," Mollie said. "He's in the middle of settling two cases. I try to put calls through and he won't even answer. I guess I could go down there and—"

"No," Kirsten said, "that's all right." She considered going next door for Mark Brumstein or one of his people, but it was Dugan she wanted.

When she got there Dugan had his back to her, looking out his office window with the phone to his ear. "Hey," she said.

He turned and waved her in, but kept talking into the phone.

"Don't be silly, Julie," he said. "My guy will prove he earned seventy thou, and if you prove he only reported thirty-five to the IRS, half the jury will ignore it and the other half will give him extra points. I mean, the guy's got five major fractures and a punctured lung, for chrissake. And three kids." He paused, obviously listening.

"Dugan," Kirsten said, "I'm in a hurry."

He grinned at her and, still listening to whoever was on the phone, gestured her toward one of his client's chairs. When she made no move to sit down, he just shrugged.

"Yeah, yeah, yeah," he finally said. "I know, I know. But if I don't hear from you in a week, Julie, I'm sending the case out to Milt Tunney to try the damn thing. You could lose big on this." He listened some more. "Uh-huh, love you too. 'Bye." He hung up, and at once his phone rang.

"Don't answer it," Kirsten said. "Period. We're getting out of here."

He stared at her, but he let the phone keep ringing and grabbed his suit coat from the back of a chair. "Yeah, I think a *nap* nap is a great i—"

"*Stop* that, dammit! I need you for something. Let's go."

On their way out Dugan told Mollie he'd be back "sometime this afternoon." Mollie just shook her head and they walked on through the suite and out into the corridor. Kirsten didn't like admitting it to herself, but she felt better—no, dammit, *safer*—in Dugan's presence. Not physically safer, exactly, but psychologically.

They waited for the elevator and Dugan said, "I know I shouldn't say this, but you seem . . . well . . . *scared,* or—"

"That's bullshit."

"I was going to say 'or *concerned.*' How's that?" She didn't answer. The elevator came and they stepped inside and rode down. "It's not too early for lunch," he said, as the doors opened onto the lobby.

"We're going to my office. I want to see if . . . if you notice anything."

It was a walk—actually, nearly a run—of only a few blocks and neither of them said anything on the way. At her office she unlocked the glass door but didn't open it. "I want you to step inside and close the door," she said. "Just stand there. See if anything's . . . unusual. And then come back out. Okay?"

"Yeah, sure." He went in and stood in one place and looked around.

When he came back out she said, "Well?"

"There's the odor, right?" She nodded and he went on. "It's . . . don't know if it's cologne . . . or perfume. But it's a pretty common smell. To me it almost smells like soap or something."

"But is it a scent I ever wear?"

"No," he said. "Maybe a cleaning person?"

"They only come in once a week. That'll be tonight." She felt a little better knowing he'd smelled it, too. She locked the door again. "Let's go get—"

"And the magazine on the table," he said. "The *Smithsonian.* Part of the cover's been cut off."

"You're right," she said, peering back in through the glass.

"So you think that's where the mailing label on your HERE I COME postcard came from?"

"I . . . I guess so."

"Is it possible the magazine's been there all along and you just overlooked it before today?"

"Not a chance."

"I believe you," he said, but she wasn't sure he did. "So then, how did it get back in there? You always lock the door when you leave, right?"

"It's not that great a lock. There's nothing in there worth stealing. But yes, I always lock it."

He took her arm. "Let's get some lunch."

She walked with him but doubted she'd be able to eat.

At the elevator he put his arm around her shoulders and pulled her close to his side. "You're probably surprised I got 'em both, huh?" he said. "The smell *and* the magazine?"

"Yes, I am," she said.

What she didn't say was that just twenty minutes earlier, when she left to get him and bring him back, there'd been no *Smithsonian* magazine on that table.

24.

ebra stood on the crowded sidewalk beneath the el tracks and watched the two of them come back out of the building. She was too far away to hear what they said, but she knew they'd been up to the bitch's office and found the magazine. The bitch was hiding it well, but she'd gone at once for her husband . . . and she was afraid. Debra smiled.

Fear was a darkness that had clouded Debra's days as a child, crept into her dreams at night. But as she grew older, the shadow of fear was slowly replaced by anger. And anger became rage that grew and glowed red, until the day came when, still in her teens, she struck for the first time to take her revenge. By then she felt no fear at all. And now, though determined not to be caught, she still felt none. Or none for herself, at least, but only for Carlo. He could not survive without her.

As she crossed the street a train roared past overhead and she closed her eyes against the grit and dust that fell from the tracks above. When she reached the sidewalk she turned and headed for where she'd parked the van. No need to follow those two now. God had already turned another disappointment into a blessing.

She had intended to take Father Stieboldt back home with her, where she could help him atone fully for the pain and terror he had inflicted. But he was cowardly, weak. While she was removing something from him to leave behind, to show that she had taken him and he hadn't just wandered off, his heart gave out and he died right there in her van. She'd been upset and angry at first, almost in tears. Then, though, she remembered that the pervert's premature death was obviously God's will, so something good would come of it.

And it did. With the pervert Stieboldt carefully wrapped in plastic in the back of the van, she'd had the time and opportunity to play with the woman's mind again. She'd very nearly been caught, too, but even then she hadn't been afraid. She would simply have killed the bitch on the spot if she'd had to. Of course, what a disappointment that would have been! One far greater than Father Stieboldt's too-hasty death.

Now, though, she had to drive home, feed the hungry hogs, and be all the way back by tomorrow morning. She had never felt stronger or more energized, and she would give these people no rest. Three priests still to go, and the woman, and time was growing short.

25.

At lunch Dugan started talking again about taking a trip some-where, but Kirsten made it clear that whatever this "here I come" business was about, the issue had to be faced. "Besides," she said, "I can't run out on my clients."

"Clients?" Dugan shook his head. "Those priests? A bunch of despicable losers who hired you by default and—"

"Stop, dammit!" She could hardly believe how angry she suddenly was. "Michael's my *uncle*. Someone wants to kill him. Don't you *get* it?"

"No, I don't '*get* it.' For one thing, you said you'd bodyguard him, and you've got Cuffs doing that."

"But that can't go on forever. Michael will never be safe until the killer's actually caught."

"Which is why we have police. Meanwhile, if you're so worried, send him to Idaho, or Ireland, or some damn place. I'll give you the money."

"Don't be ridiculous. What would he do somewhere else? He wants to stay a priest. Here. That's why he's putting up with being almost in jail, for God's sake, while he appeals to Rome. He wants them to let him act as a priest."

"Do you think he *should* act as a priest? Jesus, a child molester?"

"He did a terrible thing. But how can you keep saying he molested a *child?* What he admitted was having sex with a—" She gave up. "Look, I'm going to help him, whatever you or anyone else thinks."

"Kirsten, your uncle and those others, they created the problem they have. But you have a problem of your own right now. And you don't owe them, or your uncle, a goddamn—"

"You have no idea *what* I owe Michael." She should have woken him up in the car last night and told him about Florida. But right now she was too angry. "You just . . . you just don't understand."

"Maybe I don't," he said, "but this business of someone sneaking into your office is serious. You have to—" He stopped, then reached across the table and took her hand. "Look, I didn't mean to make you mad. You don't *have* to do anything. Not for me. I just don't want something to happen to you."

"I know." She felt her anger fading, as quickly as it came. She withdrew her hand from his. "But nothing's going to happen. I know how to keep my eyes open, watch my back." She saw the expression on his face and quickly added, "Don't say it! I know I didn't see anyone follow me to Rockford Tuesday. But . . . maybe that's because I was wrong. Maybe there wasn't anyone." She didn't believe that for a minute. "Anyway, I'll be careful, and I'm better off with someone else's problem—like Michael's—to worry about. To keep me from obsessing. Nothing bad's going to happen. Believe me."

"I guess I'll have to," he said. "And I'll also have to let you do what you do, because you're never going to change. But . . ." He shook his head.

"Yes?"

"Just don't expect me to like Michael . . . or any of those others." He waved at the waitress, asking for the check. "I don't even *want* to like people like that."

He clearly wasn't looking for a response, and she didn't give one. Those other priests, did *she* want to like them? She knew almost nothing about any of them. Only that they were priests who she had to assume had abused children . . . or minors, anyway. It was easy to despise them all. Of course, none of them had hurt her like Michael had. He should have told her what he'd done, right from the start, down in Florida. She could have absorbed it and then could have decided whether she still wanted to be his friend.

But he'd kept it from her. And now, though she *wanted* to love him like she had before, she couldn't. He'd been her hero, her friend, almost like a father. And now there was a gulf between them that couldn't be crossed. She wished she *could* cross it. She wanted her uncle back.

They went to Dugan's suite, and he gave her an empty office to work in temporarily because a crew from Renfroe Laboratories was already on its way to her own office. They'd check for signs of someone picking the lock, and they'd install a new one. They'd retrieve and examine her wayward magazine, and dust and comb and scrape the place for fingerprints, fibers, shoe residue . . . anything and everything. Renfroe even had some sort of new "sniffer" that might identify the scent. But she doubted he'd get anything more helpful than he'd get from the postcard she brought him earlier that day. Which, she was certain, would be nothing.

She would do everything possible to protect herself, short of running. But still, she wouldn't let her own concern distract her from Michael's problem. She dug into the folder with the information he'd given her about the priests. It consisted mostly of his own handwritten notes. One sheet held the same two alphabetical lists he'd put on the chalkboard in his room at Villa St. George:

VSG	OUT
Robert Carrera	John Ettinger
Anthony Ernest	~~Stanley Immel~~
George Henshaw	~~Thomas Kanowski~~
Michael Nolan	Warren Klick
Brian Rooney	Gerard Montello
Charles Smythe	Charles Murgeson
Carl Stieboldt	~~Emmett Regan~~
Aloysius Truczik	Kenneth Rembert
Robert Wren	
Curtis Wyeth	

She paused a moment, then drew a line through Carl Stieboldt's name, too. The only question was when and where his body would surface.

The *Tribune* article Michael had given her, the one that included Emmett Regan's picture, reported that Regan had been accused of unspecified "sexual abuse" involving at least ten teenagers, all boys. That was all Michael's notes said about him, too. Regarding Stieboldt, the notes said he had been accused of exposing himself to a twelve-year-old altar boy during a picnic. Stieboldt claimed he was merely changing into swimming trunks, and hadn't known the boy was nearby.

Kirsten thought a few minutes, then made a list of the victims:

#1 — OUT — 1-90 rest stop — shot dead, then stripped & slashed
#2 — OUT — Minn cottage — tied up, then stripped & slashed
#3 — OUT — Chgo apartment — slashed (tied up? stripped?)
#4 — VSG — Waukegan hospital — ?

Clearly, the killer was choosing to do his work away from Villa St. George. Stieboldt might not have been in the number four position if he hadn't been away from the retreat house. Since Regan was murdered Monday night or early Tuesday morning, the killer might have been following him when he visited Stieboldt at the hospital on Monday afternoon.

Still, grabbing a patient from a hospital, even during the evening when there were probably more visitors and fewer staff, was a greater risk than the killer had taken up until then. The previous three locations—a highway rest stop in the middle of the night, a cottage on a Minnesota lake in autumn, a second-floor apartment with an unoccupied first floor—all of those were isolated scenes.

She assumed the killer meant to search out the priests on the list and kill them all if he could. And though she didn't know yet where they all lived, for now she also assumed that at least some of the remaining five OUT targets were more easily available than a hospital patient. So what was it about Stieboldt? Why make him next in line?

There was also the matter of timing. The second murder was a week or so after the first, although the body wasn't discovered right away. Then Emmett Regan was killed late Monday night or early Tuesday morning. So, about a week between each one.

Then Stieboldt was taken on Wednesday evening, less than forty-eight hours after Regan. This rush to the fourth victim could be explained by a concern that he might not be in the hospital, away from Villa St. George, very long. Okay, but then why wait until Wednesday evening? Why not Tuesday? Did the killer need the extra day to plan his strategy? Or was he occupied elsewhere?

There were so many questions. But the most intriguing item was the woman who claimed to be "from the insurance company." Howard Arnett, the hospital's in-house counsel, had left word on Kirsten's voice mail that his search hadn't found Stieboldt, alive or dead, on hospital premises, and that the insurance claims people said they hadn't sent anyone to the hospital about Stieboldt.

So who was the woman? And why did she lie? Maybe she was a "chaser" searching out personal injury clients for a lawyer; or a thief, rifling through patients' rooms; or an addict, looking for narcotics. On the other hand, maybe she was an accomplice— unlikely for a serial killer, even if this one didn't fit Kirsten's understanding of the profile in lots of ways. Or she herself could *be* the killer—which seemed even more unlikely. Female serial killers were so rare as to be nearly off the chart of possibilities.

But the woman was certainly—

"Hey, hey!" Larry Candle burst into the office, and if he noticed Kirsten looking around for an escape route, he didn't mention it. "How ya doin', beautifolio?" She shuddered at yet another of his nicknames. "You catch that peeler yet?"

"Peeler?"

"Hey, I understand." Larry sat down in the chair across from her. "You gotta keep your business under wraps, kid. But I know you're after the guy who peels the skin off priests. 'Cause Danny Wardell told me you talked to him."

"Uh . . . Larry, I'm a little busy here and—"

"I mean, I called to remind him you *wanted* to, and he said you already *did*." A satisfied grin spread across Larry's pudgy face. "See? You need a little help, you just call on me. 'Larry Candle, the lawyer for the little guy.'" Kirsten recognized the slogan—catchy, if not very sophisticated—that Larry used to run in his ads. ". . . pretty scared, huh?" Larry was saying. His expression was grim now, which was unusual for him.

"What?" she said. "Why would I be scared?"

"I didn't say *you*, I said your uncle Michael, and the others, y'know? They gotta be peein'—I mean . . . petrified. You got Kanooski, Immel, Regan . . . and now Seebald."

"It's Ka*now*ski. And *Stieboldt*," she said, and immediately wished she hadn't. "Anyway, how do you know about—"

"It's been on the news. He disappeared from the hospital last night."

"Yes?" She could tell there was more coming.

"I like to stay on top of things, y'know? And there's this guy I know, works for the Waukegan cops. A civilian, y'know, but keeps his eyes and ears open. He told me what they found, and how they made the ID from the fingerprints."

"What . . . a body? They found a body?"

"Not really," he said. "Just a few of his fingers."

26.

Kirsten chased Larry away and got on the phone to the Winnebago County Sheriff's office. She waited a long time, but Sergeant Danny Wardell finally came on the line.

"You heard about the missing fourth priest, Carl Stieboldt?" she asked.

"I did. You got anything for me on Kanowski?"

"I went up to those porn stores after I talked to you. Nothing new. Then I went to Bunko's." She paused, then asked, "Anyone report an incident at Bunko's that night?"

"What incident?"

"Right," she said. "Anyway, the bartender told me almost everyone in the place the night in question was a familiar face— including Kanowski. The only strangers there when Kanowski was there were some college-age kids and a woman who stopped for coffee."

"I didn't hear about any woman. Told me no one paid any attention to Kanowski."

"This woman didn't, either. Drank her coffee and left."

"Stopped at a shithole like Bunko's for coffee?"

"It happens, according to the bartender. Someone's driving at night, gets drowsy, and stops at the next sign of life. Sign doesn't *say* 'shithole.' Anyway, she was headed north, to Madison."

"And he knows that because . . ."

"She told him," Kirsten said.

"Why would she tell him?"

"Why wouldn't she?"

"Is that it?" he asked.

"That's all on Kanowski. I've been checking out Stieboldt, though."

"Already? How—" He was obviously surprised. "Anyway, what?"

"Are you getting paper on *all* these killings? I mean, because they're related?"

"They're *possibly* related. But yeah, and you know I can't share that with you. What you got on Stieboldt?"

"How about just the medicals? Off the record?"

"I'll think about it. What you got?"

"First, a nurse's aide, or an L.P.N. or something, named Clara Johns, says there was a woman near Stieboldt's room looking for him not long before he disappeared."

"What woman?"

"Told the aide she was from his insurance company. I talked to the hospital lawyer, Howard Arnett. He asked the insurance company and they didn't send anyone."

"Jesus. A woman?"

"Yeah. Then I found an R.N. named Irene Delgado who IDs Emmett Regan as— You know, Regan?"

"I know, I know. Go on."

"Delgado IDs Regan from a photo as having visited Stieboldt in the hospital on Monday afternoon. The two of them were . . . friends, I guess. That's the afternoon before Regan was—"

"I know that, too." Wardell's impatience didn't surprise her. "What else you got?"

"What the hell?" she said. "Isn't that a lot?"

"It's not enough."

"How about those medicals?"

"You come up with anything else, let me know."

"Absolutely. I could even drive out there to pick them up. See your smiling—" She stopped. *Smiling?* "I just thought of something."

"Yeah?"

"It's stupid, but . . ."

"Lemme have it."

"Well, the bartender at Bunko's couldn't give much of a description of the coffee drinker. But he remembered that she smiled a lot."

"Uh-huh."

"And Clara Johns, the aide, couldn't describe the woman she talked to very well, either. Just that she smiled a lot. I mean, could it be—"

"Not likely. Is that it?"

"Those medicals?"

"I said I'd think about it."

Kirsten planned to stop at Mollie's desk on her way out. It never hurt to keep Mollie happy. She ran Dugan's office, after all, even if Dugan sometimes lapsed into thinking *he* did. Mollie was efficient and gruff, and forever busy. But like everyone else, she liked to be noticed, stroked a bit. Plus she was a nice person when you got to—

"Kirsten?" Mollie was already coming her way. "There's a fax for you."

Kirsten used Dugan's office fax number because there was someone watching his machine all day. The fax was from Leroy Renfroe, with an inventory of what they'd found at her office. Nothing.

At four-thirty Kirsten picked up her car and headed for the northwest side, around Belmont and Kedzie, where Emmett Regan had lived. By now the cops would have finished canvassing the block, and she'd give it a try herself. She told herself that surely *someone* heard or saw something.

Yeah, right. Still, it's what investigators do.

As she drove she tried all the news stations she could find, but there was no hard information about how Regan was killed, only that he was the victim of a "brutal attack." The media finally had the three murders linked together, though. And the new "breaking story" was the discovery of severed fingers from yet a fourth child-molester priest, in a plastic bag left in a mailbox near Queen of Mercy Medical Center in Waukegan.

She found Regan's street in a neighborhood of older bungalows, an area that had definitely seen better days. Gentrification was on the horizon, with skyrocketing home values, and few of the present residents would be able to pay the increased property taxes. The rich get rich, and the poor move over.

She found a place to park and walked to Regan's block. Right away she saw the cops. Three detectives in sport coats and ties— two white males, one black—spread out and going door to door. No one she recognized. Had it been *that* long since she left the department? She waited at the corner, figuring she'd spot a fourth detective any minute. She was right. He came out of the house three down from the corner, on her side. And she recognized this one.

"Yo, Barlow!" she called, hurrying his way. She'd worked with Harry Barlow, just briefly, when they were both assigned to Area Three. "Remember me?" She knew he would, if only from that afternoon he had held her feet and lowered her headfirst down into a deep, narrow construction ditch and pulled her out again . . . she bringing a screaming three-year-old up with her.

He turned. "Hey, Kirsten." He grinned. Barlow was good people, and good police. Everyone agreed he looked like Bill Cosby, only homelier.

They exchanged how-are-yous and lied a little about how things would never be as good as they used to be. "So," she said, spreading her arms to indicate the ongoing canvass, "still right on top of things, huh? This is Thursday. Didn't this Father Regan buy it two days ago?"

He stared at her. "What do *you* know about it? And what are you doing here, anyway?" Now more cop than comrade.

"I heard about it on the radio," she said. "And . . . I have friends in the neighborhood."

"Yeah? What friends?"

She smiled. "You."

She knew enough not to ask what they'd learned, and he didn't tell her. But he did verify what she'd been afraid of. "The two dicks who caught the case didn't do shit," he said. "Figuring the man's got no relatives, and it comes out pretty quick he's a pervert and the neighbors all figure, 'Fuck him, he got what he deserved.'"

"And now suddenly," she said, "the case is a heater?"

"Christ, fucking media all over the place." He looked at his watch. "Gotta go," he said, "and you should, too."

"Right. Well, you take care." She turned and walked back to her car.

———

She tried Wardell on her cell phone. Not available. She ended the call and immediately her phone rang.

It was Cuffs Radovich. "The guy who runs the seminary police force just called," he said. "Says someone told the man in charge there—the rector, he said—about him letting me watch over your babies. Says he almost lost his fucking job. This *rector* says me and my people gotta stay the hell away."

"But you're helping them," she said. "Is he crazy?"

"Guy's running a goddamn priest factory, so answer that one yourself. Anyway, this *rector*—I love that word—says he talked to the goddamn cardinal, for chrissake, and their excuse is it's an insurance thing. If me or one of my guys gets hurt . . . or hurts somebody . . . whatever. What it *really* is? They figure I'm a thug and they got no control."

"Damn," she said. Cuffs *was* a thug. But he was *her* thug.

"Don't worry about it," he said. "That other thing I been working on? I can put it on hold for a while. I'll get rid of my people and stay on the job alone."

"No way. They'll have you arrested or something."

"Bullshit. They won't even *see* me. If they do, maybe then I'll have to go, but they're not gonna lock me up, for chrissake. Meanwhile, fuck them."

"I don't . . ." But she knew pissing off authority was one of his favorite things. "Okay," she said. "And thanks, Cuffs, I really appreciate it."

"Just keep sending my fucking checks, is all."

27.

Friday morning Kirsten woke up and ran to the kitchen to catch Dugan before he left for his office. He was still sitting there, though, eating cold cereal, which he never did. She was pouring herself some coffee when he announced that from now on he was eating raisin bran every day, and that he wouldn't be flying to Asheville that afternoon, after all.

Kirsten spun around from the counter and splashed coffee down the front of the new tan "classic tee" from J. Jill she'd slept in. "Say that again?"

"Raisin bran. I saw this article in—"

"No, Dugan," she said. "You *are* going." It was a trial workshop and competition at a resort and conference center in the mountains near Asheville, North Carolina. She'd been wishing he didn't have to go; she wanted him here with her. But she wasn't about to let him not go on her account. She didn't need taking care of.

He got up and ran cold water on a dish towel until it was sopping wet. He dabbed with it at her shirt, but the area where he soaked the shirt was a good three or four inches to the right of the coffee spill. "What are you *doing?*" she said, but she knew a distraction when she felt it.

"Oh, sorry," he said, and then tried to wet her shirt over the other breast, too, but she pushed him away and sat down, with the table between them. He sat, too.

"You're just kidding, right?" she said.

"Actually, no. The fact is the workshop was Larry Candle's idea, and I don't really *want* to go."

She didn't believe him. "You're going to Asheville." She pointed to the calendar on the wall beside the clock. "It's right there. 'Trial Lawyers Association mentoring workshop,'" she read. "You told me months ago that Larry signed you up for it and said it would be good for the firm's reputation. You agreed. Plus, you said it would be a nice change of pace, a lot of fun."

"I must have been drinking at the time. I'm gonna call and tell them I'm not going."

"You're on the faculty, for God's sake. They're counting on you." She pointed at the calendar again. "Starts tonight and ends next Saturday." That was eight whole days and she didn't *want* him to go. "You're going," she said. She picked at her wet shirt, holding it out away from her skin and shaking it a little to dry it.

"Damn," Dugan said, "I like it when you—" He stopped when she gave him a dirty look. "Anyway," he said, "if I was sick, or on trial or something I couldn't go and they'd put my four students with—"

"But you're *not* sick, and you're *never* on trial. You can't back out now. The teams are probably all picked."

"But I don't want to leave you right now. With this priest killer running around, and this . . . you know . . . this postcard—"

"Forget that. The killer's not running around after *me*. Like you said yesterday, catching him is police business, and I've got Cuffs to help watch over Michael and the others. And as to the other

140

thing, I . . . well . . . let's not overreact to what could very well be a stupid prank." She studied Dugan as she spoke, and he *looked* as though he believed her. "I bet the real reason you don't want to go is because you don't *try* cases any more. It's been years, and you think you'll look bad compared to the other faculty members."

"That's bullshit. I've forgotten more than most of them will ever know."

She knew he was dying to go. Each experienced lawyer was teamed with four top students from law schools all over the country to simulate both preparing a case for trial and then the trial itself. "I think you owe it to the program to follow through," she said.

"I don't know." He scooped up some raisin bran, then stopped the spoon halfway to his mouth. "Hey! Why don't *you* come? They say the workshop's pretty intensive, but I'm sure they leave time for splashing around in the hotel pool at night. Plus, you'll have the days to yourself. You can swim, shop, do whatever."

"When you put it that way, it's tempting." And it was, especially when she considered that law school students weren't all fresh out of college, and that over half of them these days were women. She pictured Dugan and his "team" holed up together day after day, then splashing around the pool at night. "Um . . . do you have the names of the 'kids' on your team?"

"No, we don't get those until—" He stopped, and a grin broke over his face. "You're right," he said. "You better come along. You never know *what* might go on in a charged atmosphere like that."

"You're going." She set her coffee on the table and stood up. "I'm not." The part of her tee shirt Dugan had gotten to was still pretty well soaked. "And you know what?" With both hands she plucked the wet fabric out away from her skin and jiggled the shirt, and herself, again. "I'm not worried one bit."

Since he'd be going directly from his office to the airport in the afternoon, Dugan stuck around after breakfast for about an hour, packing and saying good-bye. Packing took ten minutes.

He had a twelve-thirty flight and it was past nine o'clock, so Dugan called his office and told Mollie he'd go straight to the airport from home. He said he had plenty of work in his briefcase to keep him busy while he waited. Kirsten was relieved that by the time he left he seemed truly convinced that she wasn't as spooked by the idea of someone stalking her as she'd been the day before.

In reality, though, it was more than a mere *idea,* and it bothered the hell out of her.

28.

After Dugan left, Kirsten wandered through the apartment, trying to concentrate on stalkers and serial killers and how to uncover them, but mostly thinking about herself and Dugan. She had never once worried about him straying, and she knew he didn't worry about her, either. She was the luckiest person in the world.

Which is why it bothered her so much that she'd never told him about her pregnancy in Florida, and its termination. She'd never even brought it up to her doctor, and she was wondering now whether something that had gone wrong during the abortion procedure might be the reason she hadn't gotten pregnant in the more than six months they'd been trying. She should tell Dugan the whole story when he got back from Asheville.

Why was it so hard to talk about? Being young and stupid, having sex with someone you thought cared about you, even getting pregnant . . . they weren't such shameful acts. Even the abortion wasn't something—at least not now—that she thought was so terrible. One thing that made it so difficult was that weakness and fear had driven everything she did at the time. That was something she really felt ashamed of. Back then she'd believed abortion was an evil thing, one of the worst things she could do. Yet she went ahead and did it because she was scared. Frightened to death that she might be tied down to a baby.

For that reason, and for God knew what other reasons she didn't understand, over the years Florida had become her dark secret, never revealed to anyone. Most of the time she could ignore it, but the longer she kept it to herself, the heavier it weighed, like a thick blanket smothering part of her soul.

She was restless, and she went through the motions of straightening up the apartment. The TV was on in the background, tuned to CLTV, the local cable news channel. Suddenly the word "priests" jumped out at her. It was a teaser about a press conference to be aired later that morning. The FBI and law enforcement officials from Chicago, Waukegan, and Winnebago County in Illinois, and from Crow Wing County in Minnesota, would address the recent series of killings of Catholic priests.

The so-called press conference started at eleven o'clock and originated from Chicago Police Headquarters. It was little more than a statement read by an FBI spokeswoman. Five or six police officers, one of them Danny Wardell, stood shoulder to shoulder behind her, but only the woman spoke. She announced that over a three-week period three men, all of them Chicago priests or former priests who'd been charged in the past with sexual misconduct with minors, had been murdered, and that now a fourth such man had apparently been abducted.

On behalf of all the jurisdictions, the spokeswoman entertained a few questions but refused to give any but the most general and innocuous bits of information. Her main point was clearly to stress that each jurisdiction was conducting its own "very aggressive" investigation while cooperating with, and in constant communication with, the FBI and one another. All press inquiries and briefings—even regarding the Minnesota case—would be coordinated by the feds and handled through the Chicago Police Department's Office of News Affairs. There were no suspects as yet, she said, and no physical evidence that the crimes were the work of the same person or persons. She managed to maintain a perfectly straight face as she acknowledged that "such a possibility is under consideration."

She ended the session in true government style. "Though we do not know whether these incidents are causally related, the obvious similarities in the victims' personal backgrounds lead us to conclude that even if these incidents *are* the work of a single disturbed individual or group of individuals, members of the general public have no reason to fear for their own or their children's safety from this source."

Kirsten could see that gibberish summarized in a headline in tomorrow's *Sun-Times*:

ONLY PRIEST PERVERTS IN PERIL, POLICE SAY

More importantly, the media frenzy sure to follow, and the unified police front, meant that she would have a tougher time than ever squeezing information out of anyone.

Back at the kitchen table Kirsten opened the folder with the information Michael had given her. Along with his notes was the the list she had drawn up:

#1 — OUT — 1-90 rest stop — shot dead, then stripped & slashed
#2 — OUT — Minn cottage — tied up, then stripped & slashed

#3 — OUT — Chgo apartment — slashed (tied up? stripped?)

#4 — VSG — Waukegan hospital — ?

Only the priests living at Villa St. George were her clients, and she was doing what she could, through Cuffs, to protect them. But if she could find a pattern and figure out who would be next, whether it was a Villa St. George resident or not, there was a better chance of catching the maniac.

She added "fingers severed (dead?)" to #4, Carl Stieboldt. She had already recognized the differences between Stieboldt and the first three cases. He was a VSG victim; he was attacked just two days, and not a week, after the preceding victim; and seizing him from a public place was a risk the killer hadn't taken with the others.

But there was something else, something she hadn't considered before. The other bodies had been left at the scenes where they'd been murdered, with no attempt to announce their presence. With Stieboldt, however, his fingers had been severed and placed in a mailbox that was opened every day. Thus the killer had gone out of his way—or could it possibly be *her* way?—to announce that Stieboldt hadn't simply run away, even if his body wasn't found for a long time, or ever.

Kirsten was convinced that if the killer were primarily concerned with finding victims who presented a low risk of capture, Stieboldt would not have been fourth. There were plenty of remaining non-VSG targets to choose from. So again, what was it about Stieboldt?

She took her list again, and added a new column, this one for the molestation victims. They were, in order: one boy, 11; two girls, 8 and 10; ten boys, 13 to 17; and one boy, 12. That didn't seem to lead anywhere. The murders began shortly after the publication of the *Sun-Times* list, but the specific charges against each priest weren't in the paper and it seemed unlikely the killer would have that information.

In fact, maybe there wasn't any pattern at all, just four men the killer found to be available. Or maybe Stieboldt was killed by a different person. Jesus! She stared at the four names and wondered. She shook her head and—whether it was the movement that did it or not—she suddenly thought of something. Or, more accurate, *saw* something. But it wasn't possible. It had to be a weird coincidence.

A weird, *frightening* coincidence.

She turned back to Michael's list, the one with all eighteen names. Yes, there *was* a possible fifth victim who fit the impossible pattern. And only one. He was listed in the Villa St. George column, which, taken alone, made him less likely to be the next victim. So if he *was* next, what had jumped out at her wasn't a coincidence at all, but a bizarre, calculated plan.

That would also at least begin to address the troubling question of why *two* crazies—one out to kill abusive priests and the other out to terrorize Kirsten—had crept into her life at the same time.

She had to contact—who?—which police department? Someone. Whoever it was, they might think she was crazy, but they couldn't just ignore her. They would have to throw a blanket of protection over the man she identified as the next victim. And when they did, the killer would either abandon the pattern or—as Kirsten thought more likely—lie back and wait for as long as it took until they gave up and withdrew the protection.

On the other hand, if she was right, the way to catch the killer was to have the next victim protected but *apparently* vulnerable, and then jump quickly when the maniac moved in. Yeah, right.

Propose dangling a victim out as bait? The cops would tell her she was out of her mind. Which they'd already think she was, anyway, because by then she would have told them she could predict the next victim . . . and the victim after that.

29.

anny Wardell was the one to talk to. Not just because he was the only one Kirsten knew who was personally involved in the investigation, but because she already had his confidence.

She called the Chicago Police Department, asked for the Office of News Affairs, and was transferred.

"Internal Affairs." A male voice.

"No," she said. "*News* Affairs."

"I'll transfer you." She waited through silence and then a couple of rings, until a woman's voice said, "News Affairs."

"I need to reach Sergeant Daniel Wardell," she said. "He was just—"

"Where is he assigned, ma'am?" the woman said.

"He's a criminal investigator with the Winnebago County Sheriff's Office. He was just at a press—"

"This is the Chicago Police Department, ma'am."

"I *know* that. But he just took part in a televised press conference, and I'm sure it originated there at Headquarters."

"Ma'am, I—"

"It's about the killings of those priests, and Wardell was at the press conference and I need to speak with him. He . . . he's expecting my call. It's about the murders."

"Ma'am, I'm going to transfer you. Hold on."

She was transferred twice more and by the time she got to someone who knew what she was talking about, she learned that Wardell had left just minutes ago and was presumably driving back to Rockford. "Can you reach him in his car?" she asked. "Or give me his cell phone number?"

"I'm afraid I can't, ma'am." They were long on politeness and short on what she needed. "I suggest you try his home office in Rockford."

"I don't suppose you have that number handy," she said.

"Actually, I do."

She took down the number, called Rockford, went through several transfers, and finally got someone who said Wardell would be at a meeting in downtown Chicago until about two. He said he would call Wardell and ask him to call her. She gave her cell phone number and hung up, as out of breath by that time as though the obstacle course she'd just run had been a physical one.

An hour later Kirsten was back on the road. She figured Wardell wouldn't want to hang around downtown to meet with her and then have to drive home in rush hour, so if he called she wanted to be somewhere on his route to Rockford. Meanwhile, with her free hand she paged though her notebook for the number of the cell phone she had given Michael. She'd made him promise to carry it with him and keep it turned on.

It rang several times, and she imagined him fumbling the phone out of his pocket, then trying to find the right button. Finally, he said, "Hello?" Very loudly.

150

"I can hear you," she said. "You don't have to shout."

"Is that you, Kirsten?" A *little* softer.

"Yes. Just talk normally. It'll pick up your voice."

"Okay."

"That's better," she said. "It sounds like you're in a car."

"Yes, on the way to Vernon Hills. There's a shopping mall there. I might buy a shirt. But it's mainly . . . you know . . . sort of an outing."

"Are you driving? By yourself?"

"I'm driving, but I have three guys with me. Bob Carrera, Bri—"

"Is Aloysius Truczik one of them?"

"Al? Oh no. He's—"

"Please, Michael," she said, "I'd rather the others don't know what I'm asking."

"Oh, sorry."

"Where do you think Truczik is right now? And tell me in a way that the people with you won't know what it's about, okay?"

"Why, what is it? Is something—"

"Michael! Just tell me."

"Sorry. Well . . ." He paused, apparently trying to figure out how to answer, and then said, "Not me, I don't play golf very often. Um . . . there's a course right here on the seminary grounds that's leased to a company that runs it as a public course. We priests get a discount, and they've finally added a bar and a rest—"

"You mean Truczik's playing golf there now," she said.

"Right."

So he'd be out in the open and around other people. "Until when?" she asked.

"That's why I don't play. If you go out after lunch, you don't finish until almost six o'clock. Of course, you're not stuck in a boring mall someplace looking for—"

"Almost six, I got it," she said. "What about you? When will you be back to Villa St. George?"

"Depends. We're *trying* to agree on a movie. But by about six, anyway. Is that okay? Should I be doing any—"

"No, no. Really, there's no problem. I'm just trying to figure things out, is all." She tried to sound lighthearted. "You guys have a good time."

"Thanks, although that's just about impossible. But I . . . I do what I can to help."

"Gotta run. You remember how to end a call with that thing?"

"Yes . . . I *think* so." And he was gone.

Michael hated malls, hated shopping, seldom went to movie theaters. She knew his "I do what I can" meant he was trying to help some of the others keep their spirits up.

As far as most people were concerned, these men were beyond redemption. But Michael was trying to help them. Was that only because he was one of them? And what about her? She was trying to help them, too. Because Michael was one of them and she *had* to help Michael. She was glad what he did wasn't as bad as what some of the others had done. Still, though, it was bad.

Was it bad enough to merit being tied down and having his skin and parts of his body sliced away? And Al Truczik? Is that what Al Truczik deserved?

There was at least one person out there who certainly thought so.

30.

At two o'clock Wardell called. "You looked great on TV," Kirsten told him.

He told her that after "that bullshit" he'd had to go downtown to the Dirksen Federal Building, with the cops from the other jurisdictions, to meet with an FBI profiling team. He didn't sound thrilled.

"Take a lot of notes?" Kirsten asked.

"Hey, they were full of insights. New stuff . . . if you never saw a Hannibal Lecter movie. Gotta give 'em credit, though, these are guys who've found their niche, and truly enjoy their work . . . which is mainly talking to each other."

"And you're headed back to Rockford right away?"

"Soon as I pick up my damn car." It sounded like he was walking down the street. "What you got for me?"

"Have you had lunch?"

"I've had about eight doughnuts and a gallon of coffee since ten o'clock. Just tell me whatever you got."

"We should talk in person." She hesitated, then jumped in. "I know who the next victim's going to be."

"Yeah, me too. It'll be some priest who—"

"No, I know which priest it will be. And I know the one after that, too."

"Uh-huh." He thought she'd gone over the edge, she could tell. "So, have you notified the appropriate law enforcement agency?"

"I'm notifying *you*. Like I said I would. As to the guy, he seems safe enough for the moment. We really need to talk in person."

"I just spotted the garage where my car is, and I'm sure as hell not gonna wait around and get caught in rush hour. I'll call you from the road, and—"

"You don't believe me. And you won't, not unless we sit down and go over it. If you're not interested, I'll take what I have elsewhere." As if she had some elsewhere to go. "But," she said, "I know where we can meet."

She told him and he agreed. Which was good, because she was already there, waiting for him.

"Great," Wardell said. He lifted the cup that would start him on his next gallon of coffee. "So the killer is spelling out your name with his victims. Yeah, that makes a *lot* of sense."

"I didn't say it made sense," Kirsten said. "Serial killers aren't famous for making sense. Maybe your FBI consultants failed to point that out."

"My FBI consultants pointed right up their collective—"

"Serial killers are psychotic, or psychopathic, or whatever. They're crazy, anyway. And often enough they're highly intelligent people who get drawn into fantasies and . . ." She paused. "Anyway, we don't need to get into all that stuff here."

Here was a booth in a McDonald's along I-90, just northwest of O'Hare Airport on the way to Rockford. Convenient for Wardell, which was the point. For Kirsten it was out of the way, but at least she got an edible chicken salad.

"Look," she said. She took the sheet with Michael's list of eighteen names from her folder and put it on the table between them. "The three that are dead already and the one presumed dead—presumed by me, at least—are lined out. Kanowski, Immel, Regan, and Stieboldt. That's *K-I-R* and—"

"I know the alphabet. And *you* look. This freak is almost certainly some crazy mope who was abused by one of these creepo priests as a kid. Now he's striking back. What makes you think he even knows who you are?"

"Whoever it is—and there's at least a chance it's a woman—is smart, smart enough not to leave a trace so far, at least not until Stieboldt. He also seems to know an awful lot about the men he's after."

"You just said it might be a woman."

"Thank you," she said. "So, if this person has studied the priests on the *Sun-Times* list, he or she—"

"We don't even know if the killer—and the possibility it's a woman is about zero—is working from that list."

"The killings started shortly after the list appeared," Kirsten said. "Every victim so far is from the list. Some of these men have never been identified publicly as sex abusers. So without the list how would whoever it is know that?"

"Kanowski was charged and convicted. That's public. Regan messed with about a dozen kids and the archdiocese was sued because of him. That's public."

"Immel, though," she said, "that was kept quiet. And so was Stieboldt."

"We don't even know yet that Stieboldt's dead."

Kirsten shook her head. "Now you're just arguing for the sake of argument. He's a victim, isn't he?"

"Maybe he's the psycho. Maybe he chopped off his own fingers to throw us off."

"Right. Jesus." She took a bite into her salad and thought a moment. "I think the killer's working from the list, and my uncle is on it." She pointed. "Michael Nolan."

"Uncle?" He stared at her. "You didn't tell me that."

"Yeah . . . well . . . it never came up. Anyway, my uncle's case was made public a couple of years ago in a lawsuit by the parents of the girl he . . . he had sex with. And anybody who checked could easily find out I'm his niece. Also, I helped him when he was sued."

"You helped him? A fucking child abuser?"

"You're helping him, too. Trying to catch whoever wants to kill him."

"Because that's what they pay me for. Catching bad guys. I don't give a fuck who the victims are. That's different."

"Whatever, but the killer knows who Michael Nolan is, and could easily find out I'm his niece and that I've helped him in the past. I still see him fairly often, too. Maybe the killer thinks helping an evil man is evil. So I'm evil, too, and he wants to—"

"What, you think this maniac is gonna go after all the *relatives* of these child fuckers, too? Gimme a break."

"The families of a lot of these guys probably abandoned them long ago. My own mother wouldn't even talk to her brother, my uncle. And until he got sued I never knew why. I'm just saying I'm on record as trying to help him. I got my husband to represent him in the lawsuit."

"Then your husband's nuts, too."

"My husband feels the same way you do about Michael and the rest of them, but . . . you know . . . he's my husband."

156

"Right. So that's it? That's what you got? A fucking alphabetical coincidence?"

"Coincidence? Four victims. Four last names starting with letters that start to spell out my name. The odds against that are forty-seven million to one."

"You made that up."

"I know. It's probably way higher than that. But there's something else." She took out a photocopy of the postcard, front and back, and laid it on the table in front of Wardell. "A few weeks ago I picked up my mail at my office and found this. Look at how it's addressed to me. With a label which was cut off a magazine, one that had earlier been taken from my office." She tapped her finger on the copy. "See the message? 'Here I come.' That's not creepy?"

"Creepy, maybe." He looked up from the card. "But tied to these killings? No."

"The day I got the card was the very day Kanowski was killed." She went on to tell him about someone puncturing her tire, "which happened Tuesday, the day Regan got it, and the day before Stieboldt," and about the magazine having been returned—minus its mailing label.

"You're sure it's the label from that particular magazine?" Wardell asked.

"Leroy Renfroe says it is."

"Well then, it is." Renfroe's expertise was widely respected.

"And yesterday it was returned, put back on the table . . . inside my locked office. A lock which could be picked by a ten-year-old, true. But still . . ."

"So yeah, maybe someone's trying to mess with your mind. But that still doesn't show a connection with these killings."

"K-I-R-S," Kirsten said, and tapped her finger on the list again. "K-I-R-S. And there's one T on the list and that's—"

"I *told* you . . . I know the goddamn alphabet. The only *T* is this guy Truczik." He shook his head. "Christ."

"You don't have to tell anyone you actually buy what I'm saying. But it has to be brought to someone's attention, and at least they'll *listen* to you."

"I gotta check with my boss before I say anything beyond him."

"I guess I'm not going to get any medicals, huh? Or autopsy reports?" He shook his head, and she said, "Was Regan sliced up, too?"

"Yeah."

"While he was . . . alive?"

He nodded. "Pretty bad."

"And that happened late Monday or early Tuesday, Stieboldt was taken Wednesday evening, and today is Friday. So you can't waste a lot of time thinking about what I—"

"Hey!" Wardell glared at her. "I don't need you to tell me my fucking job. Got it?"

"I'm just saying . . ." She shrugged. "Meanwhile, I'll cover Truczik. It's what, four o'clock?" She checked her watch. "He's safe for now . . . in the middle of a round of golf at a course right there at the seminary. I'll get there before he's—"

"Golf?" Wardell pointed toward the windows behind her and she turned and was shocked at how dark it was getting outside. "You oughta leave your radio on," he said. "A big thunderstorm coming out of the northwest. High winds, heavy rains, maybe some hail. Lightning, for sure. The seminary's in Mundelein, right?"

"Right." She was already on her feet. "About due north of here."

"Better hurry. That golf game's gonna be called off before you get there."

31.

No route would be a fast one at this time of day, but Kirsten chose local roads rather than face the tangled expressways. Before long, rain was pelting her windshield. Why had she wasted time meeting Wardell? She should have gone straight to the seminary. Gotten to Truczik before the storm forced the golfers off the course. Warned him. Stayed with him. Not that she'd ever care a whole lot about a guy who Michael's notes said had been accused of fondling young teenagers. Four boys in three incidents over twenty years ago, all of which he denied. Assuming the charges were true, it was hard to give a damn whether the creep lived or died. But dammit, she still didn't like the idea of *anyone* no matter what hateful things they'd done being skinned alive. Not on *her* watch, anyway.

If she'd been paying attention she'd have known about the storm. Besides, now that she thought about it, storm or not, what was so safe about letting a man wander around a golf course, even a busy one? He could have been picked off by someone hiding in the woods with a rifle and a halfway decent scope. Which wasn't at all the way this killer worked, and she knew she was just beating herself up, not being rational. Still, she should have gone straight to Truczik.

It was past five-thirty when she reached the seminary and found the golf course, called Pine Meadows. Although sundown was still over an hour away, it was very dark. Rain poured down and the sky grumbled almost nonstop with low, rolling thunder, broken periodically by fierce lightning and sharper crashes.

She sat in the car in the parking lot, with her windows fogging up, and called Michael. Again there were lots of rings before he said, "Hello?" in a stage whisper. "I'm watching the movie. Just a minute." She heard breathing and mumbling, and pictured him crawling over people to get out. "Okay," he finally said. "I'm out in the lobby. Is there a problem?"

"Not at all," she said. "Everything's fine. I'm at the golf course, looking for Aloysius Truczik. But it's raining like crazy and obviously nobody's still playing. Is he likely to be in the bar?"

"Usually not. Unless someone else is buying. Al's got money, but—"

"I don't recall meeting him by name when I was there. What does he look like?"

"Why? Is something wrong?"

"Didn't I just say everything's fine? I need to ask him something, that's all."

"If he's there you can hardly miss him. At the meeting Al was the big heavy guy with the sort of irritating voice, who kept—"

"I got it. Thanks, and don't worry. If I don't find him here I can talk to him later, or tomorrow or something." *At least I hope so,* she thought.

"Should we come back? I mean, the movie's a loser and—"

"Michael, please. Everything's okay."

She ended the call and tried Cuffs Radovich. She got his voice

160

mail. She knew he didn't check it often, but she stated where she was and that she'd try again.

She couldn't find the umbrella which should have been under her front seat. She shoved her purse under there instead and got out of the car and made a run for it, holding her jacket up over her head and splashing through deep puddles. Inside, the bar was crowded, but she didn't see Truczik. She asked for help from a woman serving drinks, and was told there was a "starter" who kept track of all the golfers and Kirsten could find him in the pro shop.

The starter was a young, cheerful Matt Damon look-alike, but in a larger size, wearing crisp blue slacks and—what else?—a golf shirt, pale yellow. "Oh yeah," he said, "Father Truczik. I was lucky today. I was able to put him with three guys who didn't already know him. He's a decent golfer for a guy his weight, but he's usually by himself looking for a foursome, and there's a lot of people who won't . . . you know . . ."

"You mean he talks too much," she said.

He grinned. "You got it."

"Anyway, he's not out—" A sharp clap of thunder startled her, and the lights went out, and then back on. "No one's out on the course, I take it."

"No way. All that lightning? A person could get killed out there."

"I was to meet him here," she said, "but I don't see him anywhere. Do you think he might . . . I don't know . . . be taking a shower or something?"

"Nah, he usually heads—" He snapped his fingers. "You know, there was a message for him to call someone and I gave it to him. I remember I wrote it on the back of . . . *something.*" He rum-

161

maged around on the cluttered counter in front of him. "Oh, yeah," he said, "he took it with him. 'Cause it had the number on it." He snapped his fingers and pointed at her. "It was a woman on the phone. It wasn't *you*, was it?"

"No. But didn't she give a name?"

"Yeah, but I don't remember. Christie? Kristen? Something like that."

"Was it . . . Kirsten?"

"Kirsten! That's it! Said she had an urgent message for Father Truczik. That's the word she used, 'urgent.'"

The starter's eyes brightened happily, and just then a deep roll of thunder shook the room. The lights went out . . . and this time they stayed out.

32.

In the dim emergency lighting the starter tapped randomly on the computer keyboard in front of him, apparently to verify that the power loss was real. "Guess this means I'll get off early," he said. "Better lock up." He turned away.

"Wait!" Kirsten said. "What about Truczik?"

He turned back. "What about him?"

"What did he do after you gave him the message?"

"Well . . . let's see. I made change for him so he could call. I remember thinking, 'How many people can there *be* who don't have a cell phone?' Not many, do you think?" He looked like he expected an answer.

"No, not many." Her mind was racing. "What was the phone number?"

His face went blank. "Jeez. I *think* it was this area code, y'know? But I got no idea what the number was. I was so darn—"

"I understand," she said. "How long ago was this?"

"Jeez. An hour and a half ago? Maybe a little more. I know he came back and asked could he borrow one of the complimentary umbrellas. You know, we have these big blue-and-white-striped umbrellas for—"

"Right," she said. "*Then* what?"

"Well, then he left. That's it. Look, I gotta—" He stopped. "It *was* kinda funny, though, because . . . he went out that way." He pointed to his right, toward a sliding glass door that was open and led out to a covered walkway. Beyond that, rain poured down on grass and distant trees.

"Why was that funny?" she asked.

"I mean, I was busy with a million other things at the time, so I didn't really think about it. But that's the way to the course, you know? He'd have to go all the way around the building to get to the parking lot. Why would he wanna walk all that way?"

"I don't know," Kirsten said. "Maybe he took a golf cart."

"That doesn't—" He stopped. "Anyway, he didn't. The cart jockey already took all the keys." He was obviously wishing she'd leave. "I better lock up."

"Okay. But hey, think I could borrow one of those umbrellas? I know you're closing up, but I'll return it, really." She smiled and made a cross-my-heart gesture.

"Uh, sure." He took a long, slim, tightly wrapped umbrella from a box near the door. "You look honest." Anything to get rid of her.

"Thanks." She took it and peered out the open door. It was still raining. "I'll just go this way. Thanks again."

"No problem," he said, and slid the door closed behind her.

She stood in the covered walkway and stared out at the golf course. The wind and rain seemed to be letting up a little, and the thunder and lightning were definitely moving eastward. Someone had dropped a used scorecard on one of the wooden benches that lined the walkway and she picked it up. An unhappy golfer had penciled "SHIT" across the scores in large dark letters. On the reverse side was a stylized map of the course, showing the holes and the yardage for each one, and indicating where there were sand traps and bridges and rain shelters.

The longer she waited, the darker it was going to get. She unsnapped the little tab and swirled the umbrella around to open it, then stepped out into the rain.

She knew it made no sense for one person to try to comb an entire golf course in the light of day, much less in the rain with night falling. Plus, this course seemed to have more wooded areas than the ones she'd seen on TV. But what else could she do? Call someone? Even if they thought she made sense, which they wouldn't, there was no way they'd organize a search tonight.

It seemed strange that Truczik would have gone out in the rain just because "Kirsten" told him to. But then she remembered that in the meeting in Michael's room, although he'd been negative to begin with, he was the first one to suggest to the others that she might be of help to them. He'd seemed to *want* to believe in her. "We have to trust *someone*," he'd said.

Even so, if he actually *did* go out to meet this other "Kirsten," where would they meet? He wouldn't have agreed to go very far, not in that storm. She consulted the map and decided to check out at least the one shelter closest to the clubhouse before it was truly dark.

She left the first tee and headed down the fairway. If she turned right when she got about halfway to the green, and cut through some trees and what looked to be deep grass, she would end up on the fifteenth fairway. On the other side of that, although she couldn't see it from where she was, there should be a shelter. The wind was down to almost nothing now, and the umbrella kept her pretty dry. From the knees down, though, her white cotton pants were soaked, and her shoes would probably never be wearable again.

About a hundred and fifty yards out she turned to head through the rough, which turned out to be more than simply deep grass, but weeds and undergrowth beneath the trees, hiding a shallow ravine. She went down, across a narrow creek of flowing rain water and up the other side, and then headed across the fifteenth fairway toward the shelter.

It was raining just softly now and, surprisingly, a few stray shafts of low-lying sunlight were streaming from the west, behind her. Up ahead the shelter looked like a rustic lean-to, with the open side away from her, facing east—the least likely direction for wind and rain to come from.

She was twenty yards away when a dog suddenly trotted out from behind the little building. It stopped, rain streaming down its matted gray flanks, and turned its head and stared at her. In the slanting sunlight its eyes shone bright yellow, and Kirsten stood perfectly still and stared back. The animal was slope-shouldered and its head hung low to the ground; it was too wild-looking to be somebody's pet. It wasn't large, and it made no move toward her, but its wildness alone held a menace that frightened her. In response she took a firm step forward. The animal jerked its head and turned aside. It was joined by a clone of itself and the two of them moved quickly away, trotting side by side, and melted like gray ghosts into the woods. Coyotes, she decided, although she'd never seen one before.

She let out her breath and moved forward again. According to the scorecard map the fifteenth hole ran along the edge of the golf course property, with a strip of woods between the fairway and a boundary fence. What was beyond that the map didn't say.

She would check out the shelter—there couldn't be anyone

there or the coyotes wouldn't have gone near it—then go back and circle around the clubhouse to the parking lot, and drive to Villa St. George. Truczik was probably back there right now, drinking somebody else's liquor and looking forward to supper.

She went around to the open side of the shelter, yelling, "Hey, hey, hey!" in case she was wrong and there were more canines hiding out from the rain. She stepped inside onto a dry concrete slab and pulled the umbrella closed. It was a little darker in here under the roof, but light enough to see that the shelter was empty.

She felt relief flood through her whole body, and her breath came out in a deep sigh. She realized, though, that she should hurry back to her car before it was too dark to see anything, and then to the retreat house to make sure Truczik was—

A dog growled somewhere. Not far off. But maybe not a dog, maybe a coyote. And then she heard it again. Low, throaty growling. Back among the trees, toward the golf course boundary. She dropped the umbrella and pushed her way forward through the wet, clinging undergrowth, and in just a few yards broke out of the trees and into the open.

There was a barbed-wire fence, and then a gravel road, and beyond that more trees. The two coyotes were trotting away along the fence line. One turned its head to glance back at her, and it had a rag or a piece of cloth in its mouth. Then they both picked up speed and were gone. She turned to head back toward the shelter. Which was when she saw Aloysius Truczik.

He was sitting upright with his back against a large tree, eyes wide open, as though amazed to see her.

33.

On the brink of being sick, Kirsten didn't really want to go any closer to Truczik, but she swallowed hard and did it. Her fingertips were damp as she leaned forward and held them for a moment under his nostrils. When she backed away again she was grateful—for his sake—that he was dead.

Grossly obese, he sat with his head tilted back against the tree behind him, his mouth taped shut with duct tape. Except for his socks he was naked, and in the fading twilight she could see blood smeared and drying everywhere across his torso. His flabby arms at first seemed to hang limp at his sides, but actually were tied at the wrists with a rope that ran around the tree. Like the arms, his legs—spread out in a V on the ground in front of him—were strangely intact and untouched by the blade that had sliced the pale skin from his sagging chest and midsection in long, straight lines, leaving it hanging in strips.

She was careful not to disturb the clothes strewn on the ground, but she didn't see any shorts, and maybe that's what one of the coyotes had taken. It appeared she'd spooked them before they'd gotten to the body itself. She was careful also not to touch the umbrella Truczik had borrowed. With its nylon material wrapped tight around the spine, the umbrella had been thrust like a sword into his groin. It might have gone all the way through and into the soft ground, because there it stayed, sticking out and angling upward. Clearly intended as a long, stiff, blue-and-white-striped phallus.

She stumbled through the trees, and back at the shelter she allowed herself to be sick on the grass. When she finished choking and spitting and was able to talk she fumbled for the cell phone in her jacket pocket and called 911.

"Don't worry," she said, when the emergency operator cautioned her to remain on the scene, "I'll be here."

It had stopped raining and the sun was down, and with what little light remained she wanted to run back to the clubhouse bar for a shot of Jack Daniels, and the hell with what she'd told the operator. But she stayed. She was unarmed—her gun was in her purse, under the front seat of her locked car—but she guessed Truczik had been dead an hour or longer, and she had no fear that the killer was still hanging around. Anything was possible with a crazy person, but this one had so far been awfully careful not to get caught.

She was more concerned that the coyotes not come back and mess up the scene, but she was confident—*pretty* confident, anyway—that they'd keep their distance if she stayed there.

There were two wide fairways, and a rough that included a stand of trees, between her and the clubhouse. Even though it was getting very dark, as far as she could tell the lights there hadn't gone back on. And it was suddenly cold—or maybe what had her shivering was a chill from inside her. She went back through the trees and stood by the body.

She waited, keeping her back to the mutilated body of the priest, straining to catch the glint of a coyote's eyes. But all she could see now were different shades of black. Finally she heard one brief wail of a siren, then no more, but she went back to the shelter and soon saw headlights, and blue and red flashing Mars lights, off in the direction of the clubhouse. Several vehicles. Beyond the trees and coming her way, bouncing over the soft, wet turf.

The groundskeeper would be pissed as hell in the morning, especially since the cops, obviously deciding they couldn't drive through the trees and the rough, turned and went all the way down one fairway to the end, and then around and back down the other toward her. That's when she suddenly remembered she should call Cuffs, to make sure he was on the job and to ask whether Michael and the others were back yet.

The buttons on the phone lit up, but her fingers were stiff and cold—and maybe still shaking just a little—as she poked at the numbers. Meanwhile police vehicles, red and blue lights flashing, roared up and stopped in a semicircle in front of her, and the lights in her eyes made it impossible for her to see anything. Car doors opened and closed, and she started toward them, stupidly waving her arms as though they might not otherwise see her.

"Hold it right there!" It was a man who shouted, and an even brighter light snapped on and she held up her hands to shield her eyes. "Drop it!" the man screamed. "Now!"

Mystified at first, she finally got it . . . and let the cell phone fall from her hand. Pumped-up cops had shot down people wielding *soup* spoons, for God's sake.

"On the ground," he called. "I mean *now,* lady! On the ground!"

Fuck you, she thought, but she didn't say it.

Instead, holding her arms out wide from her sides, she turned around very slowly and walked, head held high, back to the shelter. She sat down on the edge of the concrete, knees up, water-logged shoes sinking deep in the wet grass. She rested her fore-arms on her knees, then dropped her chin to her chest and made herself breathe deeply. In and out. In and out.

No, I will not cry. And she didn't.

She kept telling them where the body was, and they kept yelling at her for identification. She told them who she was and that her ID was in her purse, back in the car. They were obviously from several nearby jurisdictions, along with some seminary security officers, and they all did a lot of tramping through the brush and talking and milling around for what seemed like forever. They seemed mainly to be trying to figure out what to do while they waited for someone to come and order them around. After one look, most of them didn't want to go near Truczik's body. She didn't blame them.

Finally one of them had enough sense to wrap a coat around her, get her up on her feet, and walk her to a squad car to wait. On the way she picked up her phone from where she'd dropped it. As the cop opened the rear door of the squad car both of them noticed another pair of headlights bouncing toward them across the first fairway, beyond the trees.

When this new vehicle got to the trees it paused very briefly, but didn't turn aside. The engine raced and the vehicle twisted and turned, making its way through the trees and the taller grass of the rough. Its lights tipped down the incline and disappeared, and then came up again. When it finally broke out and accelerated toward them across the fairway someone put a spotlight on it and Kirsten saw that it was a Jeep—open, without a cab. She knew then who it must be, but wondered how the hell he'd known she was here.

The Jeep roared up, much too fast, and skidded on the wet grass before it finally stopped. Cuffs Radovich stepped out. He walked straight toward the spotlight and waved his huge hands up high and wide in the air—with Kirsten's purse hanging from one of them. "Hey, Harvey!" he bellowed. "Harvey Wilson! Are you out here, dammit?"

"Over here," a man called back. "Jesus, Cuffs, take it easy, for chrissake." The spotlight was lowered and a man in uniform went over and talked to Cuffs. By then there were two more pairs of headlights ripping up the grass on fairway number one, and then she heard more vehicles arriving by way of the road beyond the fence.

She got in the backseat of the squad car, sat and closed her eyes, and waited.

An hour later Kirsten was in Cuffs's jeep, headed back to pick up her own car from the parking lot. She'd given her statement three or four times and promised to be available when needed. Cuffs took a roundabout way, driving slowly and sticking to the golf cart path. She was thankful the vehicle was open to the cool night air, because she still felt nauseated.

"This Harvey Wilson," she said, "he's the person you know from the seminary police?"

"Yeah. Figured he'd be there, or at least I should show that I knew him."

"But how did you know I was—"

"Christ, I *do* check my messages sometimes, whatever you think. Anyway, what happened is I get your message that you're on your way to the golf course. You don't say to call you back, so I don't. I just go about my protect-the-pervert-priests thing. Later I hear just the touch of a siren—which you don't hear much out here in the fucking suburbs—and then a lot of cars out on the road in a big hurry. But I figure it's not my business. Then my fucking phone rings."

"Their headlights blinded me," she said, "and I didn't even know if I'd gotten through."

"Yeah? Well, so I answer but nobody says anything, for chrissake. Then I hear all this bullshit about 'Drop it,' and 'Down on the ground, lady,' and I figure it's gotta be you and maybe you could use some help."

"So you came here."

"I kept the phone line open, though, and it sounded like you lost your ID or something. I seen your car in the lot and I figured maybe you forgot your purse, left it in the goddamn car."

"I'm sure I locked it, though. I hope you didn't break my—"

"Are you kidding?" He sounded genuinely offended. "Anyway, so I slip the lock and grab the purse, and go about my save-the-lady-in-distress thing."

"What about my gun?" she asked, holding up her purse.

"Why the hell would you be needing that? It's under the seat."

By then they'd reached the clubhouse parking lot. The power was still out, obviously, and the restaurant was dark. There were two police cars parked up close to the building, and a few other cars and vans—probably employees—farther down; and otherwise just Kirsten's Celica, alone in the middle of the wet, deserted lot. Cuffs pulled up beside it.

"I'll follow you back to Villa St. George," she said. "I'm glad you wanted to help, but . . . well . . . I just hope they're all safe back there."

"Jesus! You think I just fucking walked away? Your uncle was just coming in and I told him to get all their asses into one room and stay put until I got back. If there's booze, they'll be there." He shook his head. "The fat guy, Truczik. That was him . . . with the umbrella, right?"

"Yes. I . . . I should have gotten here sooner. I could have—"

"That 'shoulda, coulda' bullshit'll drive you nuts," Cuffs said. "Besides, look on the bright side. One less creep to watch over."

34.

D ebra hid in the dark in her van and watched as the Jeep, and behind it the Celica, drove out of the parking lot. Everything was converging, as though on a divine schedule.

That morning she'd watched as the bitch's husband left home . . . later than usual, and with a traveling bag. She followed his taxi and it didn't head for the Loop, but took the Kennedy. It was obvious he was leaving town. *Where to? For how long?* When his cab veered left on the expressway toward O'Hare she hadn't followed. She would learn nothing useful at the airport. Besides, this was the day she had picked to deal with the hideous Father Truczik.

In this she had succeeded because she was bold and Truczik, the pig, was such a fool. He called her back and she answered in a hushed tone, and he never questioned who she really was, and stupidly let himself be lured to his well-deserved fate. When it was over she'd come here to the parking lot to wait and to watch— breathless, feeling the hand of God upon her.

She had seen the Celica arrive and the bitch run through the rain and inside. Later the police appeared. Then came the open

Jeep with that huge man, an oaf too stupid to care if he got rained on. He drove off across the golf course and then brought the woman back to her car, and now they were both driving away. They were surely headed for the den of the animal priests, no better than animals themselves.

Debra would go the opposite way. She had a great deal of cleaning up and disposal to do, and she'd already learned what she most needed to know. The bitch had clearly come looking for the pig Truczik, which meant she had figured out the pattern Debra was following. By now she would have pointed it out to the authorities. And everyone would think they understood.

If the quota God had set for her were her only concern, she need not have followed any pattern. She could have chosen whichever seven were most easily available. Seven was the divine number of completion, and any seven from that list would do. Her rage at her own abuse—which to her great surprise she hadn't quelled long ago by killing her own father, and then the beast Father Lasorda—would surely be put to rest now by seven additional purgings, whomever she chose. And God too would be satisfied.

But not all the dead fathers in the world could ever satisfy her rage against the bitch, this whore who'd been paid to step in and destroy the dream she and Carlo had dared to dream. And now Carlo—a broken, speechless, crippled Carlo—was coming out of the dark place, very soon, and Debra would gather up that woman and present her to him . . . a gift from his sister, his love.

She had trapped the piggish priest by letting him think he knew who was calling him on the phone, and she would trap the whore by letting her think she understood Debra's intentions. Oh, yes, Debra had a pattern she was following. But she also had a big surprise in store for everyone.

35.

When Kirsten and Cuffs arrived at Villa St. George there was a seminary security officer sitting in a patrol car out front. They walked right by him to the front entrance. He didn't say anything, but she glanced back and saw that he was speaking into his radio. The entrance door was locked, and before she could press the bell Cuffs, surprisingly, produced a key.

"Where did you come up with that?" she asked.

He didn't say anything, but gave her a look which meant she'd rather not know. He unlocked the door and pulled it open and held it for her—an even bigger surprise—but then let it close behind her without coming inside himself.

She pushed the door open and went back out again, and he was already walking away. "Hey," she said, "where are you going?"

He turned back, obviously surprised at her question. "To do the job you're paying me to do, which doesn't include having to actually *talk* to any of those . . . individuals. They're your friends, not mine."

She went back inside and down the hall to Michael's room. She was exhausted, but she straightened up and put her game face on, and stepped into the room. All heads turned her way.

The eight remaining priests were there, just as Cuffs had said they'd be, sitting on folding chairs, most with drinks in their hands. Despite the liquor, there wasn't much chatter going on and they were even more subdued than the last time she was there. Several stood up, but she waved them back into their chairs. Michael pulled a Coke and a Sprite out of the cooler on his dresser and held them out. She took the Coke, for the caffeine— although she'd still have preferred that shot of Jack Daniels she'd been wanting.

She stood there a moment, not knowing how to get started, or whether they'd heard yet about Truczik. Finally she said, "You should know that Cuffs Radovich is back outside again, keeping watch."

"When he left he told me to gather everyone here," Michael said. "We know something's happened, but we don't know what." He paused, then added, "Al Truczik's not here."

She nodded. "I know."

"He was playing golf," Michael said, "like I told you. But he never—"

"I know. He's dead."

A heavy silence settled over the room and she could tell that's what they had been fearing. "The police are on the scene," she said. "And in addition to Cuffs, there's a security guard posted out in front of your building. You'll be safe tonight."

"That's what you told us before," said one of the others, the thin, light-skinned black man. "That we'd be safe. You said you and that Mr. Radovich would protect us. You said—"

"You're wrong, Father . . . what's your name?"

"Henshaw," he said. "George Henshaw."

178

"Anyway, Father Henshaw, I know *exactly* what I said. I told you there was safety in numbers, that you shouldn't be outside this building alone if possible. I told you I made no guarantees, but that the safest place you could be, especially at night, was right inside this building. That's what I said . . . and that's what I still say."

"I'm not accusing you," Henshaw said. "I'm just . . . you know . . ."

"You're scared," she said, "and you should be. And Father Truczik might still be alive if he'd done what I suggested."

"But Kirsten, he was playing golf," Michael said. "In broad daylight, with lots of people around. And you said—"

"Right. But after the storm drove everyone inside, he let himself be talked into going back out again, alone, with no one else around. I'm not saying he's to blame. He's a victim." She looked around the room. "But you can't do what he did. Not while the killer's still out there."

"Al's pretty easily persuaded," someone else said, "but I'm surprised even *he* would do something like that." The others agreed.

"I'm not sure the police want me to tell you this," Kirsten said, "but I'll tell you anyway. There was a phone message waiting for him when he came in, from a woman who pretended to be me." A murmur went throught the room. "He called her back and whoever it was must have told him to meet her out on the golf course. So he went out there, in the storm, by himself, to a deserted spot. And . . . well . . . that wasn't a good idea."

"Are you saying it was a woman?" Henshaw asked. "You really think the killer—"

"I'm not saying who the *killer* is. I'm telling you what happened. So please, be careful. And by the way, if I leave any of you a message, I'll identify myself as 'Kirsten . . . from Kalamazoo.' Okay?"

Suddenly they were all talking at once, to each other and to her, getting louder and louder. Mostly they wanted to know when the police were going to catch whoever it was, and how hard were they trying.

"Hold on," she said, "one at a time. The police insist they're working this case very hard. I know the FBI's involved. And I know the cops have some leads they're following up on."

She went on, trying to reassure them. She didn't mention Detective Barlow's assessment that the investigators assigned to the Emmett Regan murder "didn't do shit" until the case turned into a "heater."

She didn't tell them how Truczik died, either, but otherwise she answered all their questions as well as she could. Eventually, one by one, they left the room. Finally, when only Michael was left, she sighed and dropped into the one soft chair.

"You don't look so good," he said.

"Just worn out."

"I'm sure there are empty rooms where the nuns live. I can call over there and—"

"No, really, I'm tired, but too . . . psyched up, I guess . . . for sleep." She stood up again. "Now that the storm's gone, it's actually pretty nice outside. That bench, out by the front entrance, I'm gonna go sit there a minute before I drive home. Sort of catch my breath."

"Okay," he said. "I'll sit with you."

As soon as they stepped out the front door the security officer got out of his car and met them. "Sorry," he said, speaking directly to Michael, "but they don't want you to leave the building, Father."

Kirsten pointed to a park bench overlooking the lawn, not ten yards away. "We'll just be sitting over there a few minutes. Then I'm leaving."

"I don't know," the man said. "They told me—"

"Thank you." She took Michael's arm and walked him to the bench, and the officer went back to his car.

The bench faced away from the building and they sat and she stared out across the lawn toward the darkness where she knew the trees started. She was tired and really wanted a few quiet minutes alone, but Michael had obviously wanted to come with her and she didn't have the heart to tell him no. The air was cool and refreshing, and smelled like freshly cut grass and wet wood. Neither of them spoke. She listened to the water dripping from the trees and the eaves of the building, then she gradually became aware of traffic sounds in the distance and rustlings and creakings from the nearby woods. And the chirp of what sounded like one lonely cricket.

She raised her head and the sky was black and filled with stars. "Nice night," she said.

"Yes." He looked around. "Do you think your man . . . Cuffs . . . is out there somewhere?"

"He's watching us right now, I'm sure of it. Like Santa Claus."

"Or like God," Michael said.

"I suppose."

"I prefer the God idea to Santa Claus, because God doesn't care if we've been bad or—"

"Do you *really* think that?" She felt suddenly angry, and heard the edge of it in her voice. "That God doesn't *care* if we hurt people, or kill them, or . . . whatever?"

"God cares about that."

"Well, you were just about to say that he doesn't care if we've been bad or good."

"I guess I meant he still loves us."

"Yeah, well, either he cares and it makes him mad, or he doesn't give a damn. You can't have it both ways."

"Why not?" Michael said.

"Because that's the way it is, and because . . ." She didn't *know* why not. "How did we get into this? I should get going and—"

"Wait," he said. "Don't drop it."

"Drop what?"

"The subject. Just because it's big, and it makes you—makes us *both*—nervous. That's what we've been doing all along, for two years now. Dropping what makes us nervous. Like how you feel about what I did. Ever since I got sued, and you found out, we've never talked about it. Not really."

She was way too tired to get into this, but turned to him anyway. "Fine," she said. "Great. We'll talk about it right now. It happened." She couldn't stop herself. "You were a priest. A young girl needed help. She trusted you. And you betrayed her and everything you supposedly stood for." She took a breath. "And later you betrayed *me*, too, by not telling me. I looked up to you. I thought you were . . . you know . . . like a saint or something. You should have told me." She stood up and stared out at the night, trying to catch her breath.

"I tried, Kirsten, many times. Not right away. I mean, I didn't see any reason to tell you down there in Florida when I went down to . . . when you had that problem. Why burden you with something so big right then? And we didn't even know each other all that well. Then later, when time passed and we got to be friends and . . ." He stopped and she turned to look at him, but he sat staring down at his fists, resting on his knees. "You were my niece, almost like a daughter to me, and I was afraid you'd hate me. Then the longer I kept it to myself, the harder it . . . Anyway,

I always dropped it." When she didn't answer, he said, "I know I should have told you, but I didn't."

She almost walked away, then sat down again, but not looking at him. "You were a man of God," she said. "Did you really think God didn't *care* about what you did with that girl?"

"Back then I wasn't thinking much of anything. I mostly don't even remember my thoughts. But of course I know he *did* care. A lot. It must have made him sad . . . if God gets sad."

"What do you mean, 'if'? You're the one who's supposed to *know* about God. Besides, in school we learned that God is perfect. So he can't get sad."

"Maybe not. I don't know."

His refusal to argue was frustrating, and she sat and listened awhile to the water dripping, and to the cricket. Finally she was too tired, too drained, to keep going. She stood up again and looked down at him. "There," she said, "we talked about it. And I can't see that it's changed anything. What happened is all in the past, and . . . Anyway, things can never be like they were before."

"No," he said. He looked up at her, then turned and stared out into the dark. "I wish they could, but I guess not."

Her anger was fading quietly into a deep sadness, and she suddenly had the feeling that if he stood up and turned toward her she wouldn't be able to keep from hugging him. She hoped he *would* stand up. She *wanted* to hug him.

But he didn't move, and she turned away and walked to her car

36.

It was only ten o'clock, but there was no point in driving home, so Kirsten checked into a Days Inn a few miles from the seminary. She called Dugan in Asheville. She was anxious to hear his voice, but it was probably for the best that he wasn't in. She might have said too much, and she didn't want him leaving the conference and coming back here.

Well, she'd be thrilled if he *did,* actually, but . . . She left a cheerful message and said she'd try to reach him the next day, because she was tired now and going to bed. She said she hoped he didn't get a hernia splashing around in the hotel pool with his "team," and hung up.

On Saturday morning she woke up early and had a huge, greasy, comfort-food breakfast in the hotel restaurant, then went back to her room. She was sifting through the possibilities as to who the killer might be when her cell phone rang. It was Michael. For a moment she was afraid he might try to continue the conversation from the night before. But that wasn't it. He called to say they'd just been told by the cardinal's man—the "vicar for priests," Michael called him—that if they thought they'd feel safer somewhere else, for the time being they'd be allowed to live outside Villa St. George. They would have to check in by phone on a daily basis and be able to be reached easily.

"It's funny," Michael said, "before this, we all wanted to get out of here. But now, under these circumstances, everything's changed."

He told her the cardinal was promising additional twenty-four-hour security at the retreat house, with the whole seminary being put on "heightened alert." Also, no media would be allowed anywhere on the grounds—in itself reason enough to stay. And finally, none of the priests had relatives anxious to take them in even under ordinary circumstances, and the risk that a serial killer might be a step behind was a bit too much to ask.

"So you're all staying there?" she said.

"Yes."

"Good, and . . . uh . . . Michael, let's stay in touch." She hung up.

So far, she hadn't said anything to anyone but Sergeant Wardell—and then, last night, to Cuffs—about the killer selecting victims in an order that spelled out her name. For one thing, there was no guarantee that the pattern would continue. And she didn't see how raising the issue with the priests would make them any safer. It might even make some of them relax their guard, while it would scare the hell out of both Michael, the only *N* on the list, and Anthony Ernest, the only one of the two *E*s who was staying at Villa St. George.

The second *E*, John Ettinger, was on the OUT list, and someone ought to warn him. She called the skip tracer she'd hired to find addresses for the five remaining OUTs but got a message. His office was closed for the weekend.

Next she called Cuffs to tell him what Michael had said, but he already knew. Apparently the cardinal had a real thing about him lurking around in the seminary woods, because he'd been warned that if he were found again anywhere on the premises he'd be arrested and charged with criminal trespass, and he was to inform her that she—as his employer—would be charged as well.

Cuffs said he could go back now and finish up the job he'd put on hold and make the guy who hired him stop whining. "If I pick it up again I'll have to see it through all the way to the end. But if you want me to stay on here, I will. And the whiner and the cardinal and whoever can all go fuck themselves." He said if he got caught near Villa St. George he'd deny he was working for her and say he'd gone back on his own. "If they charge me I'll tell the goddamn judge I couldn't stand to see any harm come to those poor fucking pervert priests."

She told him to go back to his other job.

When she finally checked out of the hotel it was late morning, bright and sunny. She drove around in circles for a few minutes, looking behind her, then headed for the city. On the way, she had an idea. She drove to O'Hare Airport, parked the Celica in the "long term" lot, rented a dark red Chevrolet Impala, and continued on downtown.

At her office she carried her mail to her desk and sat down to sort through it. There wasn't much. The usual catalogs, a few bills . . . and one postcard. Her name and address taped on the front this time were in embossed printing on what appeared to be thin white card stock. Again the postmark was Chicago, and again the message on the back was hand-printed in block letters: READY OR NOT.

37.

Kirsten wasn't sure how long she sat there and stared at the address taped to the postcard before she finally reached down and pulled open the bottom right drawer of her desk. Her box of business cards was there, and beside it in the drawer was what was left of one of the cards after her name and address had been cut out.

She hadn't opened that drawer in months, so the address could have been cut out, and the remnant left behind, at the same time as the *Smithsonian* was taken. Or it could have been done two days ago, when the magazine was returned.

While she was processing that, her cell phone rang. This time it was Dugan. He'd seen TV reports about Truczik's murder. From what he said it was apparent that there'd been no information given about who found the body, no mention of her at all.

"You must have heard about it, right?" Dugan said.

"Um . . . yeah. How could I miss it? It's all over the news."

"Wasn't Cuffs supposed to be out there providing security?"

"He didn't start until sundown," she said, "and he was at the retreat house. The murder was earlier, at a golf course a mile away. Was there anything on the news about Cuffs showing up?"

"No, they're not saying much of anything. *Was* he there?"

"What he told me was that he heard a siren and went to see what was going on. Anyway, he's off the case now. The cardinal doesn't want him hanging around out there, I guess."

"Really? And what about you? Are you—"

"They're promising increased security at the retreat house, and the FBI's involved. And that sheriff's investigator from Rockford . . . Wardell . . . I guess he's got some new information. So it looks like law enforcement's working this thing pretty hard. What can I do that they can't?"

"Right," he said. "And what about that postcard stuff? Anything more on that?"

She'd been hoping he wouldn't ask that because she wanted to stick to the truth, more or less. "I'm watching my back. Haven't seen anyone."

"Good, but be careful, okay? Anyway, I should get going. We'll be tied up all day out here. The weather's great, of course, but I won't see any of the outdoors till long after sundown. This program is intense, and my team— But you don't wanna hear me blab on and on about that. Talk to you later. Love you."

"You, too," she said. " 'Bye."

She *did* want to hear him blab on and on, though. About anything. She'd have spent the whole day listening to him blab.

She left the Impala downtown and took a cab home. All of the entrances to their building were quite secure and she felt safe there. So safe and snug inside, in fact, that she made herself go outside and run five miles along the lakefront in the afternoon. It was still warm and sunny, and the jogging paths were crowded.

Later she walked a mile to a Thai restaurant for supper. And walked back.

She didn't spot anyone following her. What she *felt*, though, was another matter. Frequently, and regardless of where she was, she would feel someone's eyes on her. She knew the feeling was a reaction to being stalked, certainly not based on observation and fact. And even if it were true that someone was out there somewhere, watching her, they wouldn't attack her from a distance. That would be too remote, too cold, for such a person. Anyway, she wasn't about to lock herself up in the apartment.

Inside or out, though, she did a lot of thinking, much of it fruitless, and made a few phone calls.

None of the priests turned up dead all day Saturday.

In the morning she went out for the papers and was home eating breakfast when, at five after nine, two FBI agents came. On Sunday, for God's sake. She made them wait until nine-thirty before she let them in. She didn't know if they were the same agents Wardell had spoken so disparagingly of. If not, they easily could have been, except that the whole time they were there only one of them spoke, the tall thin one. The one with the bodybuilder's physique wrote things down in a little black notebook.

"You're interfering with a police investigation," the tall one said.

"I don't believe I am," she said. "Plus, you're not police, you're—"

"We're special agents of the Federal Bureau of Investigation. We're assisting with, and coordinating, an interstate investigation being conducted by a number of police jurisdictions. Nonpolice participation is interference . . . and it's not welcome."

"What, specifically, are you asking that I stop doing?"

"It's not a request," he said. "It's a directive."

"About what, specifically? Not to talk to my own uncle? Not to bring what I believe to be helpful information to an investigating officer? Not to walk around a golf course in the rain and trip over a body? What?"

"The coincidence you pointed out to Sergeant Wardell is—"

"Jesus! The killer might change course, sure. But so far she's done *K, I, R, S,* and *T.* You think that's a coincidence?"

"She?"

"It was a woman who left the phone message for Truczik. You know that. Even *you* guys can't believe that if he called back and a *man* answered, he'd have gone out to meet him. And if you think the order these murders are following is a coincidence, tell that to Anthony Ernest. Or John Ettinger . . . wherever he is. Or to Michael Nolan, the only *N* on the list."

"What have *you* told them about this . . . theory of yours?"

"Nothing. I've told Sergeant Wardell." These guys were either amazingly stupid or deliberately avoiding the truth. "I certainly wouldn't want to *interfere* with anything an elite group of geniuses on the federal payroll dreams up."

"No ma'am, I'm sure you wouldn't." His eyes narrowed, and she knew she had crossed the line. "Keep this in mind," he said. "A five-minute phone call from one of us 'geniuses,' and you'll be getting notice from the State of Illinois that your private detective's license has been placed on probationary status. For that reason alone, I'm sure you wouldn't want to take any action that could be construed as interfering in a multiple murder investigation." He shrugged. "Am I beginning to make myself clear?"

She backed off a little, but the problem was they had their own prejudged answer to everything. When she told them about the postcards, the agent advised her that if she thought the words HERE I COME or READY OR NOT constituted a threat upon her person she should file a report at her local police station. Later he suggested that the woman who called Truczik could easily have been a man. Gay men in particular, he said, were good at imitating women's voices.

Through it all she tried to stay cool, but it wasn't easy. By the time the two men left they'd renewed their threat about her license, and she hadn't made any new promises or any new friends.

She spent the rest of Sunday much as she'd spent Saturday, including another run along the lakefront. She called Dugan and he sounded tired, but enthusiastic and caught up in his mock-trial workshop.

She resumed where she'd left off Saturday, churning the facts through her mind, trying to identify this killer who knew her name . . . and *used* it. It wasn't someone who'd learned who she was just last week, either, because whoever it was had been spelling out her name from the start. And whoever it was had to know she would eventually pick up on it. And didn't care. Maybe *wanted* her to.

She considered the phone message for Truczik a crucial factor, a turning point in helping her analyze what was going on. That phone call was so significant, in fact, that making it must have signaled a new phase in the killer's thinking, too.

In the public's mind, sexual misconduct by priests seemed to be linked almost exclusively with homosexuality, and much of what Kirsten had read and seen in the media seemed to assume the killer was a male victim of abuse. But Truczik's caller must have been a woman, whatever the FBI guys wanted to think. And the person who had shown up at Stieboldt's hospital room was a woman, too. A woman who smiled a lot, just like the woman who'd been at Bunko's when Kanowski was there. So, statistics and profiles and public perceptions notwithstanding, it appeared that this particular serial killer was probably a woman.

She concluded with even more certainty that the priest killer and her own "Here I come, ready or not" stalker were one and the same. The alternative—that two unrelated crazies knew her name, and both just happened to pick the same time to move into her world—was too big a coincidence to be credited. So it was one person with a bizarre two-item agenda: to kill abusive priests and to terrorize her. And the person was not a stranger.

Both in her years as a cop and since then, she'd made plenty of people unhappy. Ruined their lives, in fact, at least as far as *they* saw how their lives should go. Most of those people, though, were run-of-the-mill criminals pursuing their careers, and they were aware that she'd merely been pursuing hers. Many of them she couldn't even remember, and didn't need to. What she needed was a list of seriously disturbed persons with grudges against her personally. That list wouldn't be very long. And it wouldn't require a review of any records. All she needed was a sheet of paper, and her memory. She came up with a list of eleven people and then, using no tool other than her own judgment, whittled it down to six.

Four of the six were men. One of those was a cop gone bad named Walter Keegan, who might have been crazy and vengeful enough but was most assuredly dead. She didn't think she was looking for a man, and checking out the other three men would be slow going on the weekend, but using the Internet, the telephone, and some creative misrepresentations, she did the work. She was able to verify that Theodore Kopp was in a facility for the criminally insane outside Louisville, and that Carlo Morelli was a guest of the state of Illinois, in Pontiac Correctional Center. The final man, a strangely fastidious killer named Victor Utz, was unaccounted for. Utz hated Kirsten, but he was a tiny man, physically weak, and—more important—would never kill in a way that might splatter blood all over his person.

Eliminating Utz got her to where she thought she should be, because she believed the crazy in question had to be a woman. Of the two women on the list, Adele Wacker had to be well over seventy and, like Utz, was a physically small person. Again, though, Kirsten did the work, and she located Adele in a nursing home on the northwest side. That left Debra Morelli, Carlo's sister. She was a large, strong woman, psychosexually disturbed, and with ample reason to be very unhappy with Kirsten.

A mark against Debra's candidacy, of course, was that she was almost certainly dead. Still, of all those on the list—male or female—she was the one Kirsten could most easily imagine slicing off a man's skin or body parts, or impaling him with an umbrella. And unlike Walter Keegan, who was certainly dead—Kirsten had seen the bullets tear into him—Debra Morelli was only *almost* certainly dead.

No one claimed to have seen Debra die, but there was no evidence of her being alive, either; and there should have been, given the bloody circumstances surrounding her last sighting. So the cops were *assuming* she was dead. Not to mention that lots of people had been fervently *hoping* she was . . . including Kirsten.

So Kirsten knew what she had to do on Monday. But meanwhile Sunday came and went, and no priests turned up dead that day, either.

38.

A t four A.M. on Monday, Debra was on the road.

Time was racing by, but she had used her weekend well. Lots of rest, two workouts. She had never been stronger. She burned all the bloody drop cloths from the van along with the clothing, hers and that of the dead Stieboldt, and gathered up what was left of the pervert from the feeding room in the hog shed. She was fond of her two hogs and treated them kindly, but she'd learned how to withhold their food and make them very efficient. What bones they'd left she sawed up and scattered over several dumps. She was glad Stieboldt was the only one, so far, she'd had to bring home with her.

She forced herself to watch some of the media coverage, too, not because she needed validation of her efforts, but to learn what she could about public response. There was no mention of anyone mourning the dead priests, of course. Everyone knew they were animals who preyed on children. People knew, also, that they were lucky *someone* had the courage to treat those men as they deserved, as God willed.

There was no talk, either, of the order she was following. What the media stressed was that the victims were narrowly targeted, so there wasn't the general panic there'd been with the D.C. snipers, nor the outcry that would have put hundreds of police out looking for her. This time it wasn't fear that held the public spellbound, but blood and body parts, and morbid curiosity about the sexual misconduct of those priests. People were so weak, so easily drawn to sordid, sick details.

For her part, confident of God's help and with just two to go to reach the fullness of seven, she would play her cards carefully, but she would not be afraid to play. Locating Stieboldt in the hospital and catching Truczik out in the open were both the result of careful surveillance, then swift and courageous action. God helps those who help themselves.

Each purging brought its own rush of excitement and satisfaction, and she would have liked more opportunity to savor them. But she couldn't take the time. Carlo was coming out in nine days, a week from Wednesday.

It seemed so long ago, that night she'd had to run and leave him behind. That had torn her apart, and though she hadn't seen him since, everything had been for his sake. The struggle to get to Sicily, submission to the clumsy pawings of *la capra* in his compound there, the painful plastic surgeries. Then coming home, and the loneliness of hiding out. Everything was for Carlo

No one would see her, but when Carlo came out she would be watching, and she hoped to be able to gather him up at once. But she dared not contact him with advice, and he had never been smart the way she was. If he let himself be taken she had a plan. She would risk everything to save him, and with the help of God the two of them would be together again. He had never been able to function without her. She would have to protect him—and now even walk for him and talk for him. She would love him as though he were whole.

Debra drove on through the darkness, north of Chicago on I-94, the Tri-State Tollway, past the exit she always used for the seminary. Then, past the final toll booth, she exited and headed west. There were still farms up here that hadn't fallen under the developers' bulldozers.

Debra knew something about hiding out in the country and about using an alias. You couldn't create a new identity simply by moving to a new place, a rural place owned by a cousin with a different name than yours, and then calling yourself by the cousin's name.

"No," she said, "that's not enough." She was alone in the van, driving past a mailbox with the name CHRISTOPHERSON on its side, but she spoke out loud. "There's much more to it than that, my dear Father Ettinger, as you will learn."

Beyond the mailbox a driveway led up to a well-kept farmhouse. A light shone behind drawn curtains in one ground-floor window. And then, as she drove past on the road, she saw something else. Drawn up beside the house and visible in the glow of a tall, backyard pole light, sat a late-model, light-colored, four-door sedan. Not your ordinary farmer's vehicle, she thought. More like a car signed out from the pool of some governmental agency.

She cursed out loud and pounded the steering wheel with the heel of her hand . . . and drove on. But before very long she calmed herself. This setback, too, God would somehow turn into a blessing.

39.

On Monday morning Kirsten left town in the rented Impala and drove east into Indiana, then on into Michigan, headed for Detroit. It was at least a six-hour drive, and she'd struggled with whether to go that far away or not, with the killer still at large and Michael in danger. But she couldn't think of how her staying around Chicago was going to make him or the others any safer.

Besides, for them and for herself, safety lay in eliminating the source of danger, and she couldn't just sit around and hope the cops would do that. Or wait for more postcards or painted targets. Nor would she settle for calling someone three hundred miles away on the phone and hope he'd take the time to answer her questions, hope he'd open up to someone he'd probably think had gone off the deep end herself.

But she hadn't. She had spent Saturday and Sunday working out the possibilities, and had rejected the idea that the crazy who was killing priests and terrorizing her was someone completely unknown to her. First, that seemed so unlikely as to be barely possible; and second, if that were the case, and given the scarcity of evidence, there'd be nothing to do but lie back and wait . . . which was unacceptable.

So she had thought and rethought, made her list and scratched out names, logged onto Web sites, exchanged phone calls and e-mails, and became convinced it was Debra Morelli she was looking for. Born in Detroit, Debra had lived there until she moved to Chicago with her brother, Carlo. So Detroit was the place to start looking, even though it was in Chicago that Debra had dropped off the face of the earth.

It had happened four years ago. Kirsten was hired by, of all people, Larry Candle, for what seemed a simple task—find the witness who could exonerate Larry and keep the Supreme Court from pulling his law license. But Larry hadn't told Kirsten quite everything, and she and Dugan found themselves one night in a life-and-death battle with Debra and Carlo. When Debra fled, leaving Carlo behind, they didn't chase after her. She was armed, after all, and they weren't. Besides, her neck and face had been slashed and she was bleeding so badly everyone assumed she'd surface in an E.R. soon enough. She didn't, though. She never turned up anywhere. So people made another assumption: that she was dead.

Meanwhile, Carlo—the brother for whom Debra had shown a weird, domineering, sexual affection—hadn't run anywhere, because in the struggle that night he took a bullet in the thigh. Later, in custody and awaiting trial, he lost the leg in surgery. He'd still been in the hospital attached to Cook County Jail, learning to walk on crutches—or should have been—the night all hell broke out in the jail, and Carlo's throat was slit.

The feds had been trying to turn him. They were after his

mobbed-up uncle, Paolo Morelli. Paolo was called "Polly"—no one joked about that in his presence more than once—and Carlo and Debra had been cheating him in a poorly concocted drug scheme, the darker side of Larry Candle's "simple" case. The scheme failed, and the feds thought Carlo might like to help send Polly on vacation. He should have been safe in the hospital while the Justice Department jumped through the necessary hoops to get him transferred to federal custody, but a guard took him across into the jail itself. Interestingly, the guard was the only one killed that night.

Carlo survived his razor wounds, but never again spoke above a hoarse whisper. The feds didn't take him and he eventually cut a deal and went to state prison. Meanwhile, Polly Morelli continued to thrive in his mansion in Forest Park, and Debra Morelli remained among the missing.

Kirsten stopped for a sandwich in Ann Arbor and only then remembered she'd gone into the eastern time zone and it was an hour later than she thought. By the time she got to Detroit and found the police station on Clinton Street she was afraid she was too late to catch the detective she wanted to talk to. His name was John Frontera, and he was waiting for her.

"And," he said, eyeing her with frank admiration, "I'm so glad I waited."

He was a handsome, heavyset, ebony-skinned man, with a shaved head and a tiny diamond in one earlobe. The appraising look he gave her would have been offensive from anyone else, but his tone and his smile were so engaging she couldn't get properly pissed off.

After Debra fled that night in Chicago and couldn't be found, Frontera and his partner had been assigned to see whether she'd show up in Detroit. Kirsten had spoken with him on the phone several times to follow up, the last time about two years ago. He had the deep resonant voice of an opera singer, and he always sounded easygoing and charming—even flirtatious. He was cooperative, too, even though he knew she wasn't a cop. That's why she'd called and left word that she was coming to Detroit and would appreciate a meeting.

"I got your message," he said. "And if I'd been here, sugar, I'd have told you it's no sense driving clear over here if it's about Debra Morelli." He called her "sugar" easily, as though they were old friends, and she followed him to an interview room where the walls were a dirty gray and the table between them was bolted to the floor.

"Thanks for seeing me, anyway," she said. Besides the fact that a personal visit made almost everyone open up more readily, Frontera in particular was clearly the sort who enjoyed giving attention to—and getting it from—the ladies. "I'm sure if you had any news about her," she said, "you'd have notified Chicago." He nodded, and she added, "But they wouldn't have told me."

"Hey, you don't think I'd have called you myself? Just to get to talk to you?" He smiled. "Anyway, there's been no sign of her. Of course no one's *looking* for her, either. We're not short on things to do here."

"I understand," she said. "And all I'm asking is for you to maybe point me in the right direction, and . . . well . . . I'd like to keep what we talk about quiet, between you and me." His eyes widened slightly. "That is," she added, not wanting to lose him, "if I say something you *need* to talk about, you talk. I understand that."

"Right," was all he said, but she could tell he was intrigued.

"I'm reaching here," she said, "with nothing solid to back up what I'm thinking. It's about the murders of those Chicago priests, and when I mention it to the cops at home all they do is roll their eyes. In fact," and here she lowered her voice, "if it comes out I'm poking around in this, after a couple of asshole FBI agents warned me *not* to . . ." She spread her hands out, palms up. "Well . . . you know. It's probably a cage in Guantanamo for me. No lawyer, no bail."

"Yeah," he said, "I know what you mean." She had his total attention now. Cops love to hate the FBI.

"I have this belief." She shook her head. "No, really just a suspicion. I think Debra Morelli may be killing those priests."

"Ho-ly Christ!" he said. "I mean . . . when we were watching for her I read every old report I could find that had anything to do with her, and let me tell you . . . if that woman's alive, she's fucked up enough for anything."

"Right. Enough to kill her own father, I understand."

"No proof, but she did it all right. Jump-Joe Morelli. She got hold of a sawed-off somehow and blew his head from here to Windsor, and never batted an eye the whole time our people pushed her on it. And she wasn't but fifteen back then. That brother of hers . . . Franco, was it? He—"

"Carlo."

"Yeah, Carlo. Equally fucked up. But a couple years younger and under her thumb. Word was the two kids were gettin' it on together."

"I saw them together," she said, "and it looked that way to me, too."

"Anyway, the dicks figured Carlo as an accessory, but not the shooter. Of course, no one gave much of a shit about the victim. They called him Jump-Joe because he'd jump any female in sight . . . even his own little girl, I guess. The guy was an animal, and he died like one."

"The mother's dead, too, right?"

"Liver cancer. Around a year later. I guess she was a trip, too.

201

She—" Something beeped and he stopped to check a pager at his belt. "They're after me, and probably need this room," he said, but he didn't make a move to go anywhere. "So tell me, sugar, what is it you want, in particular?"

"Two things. Everyone seems convinced Debra's father abused her. But I wonder if there's any evidence of sexual abuse by a priest, too. That's one thing. The other is any suggestion about where she might be hiding if she's around. I mean, did her family have property, like a house? Does she have relatives somewhere? Anything at all. Maybe I could find something in those reports you mentioned that—"

"No way. I'm not gonna dig out any reports and hand 'em over. It'd be my ass if I did. Not unless you got proof this whacked-out bitch is alive and can pin a string of murders on her, and you wanna give me the arrest."

"I don't have that," she said. "All I have's an idea. But if I *do* turn up something—and it's around here?—I swear you'll be the first one I go to."

"Yeah, well . . ." He stood up and opened the door and yelled at someone that he'd be a few minutes longer, then closed the door again and sat down. "As to priests? There *is* something. A couple of years after her father tragically lost his head, Debra was wanted in Cincinnati for questioning in connection with a homicide there. The victim was a priest named Lasorda. I guess the killing was all over the papers in Cincy. Guy was cut up pretty bad."

"So what happened?"

"With Debra? Nothing. She gave a statement. She was about seventeen then, and she came in voluntarily. No fuss about its being an out-of-state warrant. They wanted to talk to her because the priest was known to have been a friend of the Morelli family when he was in Detroit—weird in itself for a priest. And it seems he was shipped off to Cincinnati after rumors started spreading of him messing around with little girls here. Anyway, they asked Debra and she said the rumors were ridiculous, that everyone knew he was a holy man. That was it. She was never officially a suspect. Do you think—"

"Anything's possible, but if they couldn't tie it to her at the time . . ." She paused. "The name was Lasorda?"

"Right. Same as the Dodgers' ex-manager. That's why I remember. First name Gene, or Gino or something."

She wrote it down, then said, "So . . . any ideas where Debra might hole up?"

"Not a clue. The house she was raised in was where she and Carlo lived with an aunt after their mother died. Carlo quit school and basically moped around until Debra took him to Chicago. That's after she went to college . . . and then *law* school, for chrissake. A very bright, very whacked out young lady. Somewhere in there the house was sold, and that whole block's been bulldozed since then. The Outfit guys her father hung with are scattered. You already know about the uncle in Chicago, Polly Morelli."

"Yeah, but she wouldn't go there. She and Carlo were cheating him on a drug deal when they got caught."

"That I don't know about, but he might have finally realized it was *her* who killed his brother. When it happened he insisted it had to be some local rival. Anyway, no one thought she went to Polly. She *might* have gone to Italy for a while, but that's not for sure. And there's no sign of her ever coming back into the country. Which doesn't mean she didn't."

"Coming and going was easier back then," Kirsten said. "Before nine-eleven."

"I guess. Anyway . . . property? None I know about. The aunt who took care of 'em for a while had a place in Sanilac County . . . up in the Thumb? . . . and went back there when the kids got

203

older. My partner and I went to see her when Chicago first called. Near a town called . . . what? . . . Water-something. I don't even remember going *through* the town. He drove and I slept the whole way."

"*Water*-something?"

"Yeah, like Waterville, Waterford . . . something like that. I only remember *that* much because it rained like hell that day. Anyway, it was a rundown house on a rundown farm. Not worth shit. What the aunt—her name was Angela, I think—what she was doing way up in the country I don't know, but she was a Morelli, and as mental as the rest of 'em. Old hag, three hundred pounds easy. Could hardly walk. Told us she'd 'cut the fucking slut's heart out'—those were her words—if Debra ever showed up there. The last time you called, I had someone check her out again. She went into a nursing home and her place was sold. I guess to pay the bills. She's probably dead by now." He shrugged. "'Fraid that's it, sugar. Sorry."

"Well, it's way more than I knew before," she said. "And I really appreciate it."

By this time he was standing again. "Look here," he said, "if you're staying in town overnight and you're free about eight, there's a new Japanese restaurant over on—"

"Y'know, you've been great and I'd love to," she said, "but—"

"Yeah, I thought so."

She smiled. "Right. And thanks. I mean it. Thanks a lot."

40.

Debra identified herself as "Deirdre Anzelmo" and gave her phony story. The woman on the other end of the line—"Mollie" something—sounded halfway intelligent, but Debra had her script well thought out and stayed one step ahead of her. Pleasant but insistent, that was the approach to take.

"Maybe you don't understand," Debra said. "I'm a lawyer, and my client lives here in Hartford. But her brother lives in Chicago and he suffered a serious spinal cord injury in an accident there, and my client just discovered that the lawyer she retained in Chicago has done nothing at *all* on the case. *Nothing.* This is a major, *major* case, and the statute of limitations will expire in six months."

"You've said all that already, and I *do* understand, Miss Anzelmo. If you'd give me your number, one of the attorneys in the firm will get back—"

"I *told* you, I don't *want* 'one of the attorneys.' The man who suggested your office said to speak to the head of the firm." Pleasant but insistent. "I'll call back," she said. "When will he be in?"

"He'll be out all week, but one of other lawyers, Mr. Candle, can—"

"I suppose I'll have to try a different firm." She paused. "You mean there's *nowhere* he can be reached, even on the phone?"

"He's at a trial lawyers' conference in Asheville, Miss Anzelmo. He *does* call in for messages, so if you give me your number maybe he can call you back."

"I'm a sole practitioner, and I'm in the middle of a trial, and you know how *that* is. I'll be in court all day. If I could just call his hotel, maybe sometime this evening? If he doesn't want to take the call or call me back, so be it. It's not like I don't have other names I've been given. But I have to get moving on this."

In the end Debra got the name and number of the hotel, and was sure it was the threat of their losing a "major, *major* case" that had tipped the scales in her favor. When she didn't call him that night they'd think she'd gotten impatient and contacted a different firm. There's no reason they'd be suspicious.

He was "at a trial lawyers' conference," and she could easily find out from the hotel exactly what "all week" meant. Circumstances were again causing a change of plans. One had to be both strong and flexible.

Dugan called Mollie to make sure the ship was still afloat. "Any calls?"

"Pretty slow for a Monday," Mollie said, and read him a list of about a dozen people.

"Larry can handle all of those," he said. "Anything else?"

"Some lawyer from Hartford, Connecticut, called about a case she wants to refer. A 'major, *major* case,' she says."

"Yeah, right," he said. "Aren't they all."

"This is such a *major* case," Mollie said, "that the first lawyer the family hired didn't do anything on it at all, and now the statute of limitations is about to expire. The name of the lawyer who called is Deirdre Anzelmo and I think she's a little flaky."

"Have Larry call her," Dugan said.

"Said she was on trial and couldn't be reached on the phone. But she *did* say it was a spinal cord injury, so . . . who knows? I gave her the name of your hotel. I did *not* promise you'd call her back. That's up to you."

"I won't," he said. "Anything else?"

"Nothing going on *here* but work," she said, with the clear implication that he was neglecting the office.

"Yeah, well, same thing here. We're on the go from early morning till late at night. These kids are sharp. You should scc how——"

"Y'know," Mollie said, "I got two calls waiting, so . . ."

He hung up.

Even if the case that damn Hartford lawyer called about *did* involve a bad injury, it was an old case. Stale. And probably a case where proving fault on someone's part was impossible, or where the guilty party had no insurance. He didn't need another headache.

This damn workshop was enjoyable, but it took a lot of intense work. What he needed right now was a fifteen-minute nap.

He put the Hartford lawyer and her bullshit case out of his mind.

41.

Leaving the Clinton Street police station, Kirsten hurried back to the Impala. At this point she wouldn't bother with newspaper archives about the murder of Father Lasorda. Frontera's statements that the priest was cut up pretty bad, and that there were rumors of him messing around with little girls, seemed to tell the tale. Besides, right now the big questions were: Where was Aunt Angela's farm? Who owned it? Who sold it? And to whom?

It was just past six o'clock. Traffic was heavy and it would be getting dark soon, so she just headed out of town as fast as she could. She'd never heard of Sanilac County, but she knew the "Thumb" of Michigan was straight up from Detroit.

She took I-94 northeast, got off when she'd left the city behind, and cut back west and then north. At I-69 she stopped for gas and a look at the road atlas. She found Sanilac County, and then Waterton, which had to be the town Frontera meant. It was a dot on a thin gray line with no route number. North of Decker, which was west of Sandusky. Those last two towns sounded familiar for some reason, but she couldn't think why they would.

Probably the easiest way to find Debra's aunt's old farm would be to talk to local law enforcement at Waterton. Except they'd want to know what she was up to, and word might get back somehow to the FBI and she didn't want those two idiot agents trying to get her PI license pulled. She had a little clout of her own, and didn't know how easily they could do that, but since 9/11 and the Patriot Act the feds had more power than ever and she didn't want to take a chance. So, no cops.

She had over fifty miles still to go. By the time she got up there it would be dark, and most people more easily put up with annoying questions from strangers in the light of day. The best time was in the morning, when the whole world seemed a little more open and optimistic, and a little less suspicious and hostile.

Actually, she thought, maybe all that time-of-day stuff was in her own mind. But at any rate, she was tired of driving, and she wanted a comfortable place to call Dugan from. She didn't plan to tell him where she was. He didn't have to know everything that was going on.

There were several motels near the interstate and she picked a Red Roof Inn.

It was a warm, sunny morning. Waterton was a bigger town than Kirsten had expected. The downtown was an old-fashioned square. She drove the perimeter, with stores on her right and a well-kept plot of grass with a statue of a soldier and some benches on her left. A lot of the stores were vacant, but there seemed to be a resurgence trying to take place, for the most part cutesy gift and antique stores. There was, though, a real grocery store—a Kroger's—and a drugstore, an appliance store, a diner, a hardware store, and . . . yes . . . a real estate office.

BAGGS' REALTY was painted in an arc on the window and there were a dozen photocopied notices of properties for sale, with fading black and white pictures of houses and farm buildings taped to the glass facing the sidewalk. The front door was held wide open with a piece of clothesline looped around the handle and then over a hook in the wall.

The office was very small, and the woman at the first of two desks—no one sat at the other—looked up from her computer monitor. She was maybe fifty years old, with short gray hair and a bright, helpful smile. A copy of *The Tao of Pooh* sat on the desk, and under it a *New Yorker* magazine. "May I help you?" she asked.

"I hope so," Kirsten said. "Although I have to say I'm not looking to buy or sell any property."

The eyes took on a what-else-is-new look, but the smile faded only a trace. "Rent, maybe? We handle some nice fishing cabins along the river."

"Maybe next summer," Kirsten said. She introduced herself and said she was a writer. "A freelance journalist, actually. I'm working on a story about the history of organized crime in Detroit, and about the homes in the country some of the gangsters used to have . . . to sort of get away from it all."

Before Kirsten had finished, the woman was up and walking across the little room to a coffeemaker on a table against the opposite wall. She turned. "Have a seat," she said, and nodded to a chair beside her desk. "Coffee?"

"That'd be great." Kirsten sat down and noticed a game of solitaire on the computer screen. "No cream, no sugar." She took the large white ceramic mug the woman gave her and sipped. "Wow!" she said. "That's delicious."

"Thank you." The woman sat down again and sipped her own coffee. "It *is* good. My name is Eleanor Baggs, and I don't know a thing that could help you at all in your search." She sounded refreshingly truthful, and not just trying to avoid something. "But that must be so *interesting*. To be a writer, I mean."

"I always thought so, too," Kirsten said. "But truthfully? I'm *not* one." She dug her ID out of her purse. "I'm a private investigator, from Chicago."

The woman stared, wide-eyed, at the card in the folder, then handed it back. "Oh my," she said.

Kirsten nodded. "Um . . . if you want to kick me out, Eleanor, wait until I finish this coffee, would you?"

"The part about gangsters' hideouts? That was true, right?"

"Pretty much so." Kirsten smiled. "But I'm looking for just one place. It's a—"

"Gangsters I'm not so sure of, but I moved here from New Jersey last year to help out my uncle, and found out they have more than their share of crazies around here. Militia groups, skinheads, extremists who think Armageddon's around the corner." Eleanor clearly felt like talking. "People say maybe it's something in the soil, or the water. Remember Timothy McVeigh? The Oklahoma City bomber?" When Kirsten nodded she went on. "One of his buddies lived not far from here."

"Decker," Kirsten said, knowing now why the name had seemed so familiar. The address on McVeigh's driver's license had been Decker, Michigan.

"Yes. It's a shame, too." Eleanor shook her head and sipped her coffee. "A lovely little town, and the only thing the world knows about it now is—"

"Memories fade," Kirsten said. "But I'm looking for a farm where a woman named Morelli lived. The address is Waterton."

"Is she a gangster?"

"Her brother was. I understand she had a place up here. At least she did until as late as four years ago. I'm told it's been sold since then."

As Kirsten spoke, Eleanor started typing on the keyboard, her eyes on the monitor. "Is that *M-O-R-E-L-L-I?*" she said.

"Yes. First name Angela."

Eleanor typed some more. "Can't find any Morelli at all."

"Well . . ." Kirsten thought. "Maybe she got married . . . or divorced . . . Maybe your uncle would remember something."

"My uncle doesn't remember things any more. He . . . he's getting old."

"Oh, I'm so sorry," Kirsten said. "Well, are there other real estate agents in town? Maybe someone—"

"There's Cassie Jones. She's the wife of the police chief, and she's not very—"

"Right. Well . . . how many farm sales could there be, anyway?"

"I suppose I could find *all* sales of record, and then cull out . . ." Eleanor went back to her keyboard. "I take it you don't have an address?"

"What I have is 'a rundown house on a rundown farm, near Waterton.' That's it."

Eleanor laughed. "We got *lots* of those. Is it north of here? South? What?"

"I don't know. Look, maybe I—"

"Let me try something." Eleanor seemed to be really into this search, maybe because it beat computer solitaire. "When was the sale?"

"Two or . . . let's see . . . make it within the last four years."

Twenty minutes later Eleanor Baggs had printed out a list of nine farms with Waterton mailing addresses that were bought and sold within the previous four years. Five were working farms whose owners she had either met personally or knew by reputation. Two were purchased by the same large agricultural conglomerate. "Damn them," Eleanor said. "They have no—"

"Uh-huh." Kirsten said. "What about the last two?"

"Let's see." Eleanor typed and consulted the screen. "This one was purchased three years ago, by something called the Dearborn Hunt Club." She typed some more. "And this one . . . ah . . . two and a half years ago. Seller was . . . First Bank of Waterton as trustee under trust number blah blah. Purchaser . . . Mapleleaf Bank of Toronto as trustee under trust number blah blah."

"Which means what?" Kirsten said. "Some Canadian bank holds the title, but just as a trustee? And whoever's the beneficiary of the trust is the *real* owner?"

"That's right. That's pretty common. Sometimes the beneficiary of the trust transfers his interest to someone else—essentially sells the property—and it won't show up as a sale because—"

"Because the owner of record stays the same, the bank."

"Which means," Eleanor said, "that if this Angela Morelli's farm was held in trust, she could have sold it to someone and I wouldn't be able to find the sale."

"So," Kirsten said, "I'd be better off looking around town for someone who actually knew Angela Morelli, and where her farm was."

"Maybe. But like I say, there's a lot of oddballs out there that nobody really knows. Mostly they keep to themselves, do their shopping at some place like the Wal-Mart over at Saginaw. You'll find plenty of places with fences and huge dogs and KEEP OUT signs, and you never know if it's just an ornery farmer or someone building bombs in—"

"So how many pieces of property are out there, big enough to be called a farm, that have a Waterton address?"

"That's a tough one. Around here a farm could be over a thousand acres, or just a few. People from the city see a house with a stand of corn along a country road and they call it a farm."

"So what are we talking about? Dozens of places?"

"With a Waterton address, but outside town proper? I'd say dozens, easy. Fifty, maybe. George Kleeman might know. He's the postmaster."

Postmaster, Kirsten thought. *Duh.*

42.

George Kleeman was a tall, slightly stooped over man, in maybe his midseventies. Quite thin, except under his belt, where he looked like he'd swallowed a beer keg. A long skinny neck stuck up from the collar of his white shirt, and long skinny arms stuck out from its short sleeves. His tie was dark blue and polyester and so were his pants.

Kirsten sat across from Kleeman at a wooden picnic table under a shade tree beside the small, spotless brick post office on the north edge of Waterton. "I bought and paid for this table myself," he said, "so's my people could eat their lunch out here. You ever try and get somethin' *useful* like this outta the postal service? Hah! We did better when it was the government."

Kleeman's *people* were either out on their routes or inside, sorting mail or manning the surprisingly busy window. Kirsten had been waiting about a half hour and there'd been scarcely a moment when a car wasn't driving away and another one pulling up.

She asked, again, whether Kleeman knew of an Angela Morelli or her farm.

"You asked me that three times now, cutie," he said. He was studiously wiping his wire-framed glasses with a handkerchief.

"I know," she said, "but—"

"I'm thinking, darn it. I'm not stupid, or forgetful. Hah!"

"Sorry." She sat back. "I just thought maybe you were wondering if you should answer. You know, concerned about confidentiality or something."

"So far you haven't asked me what kinda mail she got, or how often, or who it's from. What's confidential about a person having a mailbox out in front of their house? Or the mail carrier going up their walk now and then?"

"Right. I couldn't have put it better myself."

"Hah!" He put on his glasses, one wire earpiece at a time, squinting as though it were a pretty painful process. "If an Angela Morelli got mail through this office in the last thirty years," he said, "I'd remember it. Doesn't mean she wouldn't be out there if I didn't. Would just mean she never got mail that came through here. I'd remember it if she did."

"Well, then," Kirsten said, "how about—"

"Hah!"

"What?"

"Did I answer your question?" he asked.

"Well, not really. But I thought—"

"You thought I was some old fool out in the sticks didn't know squat." He smiled then, and she suddenly realized he was having a great time. Maybe, like Eleanor Baggs, he was taking a break from a game of solitaire. "Okay," he said, "the answer's no. I never heard of anyone named Morelli in my district, Angela or anything else."

She couldn't help but like this guy. "All right, then," she said, "how about a three-hundred-pound Italian woman who lived in a rundown house on a rundown farm near Waterton, and a few years ago went to a nursing home and her house was sold, and she died? How about that?"

"Does she have to be Italian?" he said.

"Are you putting me on again?"

"Nope. There was a woman like you described, lived five miles north of here. Two, three years ago she got to where she couldn't walk and had to go into a nursing home . . . or die. Said she didn't have a dime. And no relatives. *Somebody* had to take her in, and Green Meadows did, because a lawyer came and said her place was sold and paid for two months on the spot. Said the payments would keep coming, each month in advance. And they did. Cash money. By mail. Hah! Who says you can't trust the U.S. Postal Service?"

"What was the woman's name?"

"She was pretty sick by then. Heart failure, mostly. Not talking much. The lawyer *said* her name was Anna Bergstrom. She had no identification, no Social Security number, no Medicare, no nothing. Never had a visitor and only lasted six months. When she died the cash came for a cremation."

"I'm just wondering," Kirsten said. "How is it that *you* know all this?"

"Hah! Made it all up!" He obviously enjoyed the look on her face and then said, "Actually, no, I didn't. Thing is, I *own* Green Meadows Nursing Home, and a couple more, too."

She shook her head. She asked where the woman's home was and who bought it, and Kleeman gave her directions and said the place had sat empty for a long time. He thought someone was living there now, but whoever it was never got any mail.

"You about wrapped up with your questions?" he asked.

"Almost. What was this lawyer's name?"

"Hah! Who said it was a 'he'? It was a lady lawyer . . . if she

211

was a lawyer. Kinda pretty, too, but big and strong looking. *Too* big for my taste, and she had this big phony smile on her face all the time. Like she thought someone was gonna take her picture."

"What about a *name?*"

"Oh. 'Jane Adams' is what she *said.* Never left a phone number or an address. Even the cash came in an envelope with no return address. And that big old Anna didn't look much like a Bergstrom, either. Truth is, she looked more like a Morelli, now that you mention it. Anyway, she's dead now. And her bills were paid. Hah!" He stood up, obviously anxious to go.

"One more thing," Kirsten said. "If there was no way for you to contact this so-called lawyer, how did she know to send money for a cremation?"

Kleeman rested his palms on the table and leaned toward her. "You know what? I always wondered about that myself."

Kirsten had a difficult time finding her way, even with George Kleeman's crude, hand-drawn map on the passenger seat. She went past cornfields and pastures, and the occasional farmhouse, and finally came to the abandoned railroad tracks marked on the map. Just beyond that she turned onto a side road—gravel and apparently not well-traveled—and about a mile later came to the place where "Anna Bergstrom" had lived.

She had a vague notion of how big an acre was—"a little less than a football field," Dugan had once told her—and the property looked to her to be several acres, surrounded on three sides by fields from which the crops—something growing low to the ground, like beans—hadn't yet been harvested. She saw no corn on the property, but otherwise it was just the sort of place the Realtor Eleanor Baggs had described when she said city people see a house with a stand of corn along a country road and call it a farm.

She approached from the west and drove on past the house until, about four-tenths of a mile east of it by the odometer, the road first rose a little and then dipped sharply down to an old one-lane bridge over a narrow river. There were lots of trees along the river's banks, going off in both directions from the road. Past the river the road rose up again and then ended, making a T with a crossroad, also gravel.

She turned around and drove back. Away from the river the land was flat with only an occasional tree, usually near the road. The house was set back about fifty yards at the end of a straight, narrow drive. There was no fence along the road, but the entrance to the driveway was built up over a metal culvert set into a deep drainage ditch that ran alongside the road, east almost to the river and west as far as she could see. The ditch, and a chain strung across the drive between iron posts, probably barred most vehicles from the premises.

There were shade trees up near the house and, farther out, rows of evergreens that made a windbreak along the west and north sides of the property. Apparently this had been a working farm in the past, because she could see a barn—sagging now to one side, no paint at all on its weathered gray sides, a section of the roof caved in—and a few other equally tired-looking sheds. Farther out, in the corner where the two rows of evergreens met, sat a three-sided shed about the size of a two- or three-car garage, with a roof that sloped back from the open front. It lacked paint, too, but at least the walls stood up straight.

If there were any tractors or machinery or vehicles on the property at all, they were inside the barn or one of the other buildings. There were no animals in sight, either. And no people.

One indication the house was inhabited, though, was that the grass—or weeds or whatever—was mowed short all the way out to the farmer's fields. She parked and walked over for a closer look at the barricade across the drive. It was a thick heavy chain, showing no sign of rust, with each end secured to its post by a large, sturdy-looking padlock. Not much short of a tank would get through or over that barrier, and it struck her that a person would have to be pretty strong just to lift one end of the chain to fasten it in place.

She was wondering whether to walk up to the house when her cell phone rang, from the front seat of the car. She ran back and dug it out of her purse. "Hello?"

"Kirsten?" It was Michael, talking *way* too loud. "Is that *you?"*

"It is, and you don't have to shout."

"Oh, sorry." Much better. "I'm on the cell phone, out in my car so no one will hear. There's . . . there's a problem here."

"A problem? What problem?"

"It's Tony. Father Anthony Ernest. He always sleeps late and when he didn't show up for breakfast I didn't think much about it. But now it's almost eleven o'clock . . . and nobody knows where he is."

43.

Michael told her that on the previous afternoon two FBI agents had shown up at Villa St. George. "They were checking our security arrangements," he said, "but before they left they took Tony and me aside. They said it might be just a coincidence, but that the first letters of the victims' last names so far were—"

"I know. Spelling out the name 'Kirsten.'"

"Right! But why *your* name?"

"It's 'Kirsten,'" she said. "It's not necessarily me. But go on. Did the FBI say to do anything?"

"They just told the two of us to be extra careful, and then they left. Oh, they made us swear not to tell anyone else—including the other priests, so they wouldn't get careless. They don't want it to get into the media, either, and—"

"Let's get back to Anthony Ernest," she said.

"Oh . . . well . . . it's like that was the last straw for Tony. He was really scared. He'd have been better off not know—"

"Michael, what did he *do?*"

"He's gone. That's what I just said. Last night was Monday, my AA meeting night, and I told him I'd skip it and we'd stay together. But he said why make it easy for the killer to catch an *E* and the only *N* together in one place? He said if he hid somewhere, like John Ettinger—the only other *E*—he'd be safer. We'd *both* be safer, he said."

"But where would he hide?"

"He . . . he said not to tell anyone, but I *have* to tell *you*. He has this friend—or not a friend exactly. It's a man he helped a year or two ago when he was still assigned to St. Jeremiah's in Rogers Park. The man was in the country illegally and worked as a janitor at a big apartment building across from the church, and lived in the basement. Tony says he's still there and would take him in. I told him that was nonsense and he's safer here, and I was *sure* I'd talked him out of it. But now . . . now he's not anywhere around."

"Did you call the police? Have you told them about the man . . . the janitor?"

"The security people called, but the police haven't gotten here yet, so no one's asked me anything. The thing is, Tony said the man's supporting his girlfriend and their baby, who are both citizens here. But he's a Moslem—from Syria, I think—and if they find him they'll deport him, or maybe even send him to prison. That part really worries me. If Tony *did* go there, I sure wouldn't want to get the man deported . . . just for helping him, and—" He stopped, then said, "*You* won't tell anyone, will you?"

"Michael, I'm a day's drive away. I'll call you after I get back. Meanwhile, if anyone questions you—especially the FBI—you *have* to tell the truth. If you don't, you could have a big problem."

"I'm not in the habit of lying," he said. "But then, what else *is* there but problems?"

It was just past noon, and it was a good seven hours to Chicago. It made no sense for Kirsten to race back to help look for Father

Anthony Ernest, not until she finished what she'd come to Michigan to do. Although convinced that she'd found Debra Morelli's hideaway, she had to try to make sure. There was no mailbox, of course, and nothing to indicate who, if anyone, lived here.

She walked up the drive toward the house, her hand on the Colt .380 in her coat pocket. The whole time she'd been here not one car had passed by in either direction. If someone did come, they couldn't get very close without being seen. As she walked up to the house, she became more convinced that *someone* lived here. There were no broken windows; no trash was lying around.

It was a two-story frame house, white with faded green trim, and missing the covered front porch that Kirsten thought made so many farmhouses look so cozy. The basement windows were painted over on the inside. Unpleated curtains, possibly made of tan bedsheets, hung straight down at all the other windows. Four concrete steps with wrought-iron railings led up to a wide stoop and a windowless front door.

She went up the steps and saw a circle on the doorjamb where there'd once been a bell, and marks indicating hinge sites for a screen door, also gone. Still clenching the gun in her pocket with her right hand, she pounded on the door with her left. No answer. She tried the knob and it turned, but the door was locked with a keyed, turnbolt lock. She went down the steps and around to the back. That door was locked, too. As was the set of sloping cellar doors. All the locks looked sturdy and new.

The huge double doors on the front of the sagging barn were closed, but an entry door on the side was standing open. She went to the doorway and looked inside. Thin lines of sunlight streaming in through cracks in the walls, and a larger column through the hole in the roof, served more to accent the shadows than to dispel the darkness. The few windows along the side walls were coated with years of grime and illuminated nothing. She stepped farther in and ran face-first into a sticky spiderweb, and had to pick it, strand by strand, away from her skin and out of her hair. The barn was filthy and smelled strongly of rotting vegetables and the droppings of small animals. She stood and listened, but heard only the occasional flapping of the wings of birds—or bats, maybe—flitting around up near the roof.

Suddenly she heard a car approaching on the gravel road. She ran back outside and saw an old red pickup roar by at about sixty miles an hour, tossing up a wake of stones and dust. It didn't slow down as it passed the house and the parked Impala, and it quickly dipped out of view down by the river. She could still hear it, though, and could tell when it got beyond the river and came to the end of the road, slowed, and turned onto the crossroad. It accelerated again, and then the sound faded away into the distance.

She didn't go back into the barn, but checked the nearby sheds and found them equally dirty and deserted and empty. Except for one. That one had been cleaned out and had a fenced-in pen inside it, and in the pen were two pigs. Or hogs maybe, she thought, if there was a difference. They were huge, anyway, and ugly, and they didn't bother to get up on their feet when she came in. They lifted their heads and made low snorting noises, and stared at her with mean eyes that made her shudder at what they were thinking about. Apparently no one had been in to clean up for a while, because the pigs and their shed smelled even worse than the barn.

Finally she walked out to the three-sided building near the corner where the two rows of evergreens met. With its wide-open front it was easy to see that it was empty. It was an undivided space, a little wider and deeper than a two-car garage; the roof was about twelve feet high at the front and sloped down to maybe eight feet at the back. The floor was hard-packed dirt, and the tracks leading in and out showed that the shed was used for vehicles or some type of farm machinery. An unopened case of twenty-four quarts of motor oil sat up against one side wall.

With nothing more to look at, she turned and walked back to the house, and then down the drive toward the Impala. The sun was still out, so it startled her to hear distant thunder. She looked up to see storm clouds rolling in from the west.

There were no toys or swing sets in sight, or anything else indicating children lived here. And it wasn't some group of skinheads or militia types, because those would be men, and this place seemed neat and clean, as though a woman were in charge. She'd have loved to look around inside the house, but even if she'd had her tools with her it wouldn't have been easy to pick any of those locks. And she sure wasn't about to break in and leave notice to Debra—and that's who lived here, she was sure—that someone had an interest in the house and its occupants.

She could contact the Detroit detective, Frontera, and tell him she found Angela Morelli's old place and was pretty certain Debra Morelli was living there now. But as she played that conversation out in her mind she knew it wasn't a call she would make. First, she had no real proof that Debra lived here. Second, Debra wasn't a high priority on anyone's list for her part in the crimes that had sent Carlo to jail.

Nor was there any point in calling Danny Wardell in Rockford. He took her way more seriously than those two FBI idiots, but she had nothing solid to tie Debra to the priest killings. She had told Wardell about the postcards and the target on her door and her punctured tire, but from his point of view she had only a *belief* that the murderer and her unseen stalker, assuming there was one, were the same person . . . and a woman. Beyond that, he would discount Kirsten's belief that Debra Morelli matched her "profile" of who that woman must be, and say it was only a *guess*.

225

Thus, about all she would accomplish by calling any cops at this point was to line herself up in the FBI's crosshairs. No thank you. She got into the Impala and drove away. With the time difference, and a little luck, she could be back in Chicago by seven o'clock that evening.

A combination of factors made it almost midnight when Kirsten got home. Rain had started falling shortly after she left, and it got worse the farther west she went. The traffic was terrible, too, with a multicar accident on the interstate somewhere around Gary, and then construction making one lane out of the Skyway—the towering bridge that spanned the entire southeast side of Chicago from the Indiana-Illinois border to the Dan Ryan Expressway.

What delayed her more than all of that, though, was her decision to stop at every home she could find within a two or three mile radius of "Anna Bergstrom"'s place and ask whether anyone knew who lived there now. No one did. In fact, no one had ever heard of Anna Bergstrom or Angela Morelli. Basically, no one knew one damn thing they wanted to share with some strange woman from Chicago who drove around in the rain asking weird questions. She decided it wasn't a myth after all that such interviews go better on bright cheerful mornings.

When she got home it was too late to call Michael. She listened to her phone messages. One was from Dugan, who said he was exhausted and not to wake him up. The other was from Harvey Wilson, the man in charge of security at the seminary. He left his cell phone number. "Call me," he said, "no matter how late it is."

So she did, and he answered right away and sounded like a man with a lot to worry about.

"These priests," he said, "I mean, the cardinal told them they don't have to stay here. So I can't keep them here if they *wanna* leave. The problem is, I'm not set up to keep track of them unless they cooperate."

"I know." She was asleep on her feet and wondered what the hell Wilson thought she could do about anything.

"But I'm responsible here," he went on, "so if one of them disappears, how do I know he's not kidnapped, or . . . you know . . . dead or something?"

"I understand. So how do you know whether Anthony Ernest just decided to live somewhere else, or was—"

"Exactly," he said. "But the reason I called is your uncle. Father Nolan. The FBI wanted to talk to him about Father Ernest. But now Father Nolan's gone, too."

44.

Rogers Park is the last neighborhood on the north edge of the city, along the border with Evanston. Kirsten took Lake Shore Drive north to Sheridan Road, then Devon to Western Avenue. The sari shops and restaurants and other storefront businesses this far west on Devon seemed primarily Indian, but she knew there were immigrants from over a dozen different countries and three or four continents living within a half-mile radius of where she was. It was eight o'clock in the morning.

A bit farther west and two blocks south she found St. Jeremiah's. It was in a congested neighborhood, but directly across the street from the church the property lay flat and vacant. Whatever used to be there had succumbed to the wrecker's ball, and a sign on the security fence announced townhomes on the way, offering "the latest in urban luxury and convenience."

She pulled to the curb as two black-haired women in bright saris came along the sidewalk with their babies. The strollers they pushed looked about half the size of Kirsten's Impala, and she wondered how hard it would be to maneuver one of those things up and down her stairway at home. She got out of the car and approached the women. The sun was out, but there was a chill in the air, and nothing of the babies was visible beyond what must have been their noses, deep down in the folds of their blankets.

She leaned over the strollers and cooed at the noses and told the women how beautiful their children were. That must have been true, too, because both mothers were radiantly beautiful themselves. Both were just girls, really, ten to fifteen years younger than Kirsten. They smiled and thanked her, in halting English, and she was surprised to feel suddenly envious. Of their youth, to be sure. But more than that, in an ache of resentment growing deep in her abdomen, she envied them their strollers. Signs they had babies to push.

"Oh, wait!" she called, because they'd gone on by before she remembered to ask them. "Excuse me!" When they stopped and turned back, she asked, "Last year, wasn't there a big apartment building across the street here?"

They looked at each other, and she was afraid they didn't understand. But then one of them said, "Oh no, miss. That was houses there. Old houses. Not apartment building."

"A big apartment building," the other one said, pointing, "is past the church. On the other street."

"Thank you," Kirsten said, and the two of them turned away and pushed their babies on down the sidewalk.

She looked toward where the woman had pointed, but her view was blocked, so she walked that way until she could see past the church to the apartment building. It was a massive three-story structure on the corner, made of ugly yellow brick, with entrances on both streets. Probably thirty or forty apartments in there.

She wondered how Anthony Ernest thought he was going to live across the street from the side of the church, and across from the *front* of the rectory, without being seen coming and going by someone who knew him from when he worked here as a priest. If that happened—and regardless of what his actual crimes were, or how long ago they'd occurred—there would be a huge outcry that the child abuser was back, skulking around the church and school again, a predator seeking more victims.

Or maybe he planned not to come or go at all, but to stay holed up for God knows how long in some small, dingy, sunless room in the basement, probably next to the boiler. Sharing it with a man who himself lived in daily fear of exposure to the authorities.

It was a foolish plan, and dangerous. Both for himself, and for the janitor if he let him stay. But she sure hoped Anthony Ernest was here. Because otherwise he might right now be sitting somewhere else, dead. Or worse yet, still alive, with sections of his skin being peeled off in strips. Besides, whether he was here or not, this had to be where Michael had come.

If Michael had stuck around Villa St. George long enough for the police or the FBI to get there, he would have had to choose between lying to them or exposing the janitor to arrest and deportation, possibly never to see his baby or its mother again. Michael wouldn't have liked either alternative. Nor did Kirsten, which was why she hadn't told Harvey Wilson where she thought Michael might have gone to look for the missing priest.

Michael knew that Anthony Ernest's hiding out here was a dangerous idea. And since he clearly felt a responsibility to his fellow "exiles," he would have come here to try to talk him out of it. That was assuming, of course, that Michael's disappearance from Villa St. George was voluntary. Which is what she *did* assume. First, because Harvey Wilson said Michael's old white Ford Fairlane was missing from the parking lot there; and second, because any other assumption was simply unacceptable. She tried each of the five street-level entrances, but found no mailbox or doorbell marked MAINTENANCE, or MANAGER, or anything like it. She went around to the alley and to the rear of the building. The space within the L formed by the two wings was paved, and there were several cars parked there. Two were taxis; none was Michael's Fairlane.

A set of concrete steps led down to a basement entrance, right at the angle where the two wings met. The door was wooden and covered with what looked like fifty coats of black paint. It was locked, so she pressed the button and heard a loud buzz from inside. No one answered. She tried again and still got no response, so she just pressed her finger to the button and let the buzzer go on and on. Finally a door opened on a wooden porch a little to her right, and about five feet above ground level. She took her finger off the buzzer.

The door was the back door of a first-floor apartment. A dark man in an undershirt and gray pants came out, yelling in an angry voice. The language must have been Arabic, but the message was clear: that damn basement buzzer was driving him crazy.

"Where's the janitor?" she yelled back.

"What?" He stared in her direction, blinking as though she'd woken him up. Then he ducked out of sight and returned almost at once, wearing thick, black-rimmed glasses. "What you want?" he asked, leaning forward with his hands on the porch railing.

"The janitor," she said. "He's not answering."

"So then . . . go away."

"Do you think he's down there?" she asked. "Because—"

"I don't know nothing. Go away." The man went back inside and slammed the door.

She turned to go and almost tripped over a boy, maybe six years old. "He went to the Elks Club," the boy said. He looked Middle Eastern, too, but his English was perfect. He had wide, serious eyes that gazed up at her under lots of curly black hair, and his backpack said he was on his way to school. "He took the American man to the Elks Club," he said, then added, "What is an Elks Club?"

231

"Who took who?" she asked. "What man?"

"The janitor, Habi." The name sounded like *hobby*. "He took the sick American man in the sick man's car. That was not so long ago." He frowned. "I'm American, too. Did you know that?"

"No," she said. "But how do you know the man was sick?"

"I heard him. He said he felt terrible and gave Habi his car keys. Habi said the Elks Club is on . . . I think . . . Foster Street?"

"Foster *Avenue?*" she suggested.

"Oh yes, Foster Avenue. I'm American because I was born here, and anyone who is born in America is—"

"Just *one* American man? What kind of car? How did—" She stopped, not wanting to scare the boy off.

"Just one. And Habi, the janitor. It was an old white car and they—" A late-model SUV pulled into the alley, and the boy swung around. "Oh, I must not be late," he cried, and ran to the SUV and was gone.

45.

It took just two phone calls for Kirsten to get the address of an Elks Club on Foster Avenue near Kedzie, a couple of miles away. The old white car the boy spoke of had to be Michael's Fairlane, but was Michael ill? And even if a fraternal organization was open this early on a Wednesday morning, why would anyone take a sick man there?

When she got there she had to park a block away and walk back. It was a storefront building, with a Thai restaurant on one side and a printing shop on the other. Horizontal venetian blinds were closed behind the large window along the sidewalk, and ELKS CLUB was painted on the window. A piece of paper taped to the inside of the glass door said simply: MEETING WED. 8:00 A.M. She knew at once what that meant.

She pulled on the door and it wasn't locked. She stepped inside into a small room with a desk and a couple of chairs, but no people. In the opposite wall was an open doorway. She couldn't see into the room beyond, but the lights were on in there and she could smell overheated coffee and cigarette smoke. She started that way and just then heard a brief burst of applause, then the scraping of metal chairs on a tile floor, then people talking and laughing. The meeting was obviously just breaking up.

She went through the doorway and into a room about the size of a large classroom. Set up at the end near her were four or five round tables with chairs, and more tables and chairs that were folded up and leaning against the wall. Across the far end was a small bar, and in front of the bar was a rectangular conference table with more folding chairs. Twelve or fifteen people of various ages, three of them women, were up near that table. The meeting was over, and some were slipping into their coats, while others—including Michael, in wrinkled tan pants and a dark blue windbreaker—stood around in groups of two or three, drinking coffee from polystyrene cups. Most of them were smoking, but not Michael.

Kirsten stepped aside as a woman slipped past her and left, not speaking or even looking at her. A man in a sport coat and tie was gathering papers from the table near the bar and looked up and caught her eye. "Good morning!" he called, in a deep pleasant voice. "Can we help you?" All heads turned her way.

"No thanks," she called back. "I'm just . . . ah . . . just here to pick someone up."

"That's my niece," Michael said. He disengaged himself from the group and hurried toward her. "Kirsten, how in the world did you *find* me?"

She didn't answer, but just stared at him. Gray stubble covered his cheeks and chin, and his thin grey hair was matted and uncombed. His face was even more pale than usual, and his eyes were bloodshot. Walking as though his knees were stiff, he carried a cup of steaming coffee at arm's length, taking great care not to spill . . . the way a drunk carries his drink.

Michael wasn't drunk, though. Not now. But this had been an AA meeting, and it was clear why that young boy heard him say he felt "terrible."

234

"Where's Habi?" she asked, when he stopped in front of her.

"Habi? How do you—"

"The janitor." Despite the coffee, she could smell alcohol on his breath . . . or maybe he'd spilled it on his clothes. "Didn't he bring you here?"

"Yes . . . but he didn't stay. He insisted he'd take a bus back home and—" He stopped. "But how do you know Habi? I mean . . . I guess I don't know *what* I mean. Anyway, I'm glad to see you."

"Where is Anthony Ernest?"

"He's . . . I promised not to tell anybody, but Tony's determined to stay in that janitor's room, Habi's room, as long as he has to. I went there to talk him out of it, but I couldn't. Then it got late and I was afraid to go home and . . . well . . . I spent the night with them. Habi had some apricot brandy—I guess he's not a practicing Moslem—and a jug of cheap wine, and—"

"And you got drunk."

"Yes. And then sick as a dog. That hasn't happened in ten years."

"Ten years? I thought you hadn't been drinking since . . . since the time of the girl, and—"

"Not often, but I've had my lapses. Three or four. I guess just to . . . to remind me I have a disease." He shook his head. "But this time I was lucky. Those other times I drank for days, sometimes weeks, before I stopped. But this time Habi—he's Syrian, and I don't think that's his *real* name—anyway, we shared the brandy and then he watched me knock down the better part of that jug of wine before he realized I . . . I had a real problem. When it was gone I'd have run out for more, but he wouldn't let me. He's a pretty strong guy. I didn't sleep much, and this morning he brought me here. And now it's over." She heard a strange gurgling noise, and realized it was Michael's stomach growling.

"And I'm sober again. I haven't touched a drop in . . . what? . . . eight hours?"

She could tell he wasn't joking, just calculating his latest period of sobriety.

All Kirsten wanted to do was get Michael back to Villa St. George, but she knew he should eat something. She walked him to a nearby diner and ordered coffee for herself and bacon and eggs for Michael.

He seemed terribly embarrassed. "I must look like a bum, huh?"

"Actually, you do." She wasn't kidding. All those years she'd had a wonderful uncle, a priest. A hero. Kind, but also strong enough to overcome his alcoholism. Then two years ago she discovered he was a man who had betrayed everything he stood for. And now? A drunk. "You smell of alcohol," she said.

"I'm not surprised. It's . . ." He sighed. "How did you find me at that Elks Club?"

"It's one of the things I do, you know? My job."

He shook his head. "It's strange. Why last night? I mean, I stayed sober even two years ago when I . . . when I was sued, and everything bad came out. Of course I went to an awful lot of AA meetings during that time, and talked an arm and a leg off my sponsor—you know, the AA person you sort of latch onto for support? And I managed to stay sober through the worst time of my life. Losing all I had left of my family. Losing *you*. And still I stayed—"

"So this . . . this sponsor," she said, "did he— Was it a man?"

"Yes."

"Did you tell him about . . . you know . . . about the girl, and that you were a priest? And all of it?"

236

"I did. I told him." The waitress brought his food, and when she left he said, "I've had different AA sponsors through the years, and I told them all. That goes along with making amends, and the whole AA program. I did it all."

"Really? You told all those damn strangers? But you never told *me*? Your only so-called 'family'?"

"No, I—"

"Do you know how upset I was when I learned you were named in that lawsuit? I said it couldn't be true, and got Dugan to help you. And then . . . and then . . . I *hated* you for what you'd done. And for never telling me."

"That's what I was afraid would happen . . . that you'd hate me. That's why I never told you."

"Right, but you told these 'sponsors.' What did *they* think? What did *they* say?"

"They thought it was a terrible thing . . . but they'd all seen a lot of terrible things, a lot of lives ruined. They'd all seen a lot of drunks, and the horrible, disgusting things some of us do. They—"

"Wait a minute. Are you saying you had sex with that girl, got her pregnant, because you were an alcoholic? Jesus, is that your excuse? 'Don't blame *me*, 'cause I was drunk!' Is that it?"

He pulled back as though she'd slapped him, then slowly leaned forward again. "I wasn't drunk when we . . . when it happened. I was drinking every day, but I wasn't always drunk. There *was* no excuse. She was . . . she seemed older . . . but I knew she was seventeen. She had problems, and I thought I was helping her. I was going on thirty, and I'd been out of the seminary five years and I might as well have been *fifteen* myself, for all the experience with women I'd had. A few months went by and I thought I was in love, you know? Stupid, but inside me I was thinking I might leave the priesthood and we'd get married. I never realized how much she must be looking *up* to me. I thought we were just . . . equals, some-how. I thought we loved each other and . . . and then one night we slept together." He stared down at his untouched breakfast. "And then I got really guilty and I went on a binge, and I lost track of everything and . . . and the next thing I knew she was dead."

"You didn't know she looked *up* to you? She was a kid and you were her *priest*, for God's sake. You didn't know she trusted you? You didn't know she thought—"

"All those things are so obvious . . . now." He sat back, his shoulders sagging. "What I did was wrong, Kirsten. I had no excuse then, and I don't have one now. But you asked me, and I—"

"I wasn't asking for explanations. I was just—" She drank some coffee and it was cold. "Eat your eggs and let's get the hell out of here."

After breakfast Michael still looked exhausted, but he swore he couldn't fall asleep now if he wanted to, so Kirsten let him drive his car. She drove behind him all the way and went over their conversation a hundred times in her mind. She'd never before actually told him that she'd hated him. But she'd also never given him an opening to talk about what had happened with him and the girl. Maybe she should have.

When they got to Villa St. George they parked in the lot and she walked him into the building. There was a security guard in a patrol car out front, but otherwise there didn't seem to be anybody around.

When they reached his door he opened it, then turned to face her. "Look, Kirsten, I'm sorry," he said. "I really am." He looked gray, and old . . . and small.

Without thinking, she reached out and laid her hand on his shoulder. "I know you are," she said. She squeezed his shoulder and could feel his bones through the thin jacket. He stood there, stiff, as though not daring to move, and it struck her that she hadn't touched him—not once—in over two years. Not since he admitted what he'd done.

"Thanks," he said, finally. He was trying to smile, and she felt a strong urge again to hug him . . . to tell him everything was okay.

But instead, she withdrew her hand and slipped it into her coat pocket. "Talk to you later," she said.

The guard out in front lowered his window and told her she'd find Harvey Wilson in the "Administration Building," and directed her there.

She walked into Wilson's office and told him, "I brought my uncle back."

"Man, that's a relief," he said. "The FBI's not around, but I should talk to him. Maybe he knows where Father Ernest went."

"Forget it. He can't help you on that. He's an alcoholic, you know? He went on a binge. Or at least he started a binge, but luckily he didn't get far. He's in his room, not in very good shape. Anyway, he had nothing to do with Anthony Ernest's leaving." All of which was true. "And he has no idea where Ernest is." Which *wasn't* true.

But it also wasn't up to her to get a man picked up and deported after he'd gone so far out of his way to help both Anthony Ernest and Michael. Nor was it up to her to give away Ernest's hiding place when she couldn't guarantee he'd be safer where *she* thought he should hide. Besides, if the guy could resist answering when she rang the hell out of that buzzer, maybe he knew how to stay out of sight.

When she got home there was a phone message from the doctor's office, reminding her she had an appointment the next day, Thursday, and asking her to call back and confirm. She'd put the appointment off before, a couple of times, citing an overbooked schedule—not that the gynecologist needed an excuse, but Kirsten did.

Tomorrow really wasn't a good day, either, not for the examination and tests and consultation, and possibly discussing and scheduling some additional tests. So she picked up the phone and called the number to cancel. A woman answered and put her on hold, and while she waited her mind drifted to those two beautiful women in bright saris, and the shy, proud smiles on their faces . . . and their strollers. And that ache in her belly was back again.

The woman came on the line and apologized for making her wait, and probably didn't believe Kirsten when she promised she'd keep her appointment this time.

46.

Kirsten took a cab home late Thursday afternoon. She dragged herself up the stairs, and checked for phone messages. There was only one, from Dugan, calling to leave word that he was alive and well. She could tell he was on a high. His team had made it to the semifinals and she shouldn't try to reach him until tomorrow evening because they'd be practicing late tonight and doing their mock trial all the next day.

It was just as well. She'd have something comforting to eat, take a bubble bath if she could stay awake long enough, and then go to bed.

She'd spent the afternoon at her gynecologist's office. The doctor had been late and got way behind, and Kirsten sat in the waiting room reading *People* and *Family Circle*, and smiling at radiant, round-bellied women and the noisy, inquisitive toddlers it seemed they all hauled around with them.

She finally saw the doctor and was examined and answered a million questions—including telling another human being about what happened to her in Florida for the first time since Michael had come to her rescue and taken her home. She was amazed at how *ordinary* the whole incident sounded, telling it to a doctor she really didn't know very well. But still . . . she broke into tears at the end.

Then she'd scheduled some further procedures, primarily a laparoscopy. Her doctor said they wouldn't ordinarily go ahead with these invasive tests until after they'd ruled out the husband as being the source of the difficulty. Kirsten's response—as far as she could remember it—had been vague and probably made no sense. She doubted the doctor believed her, but Kirsten could be hard to say no to when her mind was made up.

Then she found out the laparoscopy would be done in the hospital and was apparently a bigger deal than she had thought. At first she said she'd call back in a week or so to schedule it for a more convenient time. But the doctor—as sweet as she could be, but equally difficult to contradict—said there'd be a two-week wait anyway, and convinced her there'd never be a really convenient time. "And Kirsten," she said, "if you're *serious* about wanting to conceive . . ." So a date was set.

While she'd been waiting she checked in with Harvey Wilson a few times, but nothing happened to give her any excuse to run away. Her big concern, actually, wasn't that she was taking time to do something for herself while Michael was in danger. It wasn't even apprehension about what all these exams and tests might reveal. The main thing was guilt, because she hadn't told Dugan about any of this and, in fact, was taking advantage of his being out of town. What kind of wife kept such secrets?

She hadn't been getting enough sleep and the whole doctor thing exhausted her, but finally it was over and they called her a cab. When she got home she had a bowl of oatmeal and some toast. She took her bath, too, and that was wonderful. And then she fell into bed to sleep off the fatigue and the stress and, yes, the guilt.

She vowed she'd tell Dugan everything the minute he got home from Asheville. About seeing the doctor and scheduling the laparoscopy, about the pregnancy and the botched abortion in Florida, about how selfless and kind Michael had been . . . about everything. It was so clear now that she had been foolish not to tell him, and she knew she wouldn't flinch this time.

She woke up Friday morning feeling more rested and hopeful than she had in weeks. She was hungry, too, and decided to go out for waffles and sausage. She would walk to and from the restaurant, to make it easier to convince herself that her hips were probably smaller, not larger, than they'd been before breakfast.

She went downstairs and out the door into bright sunshine. She'd persuaded the owners on the first and second floors that they should all keep the wrought-iron gate locked, which meant she had to lock it herself. So she did, and when she turned around all the hope she'd woken up with drained away, as if someone had pulled the plug.

The sidewalk was blocked by two tall, clean-cut young men in dark suits and ties, showing her their FBI credentials.

"What happened?" she managed. "What's wrong? Is somebody—"

"You'll have to come with us, ma'am," the darker agent said. He took a sheet of paper from his breast pocket and waved it at her. "I have here a warrant for your arrest."

She ignored the paper and pulled her phone from her jacket pocket.

"I'm afraid you'll have to give that to me, ma'am," he said.

"Yeah? Well, I'm afraid I'll have to call my lawyer first." She started entering the number, but the man snatched the phone from her hand.

"Sorry about this," the other man said, as he snapped cuffs on her wrists. "I'm sure the special agents who obtained the warrant will afford you all of your rights."

"Which agents?"

"We're transporting you to the offices of the FBI, ma'am. Dirksen Building. Downtown."

They were the same two agents who'd shown up at Kirsten's on Sunday morning. Again the thin one did the talking, starting with, "Do you remember my telling you to keep your nose out of this investigation?"

"Am I under arrest?" she asked.

"Did they show you the warrant?"

"I want to call my lawyer."

"You don't need a lawyer," he said. "We've conferred further, and decided not to charge you . . . at this time."

"Not charge me with what?"

"Not with anything . . . at this time. A brief chat should be sufficient."

"I'm not giving any statements," she said, "or answering any questions. Not without my lawyer present."

"I don't need to ask you any questions. Here's the story. Wednesday morning you learned that a man named Anthony Ernest had sequestered himself in a certain basement apartment in Chicago, with another male individual." He waited, but when she didn't comment he continued. "You knew this because you were continuing to pursue an investigation, contrary to the direction of an agent of the federal government—namely, myself."

"I was looking for my uncle, not pursuing an investigation."

"Uh-huh. So you agree you went to the building. At any rate, you came into possession of, and did not reveal, information which you knew or should have known would be useful to law enforcement authorities." His tone was flat, as though he were reading. "Information relevant to the possible identification and apprehension of the individual or individuals responsible for a series of homicides of priests and former priests."

She stood up. "If I'm not being charged with any crime, I'm leaving."

"Fine," the man said. "But criminal charges or not, actions have consequences." He stared at her. "Maybe you considered that janitor to be just another illegal alien of Arab descent, and Anthony Ernest to be a worthless individual who'd done sick, repugnant things. But if you hadn't withheld information, and in addition lied about what your uncle knew, and instead had acted responsibly, a serial killer might have been apprehended."

"What?"

"And those two men might still be alive."

The FBI agents had shown Kirsten the door at that point. They told her that "further interference" by her would result in charges including "obstruction of justice." They said she'd be hearing from the State of Illinois about her PI license. They refused to tell her anything else about the deaths of Anthony Ernest and the janitor who had taken him in.

The rest of the day was a nightmare. Even Danny Wardell in Rockford wouldn't take her calls, and she had to learn what she could from news reports. She drove up to the seminary and spoke with Michael. He'd been woken up in the middle of the night and had told the police about his finding Anthony Ernest, and about Kirsten coming to get him. He was feeling as bad as she was, blaming himself for the two deaths.

He was sure the killer must have followed him to Rogers Park, and since she was certain no one followed *her*, she thought so, too. But she didn't say so. Nor did she tell him that even though in hindsight it seemed their silence may have aided the killer, she wondered if she wouldn't do the same thing over again, given similar circumstances. She told Michael she was the one, not he, whom the FBI blamed for not telling the police where Father Ernest was hiding.

The two bodies had been discovered by the owner of the apartment building Thursday evening. He had been looking for Habi, who hadn't shown his face all that day, despite repeated calls from tenants seeking services, tenants who then turned their ire on the owner.

According to media reports, which were sketchy, the homicide scene was a bloody one. Police verified that an Arab man had died of a gunshot wound to the head, and that the priest died of wounds "inflicted with a knife." Reporters were speculating that the Arab had been killed quickly, to get him out of the way so that the real havoc could be worked on the priest, a known sex offender. Police, however, refused to join in that speculation or to describe more specifically the knife wounds.

Kirsten would have called Dugan, but there was no point in dragging him away from the trial competition. There was nothing he could do, other than try to convince her that she wasn't personally responsible for the deaths of the two men . . . as she had tried to convince Michael.

By five-thirty she was back home. There was a phone message

from the Illinois Department of Registration advising her that her private detective's license had been placed on probationary status and giving a number she could call for further information. At least the license hadn't been revoked . . . yet.

The only other call was from Dugan. "Call me," he said, so she tried. But all she got was voice mail.

47.

It was Friday evening and Dugan sat at the bar with his second scotch on the rocks. He knew he shouldn't be taking the loss so hard. His team members—four women from the Law Center at Georgetown—were being better sports about it than he was. "Hey," one of them said, "this way we'll have Saturday free. We can visit the Biltmore Estate."

But litigation wasn't about being a good sport. It was about winning. And they'd lost. In the semifinals. It was only a competition, but what the hell, his team was the best. Smart and aggressive, their cross-examinations were tough, their objections were incisive, and one of them ought to be right up there for "Best Final Argument."

The team they'd lost to was just so-so. Two men and two women from Virginia State. Basically plodders, with smooth Southern drawls, who never rose above the ordinary. But they won, and so far two different people had suggested—without quite saying it—that the reason Dugan's team lost was that they were all women. "They came off as a little too . . . well . . . *bitchy*," was the way the lawyer from Denver put it.

"That's bullshit," Dugan said. "They were aggressive, and they're better than either of those half-ass teams that made the finals." He waved for another scotch, and Denver said he had to run. When he was gone, someone reminded Dugan that Denver's team was one that made the finals.

Then, a little later, a similar comment. "I believe the judges thought your people were too much . . . well . . . *in-your-face*," a lawyer from Kansas City explained.

"Fuck that," Dugan said, surprised at how loud it came out. "They were just too damn good, and people didn't like it." Kansas City drifted away, too, and Dugan ordered another drink.

He'd called Kirsten about five. She hadn't called back yet, and he realized he must have left his cell phone up in his room. He'd try again later. Meanwhile, time went by and people seemed to be avoiding him now. Maybe they knew his team flat out got a bad deal, and were tired of making up bullshit excuses. On the other hand he was taking this thing way too seriously. Plus, he hadn't been away from Kirsten for this long since the day they met.

He struck up a conversation with anyone he could find who was part of the workshop, so he wouldn't have to drink alone. Most of them had plans for dinner, but he didn't feel much like eating . . . and no one invited him. He wasn't so drunk that he didn't know he wasn't very good company.

By eight-thirty or so there was no one left in the bar that he recognized. He hadn't eaten since lunch, and he hadn't had this much to drink since—what?—college? He decided to have one more, then go up to bed. Maybe go home tomorrow. Fuck the damn finals. And fuck the awards banquet, too.

Kirsten could tell the woman on the phone was struggling not to lose patience. "I'm really sorry, ma'am," the woman said, "but that's the best I can do. The guest is not answering and we can't—"

"For God's sake," Kirsten said, "he's my *husband*. I've tried his cell phone and his room, and left two messages in both voice mails, and he hasn't called back. That's not like him. I mean . . . he's still there, right? Surely you can tell me *that* much."

"Um . . . would you mind holding a moment? For my manager?"

"Thank you."

Under ordinary circumstances Dugan's being suddenly unavailable might not have bothered her so much. He'd told her the final trial competition was Saturday, and that he knew his team would be a finalist. So maybe they were working late, getting ready. Or maybe he'd been overly optimistic and they'd been eliminated today, and he got pissed off and decided to come home early. But wouldn't he—

"Hello?" It was the manager, who reluctantly admitted that Dugan was scheduled to depart the following day, and hadn't checked out early. "But you must understand that we don't track the whereabouts of our—"

"What if he's unconscious in his room, for God's sake?"

"Oh. Well . . . does he have a medical problem that might—"

"No," she said. "I mean . . . *yes!*" Her mind raced. "He has . . . diabetes, and he has trouble controlling his blood sugar level. He could be in a diabetic coma right now. What's the problem with knocking on his door, announcing yourself, and then going in if he doesn't answer? At least we'd know that he isn't . . . you know . . ." She let it hang there.

The manager agreed to send someone up. "You're his wife? So can you verify the home number he gave us?"

Kirsten recited the number. "I'll hang up and you can call and I'll pick it up. Jesus!"

"That won't be necessary. I'm going to put you on hold. Don't go away."

She had to admit that she was less *worried* about Dugan than pissed off at him. Why choose this particular time to suddenly become incommunicado? Of course *she* was the one who had talked him into going after he decided not to, and all week on the phone she'd kept assuring him everything was fine. Still, he ought to stay in touch. She waited, beating up on herself and Dugan alternately, until a man came on the line and said he was with hotel security.

"So," she said, "is he there?"

"Three-oh-five is not in his room, ma'am."

"Are you sure? Is everything all right?"

"I'm in the room now, ma'am. Everything's fine here. From all the papers spread out everywhere, he's probably been working real hard and went out for a snack. His cell phone's on the table, and his room phone's message light is blinking, so I'm sure he'll call when he gets in."

"Is the hotel pool still open?" He better not be splashing around with his goddamn *team*.

"Yes, ma'am. But I walked right by the pool area when I was on my way up here and there was nobody there at—"

"Thanks for all your trouble."

"No problem."

She hoped so. Worry was getting the upper hand over anger now, and she didn't really know why.

———

Dugan had his billfold out. Concentrating, trying to figure out how much to tip the bartender. The bar was nearly empty. Just a woman down at the far end. Tall, attractive, but somehow hard-looking, too. She turned and caught him eyeing her . . . and smiled. A wide phony smile. She swung off her stool and came his way, carrying her drink with her. She looked familiar, but he couldn't place her. Christ, all he needed now was some damn woman thinking he was looking for fun.

He slammed a few bills onto the bar and turned away. He felt incredibly stupid. One more drink and he'd never have made it to his room without falling down. Even now, it was questionable. The bar had one exit leading directly into the hotel lobby, but he took the other one, the door that led outside. From there it was an easy walk back to the hotel entrance, and it was actually shorter this way to the elevators. Besides, the cool air felt—

"Hi there, big fella." That damn woman from the bar. Shit. Right beside him.

"Beat it," he said, and waved her away.

"Hey," she said, "be nice. I'm not gonna hurt you." She flashed the phony smile again. "I promise."

The phone finally rang. And rang. The *cell* phone. It took Kirsten forever to climb out of her sleep and find the damn thing. It was almost five A.M. "Hello? Dugan?"

"It's me," he said. "You should—"

"Jesus, where've you *been*, for chrissake?" He didn't answer, so she said, "Hey, sorry. I'm not *mad*. Just . . . worried. How's it going?"

Still no answer.

"Dugan?"

252

"He can't talk on the phone right now." A woman's voice. "You'll hear from us again, though, in a few days."

"What are—"

"And no cops, bitch. Got it? No cops. Or I skin this man alive."

48.

Kirsten's hands were shaking as she keyed in the number.

"Yeah? Who is it?" His voice was thick and it struck her that she'd never pictured him sleeping.

"Cuffs?"

"Chrissake, Kirsten," he managed, "it's kinda fucking early."

"Yeah, but it's important." She'd barely moved in the fifteen minutes since the call from Dugan. "Look, I know you're on another job. But I have . . . a problem."

"Uh-huh," he said. "Do you know the Tree Top?"

The Tree Top Grill was a twenty-four-hour restaurant on Irving Park Road, a busy, old-fashioned place with big comfortable booths. Cuffs had assured her it wouldn't be crowded yet by six o'clock on a Saturday, which proved to be true. He waved aside the menu the waitress offered and said he'd have a pot of hot chocolate, two three-egg Southwestern omelets with sourdough toast, and two grapefruit halves. Kirsten ordered coffee and a toasted English muffin.

"Jesus," Cuffs said when the waitress left, "you look like hell."

"I feel worse than that," she said. She told him about Dugan's trial workshop in Asheville, how she couldn't reach him the night before, and then the phone call that woke her up. She said she was sure it was Debra Morelli with him on the phone, and that Debra was behind the postcards and the target on her front door and her punctured tire. "And," she added, "I think she's the one killing the priests, too."

Cuffs stared at her. "I guess you already know how crazy that sounds," he said, "so I'll just ask. What the hell's your proof Debra's killing pervert priests?"

"I don't have real proof. But I talked to a homicide dick in Detroit, and it looks like when Debra was a kid she was abused by a priest. The priest got transferred to Cincinnati, and a few years later he was murdered. I don't have the details, but he was slashed and cut, like the priests here, and—"

"And it still sounds crazy," he said.

"Fine, but I didn't call you so we could debate it. I called because of Dugan. He—" She stopped because the waitress was there with their food. When she was gone Kirsten looked down at her English muffin and wondered why she'd ordered it.

Cuffs dug into his grapefruit. "So . . . go on," he said. "Tell me about Dugan."

"Just before I left to come here," she said, "I called his hotel again. This time they said he'd checked out during the night, and left nothing in his room."

"Probably some kind of express checkout," Cuffs said, "so nobody actually *saw* him."

She nodded. "The thing is, I've been focusing on the killer spelling out my name, and on which priest would be the next victim. That's what she *wanted* me to be thinking about, and then she went after Dugan. And it's my fault."

"That's bullshit. He's off some place in North Carolina . . . why would you have been worrying about him?"

"The thing is, I'm the one who made him go. He'd changed his mind and wanted to stay here, and—"

"Christ, that's bullshit, too. He probably wanted to go, and just let you *think* you talked him into it."

"What?"

"Jesus, he's *your* husband. Don't you know him well enough to—"

"That's not important," she said. "What's important is what to do."

"My point, exactly." He squeezed the juice from his two empty grapefruit rinds into one bowl and drank from the bowl. "You sure it was Debra Morelli on the phone? Because if she's around, the cops would like to know it. Plus, her uncle Polly would, too. Polly Morelli. Fucking sadistic creep. He'd love to watch her die a slow and painful death."

"Really?"

"Yeah," Cuffs said. "When Debra was a teenager her old man—Polly's brother—got his brain splattered and—"

"I know about all that."

"Yeah? Well, Polly believed her when she said she didn't know anything about who did it. But when her and Carlo tried to screw him in that drug deal, that got him to thinking over the whole thing again and he decided it was her—and probably Carlo, too—that whacked his brother."

"That's what the Detroit cops think, too," she said. "But how do *you* know all this?"

"I know . . . well, shit, it's well-known. I hear stuff from people. I mean, Debra and Carlo's old man was Polly's twin brother, for chrissake, and Polly's not gonna—"

"His *twin?* Jesus, I never heard they were twins."

256

"Well, twins is what they were, and if Polly gets hold of her he'll slice off both her—" He dropped it. "That's her problem. You're sure it was her who called? I mean, how would she even know Dugan went to Asheville?"

"I don't know, but I know she's been watching me. Or *us*, I guess."

"If she's doing all you say, she's a busy woman. Asheville's pretty far away. Could it have been someone else? Someone working with her?"

"It was Debra on the phone," Kirsten insisted. "Besides, she's a raging psycho. Who'd work with her?"

"Some other psycho, I guess. Back when you and her had your *last* run-in, she sure had a partner."

"Yes, but that woman had no idea how crazy Debra was."

"Jesus, not her *law* partner." Cuffs spoke through a mouthful of toast. "I mean her goddamn brother."

"Oh." Her mind wasn't working. "Well, it sure wasn't a *man* on the phone. Plus, the Department of Corrections has a Web site, and I looked Carlo up on it. He's still in prison, down in—"

"I know," Cuffs said. "In Pontiac. I wasn't saying it was him on the phone. Although he's set to get out in a week or two."

Kirsten had seen that on the DOC Web site, too, but she wondered again how Cuffs knew so much. "Carlo got a pretty short sentence," she said. "Do you think he opened up to the feds about his uncle Polly?"

"Carlo's so damn stupid he—" He shook his head. "How the hell would I know if he did?"

"I don't know," she said, "but even if he didn't, he better have a plan for when he gets out. If Polly's after Debra, he'll be after Carlo, too. Even if it's just to see if he knows where Debra is."

"A plan? The guy's not real bright, y'know? And he's got no friends. Just a sister who's got the hots for him." He shook his head. "Jesus, doesn't *that* turn your stomach?" He crammed more toast into his mouth and poured more hot chocolate into his mug. "You know where we goin' with this? I thought we were talking about Dugan, and what to do."

"We are. I mean . . . I guess I'm just flailing around." She leaned across the table toward Cuffs. "I'm scared to death," she said, "of what she might do to Dugan."

"Right." He stirred up his hot chocolate. "I hate the way this shit separates out." Then he looked at her and said, "You could call the cops, or the FBI. But . . ." He shrugged.

"I know. They'd say I have no proof that Debra kidnapped him. But I know it's her, and I *think* I know where she might take him. It's in Michigan." She told Cuffs about Waterton, and the postmaster, and the farm she was sure was Debra's. "The thing is," she said, "wherever they are, if Dugan's still alive and she smells cops closing in, she *will* keep her promise. She'll peel off his skin. I know she will."

"There's always that," he said. "So here's what I think. *A,* she'll keep him safe until she gets what she wants, because if she only wanted to kill him, she would have. *B,* she grabbed him last night and from Asheville it's . . . what? . . . at least one long day to this place in Michigan if she's driving. And she sure as shit isn't gonna buy him a ticket on a plane." He stopped and took a huge bite of toast.

"So . . . dammit," she said, waiting, "what do I do?"

He took his time swallowing, and then said, "*C,* if you don't wanna bring in the cops? All you can do is keep your cell phone on and wait for another call. See what she's got in mind." He returned to his meal, pushing a mountain of eggs onto his fork with his toast.

"I guess you're right, except how can I—" But watching him stuff his mouth full, she finally couldn't take it any more. "God damn it, Cuffs, how the hell can you sit there and shovel food in like that? I mean . . . while Dugan's out there with—"

"Hold it." He held his huge palm out to shut her up until he could finish chewing and swallowing. Then he said, "Dugan's a decent guy. I like him. But I gotta tell ya." He slurped hot chocolate from his mug. "*My* life doesn't fucking revolve around *his*."

49.

Kirsten was too full of anger at Cuffs and fear for Dugan to say anything for a long time. Cuffs finished his breakfast and while they waited for the check she suddenly remembered Michael, and she dug out her cell phone and called him to see how he was holding up. He was clearly still shaken. After all, he seemed to be next on the killer's list, and he couldn't get over feeling responsible for the most recent two killings. But there was something else, too.

"I probably shouldn't even bother you with this," he said, "but do you know one of the things I'm most scared of?"

"What?"

"That I'll start drinking again. I'm so scared, and so guilty, and so . . . I don't know . . . just so everything. Of course, I'm too frightened to go out and get some, but there's liquor all over the place here, and—"

"Can't you tell the others to keep it away from you?"

"I did that already," he said. "Anyway, I'll be okay. It just sometimes helps to tell someone." He went on to say that the other priests were more afraid than ever. Even if he was next in line, no one thought the killing would stop there. "But one thing: security here is tighter than ever."

Kirsten asked Cuffs and he agreed that the priests were all probably safer at Villa St. George than anywhere else. Harvey Wilson had gotten authority to hire extra help, and they were men Cuffs handpicked for him. "One thing's clear, though," Cuffs said. "Harvey sure isn't gonna let *me* sneak back in. He's worried about his fucking job."

"That's understandable," Kirsten said, thinking Cuffs was offering to help. "So maybe you and I could—"

"Uh-uh. I told you I'm back on this other job, and I gotta finish it up. Fact is, things have kinda gotten outta hand, and the shit's about to fly, and I have to go to Cleveland for a couple days."

"Fine, go ahead," she said. "Nothing important's going on here. Not important to *you*. After all, Dugan's life doesn't revolve—"

"Hey! How the fuck did I know *this* was gonna happen? I told you what was up and you gave the okay. Now I swore I'd see this goddamn Cleveland thing through, and that's what I'm gonna do. Other people got problems, too."

"I said 'fine,' didn't I?"

"Anyway, you don't even know where Dugan is. She *might* be taking him where you said, but who knows? Right now she's probably on the road somewhere. All you can do is wait. I should be finished in Cleveland . . . oh . . . Tuesday, I hope."

Kirsten headed for home, and that early on a Saturday morning the drive was a quick one. On the way she concentrated on taking slow, deep breaths. She would *not* let herself get to where she couldn't think straight.

At least Michael was being taken care of. She realized she should be grateful Cuffs knew the seminary security chief and was providing him with good people. She was pissed as hell at him for leaving town, but he had his own responsibilities. Right now there was someone in Cleveland who was as happy as she was mad that Cuffs didn't let his feelings interfere with his work. Or rather, that he *had* no feelings.

She would control her own emotions and stay calm. Getting Dugan was all that mattered. If she went to the cops she'd bring an army of law enforcement into the picture and that scared her. On the other hand, she couldn't just sit by and wait for another call from Debra. Why she had thought Cuffs might come up with a better idea she didn't know.

Then again, he *had* given her something.

It was an idea, or at least the beginning of an idea. There was someone she had to talk to. But she knew this someone was, for all practical purposes, unreachable. She needed a contact, and she could think of only two possibilities.

"Hey, beautifolio," Larry Candle said, once he finally woke up and answered his phone. "What's up? Whaddaya hear from Doogie boy?"

"Uh . . . I couldn't reach him last night. I guess it's a pretty intense workshop." She took a deep breath, then pushed on. "Listen, Larry, when I talked to Danny Wardell he told me what a great job you did for him, back there in Cicero. Said you had a way of getting through to the right people."

"Yeah, well," Larry said, "ya gotta know the territory."

"I guess you know an awful lot of . . . uh . . . influential people, right?"

"Yeah, well, ya gotta stay in touch." She didn't need a video-phone to know he was puffing up. "Why?" he said. "You need an intro?"

"Yes."

"You can count on me, y'know? 'Larry Candle, the lawyer for the little—'"

"Right. Okay, I want a meeting with Polly Morelli."

"What?"

"I want a meet—"

"I heard you. Sorry, kiddo. No can do. I may know some guys, and they may know a few other guys. But I can't get you that far up the food chain."

Maybe she didn't actually *like* Larry, but she knew he was telling the truth. If he had a way in, he wouldn't have been able to resist showing it off. "Well," she said, "thanks anyway."

"Hey, Kirsten?" he said. "Whatever you're up to? Believe me, you're better off leaving Polly out of it. He's a bad, bad—"

She hung up. One miss, one to go.

She got half a dozen busy signals, but kept trying until she finally got through.

"Jesus," Cuffs said, "I been on the line since we left the Tree Top, making sure my guys don't walk away from watching over your uncle and the rest of those creepy mopes they'd rather be kicking the shit out of. The seminary's not paying 'em what they're used to, either, so I'm having to add a little incentive myself."

"Don't worry, I'll cover it."

"You got that right," he said. "Except that's just the money part. The motivation, that's the hard part. Anyway, what is it? I hope you didn't hear from that crazy cun—woman—again already. 'Cause I told you. I can't—"

"No, no. It's just . . . there's someone I need to talk to," Kirsten said, "and from our conversation this morning I realized that you could . . . you know . . . be my contact."

"Yeah? Contact with who?"

"Polly Morelli."

"Try directory assistance," he said, and hung up on her.

She redialed and asked him again. "Just get me a meeting. So I can tell him what I want. The worst he can do is say no."

"Wrong. No way that's the worst he can do. You roll around in the barnyard with Polly and what you get is covered with shit."

"Look, I need him. It's pretty clear *you* sometimes deal with him."

"I do . . . different things . . . for lots of different people. I got nothing going with Polly."

"But sometimes you do," she said. "You *know* him; you've *dealt* with him. Why shouldn't I do the same?"

"I'm not saying I ever have. But even if I did, there's a hell of a difference between me and you. For one thing, I would never ask a fucker like Polly to do a favor for me. Not anything, not even just to meet with a friend of mine."

"Why? He can tell you no if he wants to. What's the down-side?"

"The downside is he might fucking say yes. And then I owe him. And I don't wanna owe Polly Morelli. Ever. For anything."

"Cuffs, please. For my sake. For Dugan's sake."

"The answer's no."

"*Damn* you, Cuffs. You're a selfish, heartless bastard. You don't care about Dugan. Or me, or anybody. Everything's just a job to you."

"Uh-huh. Well, I gotta get back to my job twisting arms to keep my guys from walking away from your pervert uncle and his pervert friends. You just keep those fucking checks coming." He hung up.

50.

Kirsten put the phone down. She felt a ball of fear form deep in her belly, then felt it expanding like a tumor. And now the fear itself frightened her. She had to get rid of it before it got so big it made her explode. She wanted to scream . . . at Debra Morelli, at Cuffs, at Larry Candle. Even at Dugan, for God's sake! How could he have been so—

The phone rang. It was their cable service, wanting to tell her how to save money by spending more. She listened, declined, and hung up.

Maybe it was the plainness of it, this unknown person out there spending his Saturday at his thankless job, but somehow the call calmed her. There was no ball growing inside her anymore. She was on her own and she was scared. That was all. And she still had her idea. She needed to talk to Polly Morelli, and she'd have to make her own introduction.

She drove down a street lined with large homes under a canopy of trees, in a suburb west of the city. She'd called a former crime reporter she did a favor for once, and he directed her here, to a world deceptively bright and early-autumn peaceful. It was Saturday afternoon and three boys chased each other on in-line skates down the sidewalk. A man ran beside a little girl on a bicycle with training wheels. Everyone was laughing. No one was thinking about monsters who would snatch up their loved ones and peel off their skins. No one but Kirsten.

Two blocks later the street dead-ended and she turned left into a cul-de-sac that led, some twenty yards ahead, to a tall iron gate set between brick pillars. She pulled close and parked. Beyond the gate an asphalt driveway, lined with evergreen trees, curved to the right, presumably toward a house that was hidden from view. Set into one of the pillars was a metal plate with a push button, and beside the button was a set of five horizontal slits.

She walked over and before she could press the button a man's voice came from a speaker behind the slits. "State your business, miss." Firm, not *quite* hostile.

She leaned toward the intercom and stated her name, then added, "I'm a private investigator and Mr. Morelli wants to talk to me."

There was a pause, and then, "You don't have an appointment. You can't—"

"I didn't say I had an appointment." Not backing off. "I said he wants to *talk* to me. It's about his nephew . . . and his niece. I know Carlo's getting out, and I'm . . . I'm in contact with Debra. Mr. Morelli wants to hear what I have to say."

"You can tell me, and I'll—"

"You know what?" she said. "You're absolutely right. I could tell anyone. You, or the FBI, or the Department of Homeland Security, or—"

"Hold on."

"—or the cops, or Channel Nine, or Larry King, or Oprah, or—"

"Hey, shut up!"

"Just give him my goddamn message."

"Yeah, well, wait there a minute."

It was more like ten minutes, but finally she heard a small whirring noise, and a slip of paper came sliding out through the bottom of the five slits, like a receipt from a self-serve gas pump. She tore it off and read the computer-printed message: SEVEN O'CLOCK. HOLY NAME CATHEDRAL.

She leaned again toward the intercom. "Is that *tonight*, or tomorrow, or what?"

There was no answer.

It was a cool, clear evening so Kirsten chose a sweater, boot-cut jeans, and her brown suede jacket. Her cell phone had been on all day, and there'd been no further calls. Her cab headed west on Chicago Avenue from Michigan Avenue, and she got out at State Street at six-forty-five. On a Saturday night she was surprised to find limos lining the curbs in front of the cathedral on both sides of State for the whole block. There were lots of blue and white patrol cars around, too, and uniformed cops directing traffic, and a few in plainclothes standing around talking to one another.

People were arriving from every direction, the women in furs and ankle-length gowns and the men in tuxedos, heading up the cathedral steps toward the three sets of ornate bronze doors. Feeling more than a little conspicuous, she joined them. The vestibule was crowded, with guests maneuvering past whispering, primping bridesmaids and family. Kirsten went through another set of doors and into the church itself. It seemed a strange time for a wedding, seven o'clock in the evening, but whoever it was obviously had enough money and clout to write their own schedule.

It was a large event, certainly, but the cathedral could have held three or four times the number of guests, and they were all being ushered up to the pews in the front, near the altar. The place hadn't been closed to the public, though, and there were maybe twenty other people—people not dressed for a wedding— scattered around the rear section, kneeling or sitting. Kirsten had been in here before, and she immediately noticed one group that was *not* present. Obviously evicted for this event was the usual assortment of shabbily dressed—often rather pungent—street people.

Now what? Was Polly Morelli a wedding guest? Did the note mean seven P.M. or seven A.M.? Or had it just been something to make her go away from his house? She moved to the wall on her left and then forward along the aisle. About five rows up from the back she slipped into an empty pew and sat down. She waited, listening to a gentle Bach cantata on the organ and watching elegant people be ushered forward to their seats. She had no idea what Polly Morelli looked like. No one looked back at her. No one paid any attention to her at all.

At five after seven the music faded and the sudden silence caused the murmuring crowd to grow still. A group of three priests came out from somewhere and stood at the front, facing down the center aisle. The one in the middle she recognized as the cardinal. Even from this distance he didn't look especially happy, and she wondered how often he thought about the little flock of priests who had disgraced his church and now wouldn't go away.

The priest to the cardinal's right gave a nod and the organ, joined by a trumpet, launched into a ceremonial piece familiar to Kirsten from other weddings. She couldn't have cared less about this event, but the bridal party was about to start down the aisle, and she automatically shifted around to watch.

"Come with me, miss." The soft voice and the tap on her shoulder made her heart stop.

"What?" Twisting around.

"I said come with me." It was a tall, black, female police officer.

"This is a public place of prayer," Kirsten whispered, "and I'm not going anywhere."

The uniformed woman glanced this way and that, obviously startled by the response, then leaned in. "If you came in here to pray, then fine. If you came for something else, let's go."

51.

Kirsten got up and followed the officer toward the rear of the church. Past the final pew and just short of the door out to the vestibule, the cop turned sharply to her left and headed to an open stairway—marble steps and brass bannisters—leading down. Kirsten walked behind her and when they reached the bottom she saw, about fifteen feet in front of her, an identical stairway that led back up to ground level on the opposite side of the church.

The cop turned and Kirsten followed her down a short, carpeted corridor, between the men's and women's restrooms, to a closed door. The cop opened the door and, when Kirsten passed through into a brightly lit room, she came in behind her and pulled the door closed. She did a thorough search of Kirsten, using an electronic wand that had been leaning against the wall just inside the door. Finally she went through Kirsten's handbag—the Colt was safely back at home—and then turned and left, taking the wand with her.

Kirsten was alone in a carpeted classroom with fluorescent lights and no windows, set up as a day care or a Sunday School, with two teacher's chairs sitting side by side, and about a dozen kid's chairs arranged in a semicircle in front of them. There were a couple of tricycles and a plastic ride-around automobile, and shelves full of smaller toys and games and books and videos, and a TV set on a rolling cart.

She waited maybe a minute and, when nothing happened, turned to leave. The door she'd come in by was locked. There was another door at the other end of the room and just as she started that way it opened and two men in tuxedoes came in. One had to be the bodyguard, thin and young and slick-haired. His broad forehead sloped backward above nervous, bulging eyes, and he reminded her of a snake. No, she decided, a lizard.

The lizard closed the door the two had come through and stood with his back against it, the jacket of his tux hanging open to show the butt of his pistol. The other man was square-jawed and still handsome, though obviously into his seventies. Deeply tanned, five-ten, maybe thirty pounds overweight, he wore black-framed, amber-tinted glasses. His hair, combed straight back from his forehead without a part, was thick and too black to look natural for a man his age. A sign of human frailty, Kirsten thought. A sign she was happy to see.

His demeanor was calm, almost gentle, while at the same time his eyes were strangely cruel and menacing. He called her by her name and she shivered when he said he hoped Dugan's law practice was flourishing, and hoped she was doing well and had finally found her niche since leaving the police department.

"You're Polly Morelli?" she asked.

He didn't answer, but busied himself arranging the two larger chairs to face each other. "Sit down," he said, gesturing toward one of the chairs. She sat, and so did he.

"Must be a new day," she said. "Trusting a woman to perform a search."

He just stared at her, and when she didn't say anything else for a few seconds he looked at his watch, then pointed upward. "The bride's the granddaughter of a dear friend. So . . ." He stood up.

"Wait," Kirsten said. "I have something to ask."

He smiled. "Ah," he said, and sat back down. It was a mean smile.

"Your nephew, Carlo, he gets out of Pontiac on Wednesday."

The smile faded, but he said nothing and she decided that, despite the search that surely would have picked up any wire she was wearing, he meant to be careful about what he put into words.

"You want Carlo," she said. "I think you'll have someone there to meet him when he comes out." He merely shrugged, and she went on. "I want him, too. And I can use him to get to the one you want even more."

This clearly surprised him, but he recovered quickly and shrugged again.

"The one you really want is Debra, more than Carlo. Otherwise, you and I wouldn't be sitting here."

"Debra?" he said. "Who even knows if she's living or dead?"

She could tell he was more interested than he was trying to appear. "She's alive, all right," she said. "I mentioned earlier today that I'm in touch with her. But it's more accurate to say that she's been in touch with me. She intends to kill me."

If that meant anything at all to him, he didn't show it. He stood up and walked away from her, toward his bodyguard and the door. She wanted to call him back, but though she'd disregarded Cuffs's advice and asked Polly Morelli for help, she wouldn't go so far as to beg him. She said nothing.

He didn't leave, after all. Instead, he whispered to the lizard, who left the room and closed the door behind him. Polly came back and sat down. "Okay," he said, "tell me what you're talking about. And include what's in it for me." With him suddenly speaking more openly, she wondered if maybe the lizard was the one who was wired.

"You have a big score to settle with Debra. You know she's far more responsible for anything she and Carlo did than he is. But you have no idea where she is, and no real hope of ever finding her."

"And you do?" Behind his phony blank expression she sensed excitement, anticipation.

"Debra wants revenge against me," she said, "and killing's not enough for her. She's toying with me. Sending weird messages. She hopes I'll freeze up. Instead, I'm going after her."

"So? How does Carlo fit in?"

"Carlo's the one person Debra cares about in this world," she said. "I'll use him to draw her out into the open."

"Really. And why would he cooperate?"

"Because I'll be offering him an alternative to you, the uncle who hates him. Once you make sure he doesn't know where Debra is—and we both know he probably doesn't—Carlo's life is over. He's not very bright, but even *he* knows that."

Polly didn't bother to deny it, but said, "I still say why would he trust *you*, the one who lost him his leg and sent him to prison?"

"Because you'll help me create that trust." She went on to tell him what she had in mind for the day of Carlo's release. When she finished she said, "If it's done right, he'll be thrilled that I showed up."

"Maybe," he said. "But you haven't said yet how you'd actually catch Debra, after you 'draw her out,' as you say. And what about the cops?"

"This will be my party. No cops invited. Not you, either. In fact, wherever she is, if anyone follows me I won't go."

"Which means," he said, "that there are complications, that there's a lot you're not telling me. Right?"

"Wrong." But in fact she wasn't telling him about Dugan, or her plan to trade Carlo for Dugan, or that capturing Debra would be a bonus she didn't have high hopes for. "It's not complicated at all. It's simple. It's just that it's gotten to be . . . a personal thing." Something this psychopath might relate to. "Between her and me."

He seemed to consider that for a moment. "My niece," he finally said, "is a formidable woman."

"Uh-huh, but so am I. And I'll never be able to walk down the street in peace until I get her out of my life."

"If you kill her," he said, "you'll deprive me of a certain . . . satisfaction. So, like I said, what's in it for me?"

"I'm not out to kill anyone. I'll use Carlo to make her careless, to get her to show herself." She's the one who was lying now, but she knew no other way. "When she does, I'll grab her."

"And then?"

"Then, after I've shown her who's more . . . formidable, I'll hand her over to the cops. That's the part they'll play, in answer to your earlier question."

"And that's what's in it for *me?*" He shook his head. "I don't think so."

"You'll know where she is. You can . . . follow up however you like. You didn't seem to have a problem getting close to Carlo in jail."

"That's not enough," he said.

"It's what I can offer."

He stared at her in silence for a few seconds and then said, "I'll play the game the way you suggested, and let you take Carlo. And then, if you *do* capture Debra, you'll bring her to *me,* not the cops."

"Sorry," she said. "You know I can't—"

"That's the first alternative. And because, like I said, there's a lot you're not telling me, here's the second alternative. If you *don't* capture Debra, then you'll return *Carlo* to me." He was watching her, and maybe he saw something in her face, because he said, "And if you don't bring one of them back, and you're still alive? Then I'll deal with you in a way that would make Debra proud. I guarantee it."

"Look, you can't—"

"Take Carlo or don't," he said. "You decide. And oh . . . by the way, his release date has been moved up from Wednesday. It's Monday now."

"What?"

"They made an error in calculating the days to chop off for good behavior. I had a lawyer check the date, and he caught it."

"The day after tomorrow? I don't—"

"The wedding," he said, "it's taking place during Mass." He stood and pointed up toward the church above them. "And I don't like to miss taking Holy Communion."

52.

Kirsten called Cuffs's number the minute she got home from the cathedral. She didn't want to. Right then she probably hated pleading with Cuffs more than Cuffs hated pleading with Polly Morelli. But she needed him. *Dugan* needed him. What she got was his voice mail.

The message said he'd be away and unreachable for a few days, but to leave a name and number after the beep and he'd return the call when he got back. Then, after the beep, a disembodied female voice said, "This mailbox is full."

She forced herself to eat something. And to slow down her mind and think. It hadn't been sixteen hours yet since that morning's phone call, and Debra said she'd call again "in a few days." Cuffs was right. If she was holding Dugan against his will she couldn't take a commercial flight, and chartering a plane seemed equally unlikely. So she was almost certainly driving. It would have taken her this whole day to get from Asheville to Chicago, and it would be about the same to Detroit. And a couple of hours more to the farm—if that's where she was going.

The farm was the best bet, Kirsten thought, and surprise was her best weapon, so she would go there, too. She'd have Carlo with her if things went her way—which meant she'd have her own transport-of-prisoner issues, so she called Leroy Renfroe at home. It was Saturday night and he was out, but her message was one he couldn't ignore, and he called her back about midnight. He obviously wished he hadn't when he heard what she wanted.

"The car's one thing," he said. "And the shotgun I can arrange for you to pick up. But the Panther baton, that's a real problem. I keep some on hand for testing purposes, but they're—"

"By tomorrow afternoon, then?"

"The problem is their use is legally restricted, and—"

"Leroy, listen to me. I *need* this." She went on to lay a little guilt on him, and he finally agreed. "And about the car," she added, "how long will it take your guy to disengage the thing? And to make sure it can't be reconnected somehow . . . or opened some other way?"

"Forget about my *guy*. It'll be Sunday afternoon and I'll have to do it myself. An Impala? Fifteen minutes, I guess. But Jesus, a rental car?"

"You can reverse it before I take it back," she said. "And if you can't, I'll buy them a *new* goddamn car. I can't tell you why, Leroy, but it's that important. Really."

"Okay, okay." He must have realized she wasn't going to give up. "Tomorrow at three. Go to the bay doors, around back. I'll be there."

And she knew he would. She'd been there for him when he needed it. Besides, he secretly loved this clandestine stuff. She hung up, exhausted, wondering if she could sleep. Ever again, until this was over.

She went to the living room window and looked down at the street. She walked back and sat at the kitchen table and disassembled the Colt .380, cleaned and oiled it, and put it back together. She packed a few clothes in a backpack and put it, and a Kevlar vest, by the door. Then she took a long, warm, aromatic bath . . . and came out just as tense as when she'd gone in.

An hour later she was still wandering around the apartment. She forced herself to sit down. She did her fingernails, very carefully, as though it were important. And then her toenails. She tried the herb tea and the scented candles that always had a soothing effect, but that night they only made Dugan's absence more acute.

A glass of wine might help her sleep, but she was afraid she wouldn't stop at a glass. She'd never felt so alone. She had brothers, yes, but they weren't that close, and she wouldn't even *hint* at any of this to them. When she became a cop she'd drifted apart from her high school and college girlfriends, until now they were little more than names on a Christmas card list. And when she left the department she left behind the people she'd known there. She'd been close only to Dugan . . . and Michael. And then just Dugan.

Now she was desperate for someone to talk to, and there *was* no one. Not even Cuffs, for God's sake. And not Michael, either. What could she do but encourage him not to drink and warn him again to be careful? Telling him about Dugan would only disturb him, and he might tell someone else, or even alert the police—and she had to avoid that. No, Michael was safe for now, and she wouldn't call him until Dugan was safe, too.

Getting Dugan back was all that mattered. She would trade Carlo for him. If she succeeded, she wouldn't have Carlo to bring back to Polly Morelli. And even if she managed somehow to capture Debra in the process, no way would she deliver either one of them to that creep. Debra she'd take to the cops so they could pin the priest killings on her. And Carlo could go . . . wherever. She'd have to figure out how to deal with Polly.

But that was a problem for later. Right now everything depended on him. He was a stinking chunk of waste, wending his way through society's sewer. Still, she was counting on him to keep his word. And she? With Dugan's life in the balance, she had no intention at all of keeping hers.

53.

On Monday morning Kirsten drove through the rain down I-55, headed for the Pontiac Correctional Center, about a hundred miles southwest of Chicago. The previous afternoon Renfroe had done his thing on the Impala and loaned her a Panther baton with a belt holster. He'd arranged a shotgun for her, too, and on her way she picked it up at a gun shop in Lyons.

The prison was an eyesore squatting in the heart of corn country, built during the first term of President Ulysses S. Grant. The designation "Correctional Center" fooled no one. It was a place to lock people up and brutally punish them. It may have provided jobs and revenue for the town of Pontiac, but it held little in the way of correction for anyone. Maybe Carlo felt at home there.

She remembered Carlo as a tall, broad-shouldered man, with large hands and a dark complexion that showed scars from a bad case of acne. His black hair had been pulled into a ponytail back then, but mostly she remembered his eyes. They were frightening eyes, because they held no expression at all. At their first meeting he had forced her out of a room with little more than a stare. But she'd seen him again just a few days later, sitting on the floor with his hands pressed to his thigh to keep the blood from spurting out, screaming, begging his sister Debra to help him. And Debra, bleeding herself, had left him and fled into the night.

Kirsten stopped at a gated guardhouse and was directed to parking area C. When she got there she went to the opposite end of the lot from where she was told friends and family members would gather. The prisoners were scheduled for release shortly after noon and she arrived at eleven-fifteen, before any of the others. The cold, constant rain had faded into a gray drizzle. With binoculars she scanned each vehicle as it came into the lot. Eventually there were ten of them, parked just this side of a guardrail separating them from a wide road that ran along the brick wall of the prison building.

Debra was a fugitive. Kirsten didn't expect her to be there, and she didn't see her. She did spot the car she was looking for, though. It was a four-door sedan, a blue BMW 7-Series, with two men in it, and the one in the driver's seat was Polly Morelli's tough guy, the lizard. She was confident Polly would have instructed his men, but she wouldn't know whether her plan would work until she made her move.

Noon came and went, and at twelve-twenty a white Dodge van, with STATE OF ILLINOIS, D.O.C. stenciled on its side, drove up along the prison wall and joined the group. Directly across the road was an opening that looked about ten feet tall and twenty feet wide in the otherwise solid two-story wall. The gate the prisoners would come through was set in a section of chain-link fence that stretched across that opening. Kirsten stayed put, occasionally raising her binoculars to her eyes.

Pontiac was one of the ten oldest—and without a doubt, she thought, ten ugliest—prisons in the country. It housed about fifteen hundred prisoners, all men, primarily problem offenders. But it also had a so-called "Level 4 Medium-Security Unit." That was probably where Carlo did his time, away from the murderous Chicago street gangs that roamed the rest of the facility.

At twelve-thirty, two uniformed guards and about a dozen prisoners finally appeared behind the gate. The prisoners, wearing jeans and brown, hip-length jackets and carrying gym bags, stood in a tight, single-file line. They shifted from one foot to the other, apparently not interested in conversation. Most of them were dark-skinned: African-American or Hispanic. The three who were obviously white were at the end of the line and she couldn't see well enough to tell whether Carlo was one of them.

Suddenly there was a short burst from what sounded like a very loud school recess bell, and one of the guards unlocked the door-sized gate in the fence and pulled it inward. A chain at the top of the gate kept it from opening very wide and the now former prisoners came out one at a time, turning sideways to slip through the narrow gap.

By then people were out of their cars and up at the guardrail. Like Kirsten, they must all have been warned when they came in not to go nearer the gate than that, but they waved and called to friends and family members among the men coming their way. Kirsten sat with the binoculars glued to her eyes.

The last one through the gate was Carlo. She was sure of that now, although he looked different than she remembered. Thinner, paler, his hair cut army-short. She couldn't see his eyes very well, but she doubted they'd have changed. It surprised her how slight his limp was, even though he'd lost his left leg somewhere above the knee.

Carlo ignored the welcoming committee and headed straight toward the van, which Kirsten knew was a shuttle to the bus station in town. He was just about to climb in when the lizard's partner got to his side. They had a brief conversation, after which the thug took Carlo's arm and guided him to the BMW and both of them got into the back seat.

The vehicles started filing out, and she slipped into line two cars behind the BMW. They drove out of the lot, went under the raised barrier at the guardhouse, and left the prison grounds. The drizzle had turned back into rain, and it was so dark that headlights were a necessity.

In a few minutes she was trailing the BMW along the northbound entrance ramp onto I-55, headed back toward Chicago. But two exits later, they abruptly left the interstate. She followed them as they drove past the only reasons anyone but a local would ever have exited there, a chicken restaurant and a gas station. Then, on a long, straight stretch of paved road with cornfields on both sides, she drew up close behind the BMW, flashing her headlights and sounding her horn. The Beemer slowed, went another hundred yards, and pulled off where the shoulder widened into a gravel parking area. They were by one of those little fenced-in-squares where a natural gas pipeline poked up out of the ground for inspection and service.

Kirsten pulled behind the stopped car and her hand started toward the button to open the trunk. But of course Renfroe had disengaged the opener, so she hurried back and unlocked it with the key, then ran up to the BMW on the driver's side. The lizard lowered his window and she flashed him an ID case which held nothing but her driver's license.

"FBI," she yelled. "Stay in your car, sir. It's Mr. Morelli we want."

She saw Carlo staring at her, and could tell he recognized her. When he spoke—a raspy, half-whispered version of speech—she couldn't hear what he was saying beyond "lying bitch."

The lizard answered Carlo without even turning his head.

"Whoever the fuck *you* think she is, crip, her badge says fucking FBI, and I'm not going down for an asshole like you. Polly waited this long to cut off your other leg, he'll wait a little longer. Get the fuck outta the car."

By that time she had the back door open and Carlo had no choice. The man beside him pushed him out and she met him, the Colt in her right hand.

"Hey, crip!" the lizard called, and Carlo turned toward him. "Sorry we didn't get to have our little chat, but we're not through with you, okay? And Polly's not, either. You're gonna—"

"Federal officer!" Kirsten yelled. "Shut up and move on!" She slammed the back door and the lizard turned the Beemer around and sped off toward I-55. She'd managed to seize the one chance she had to save Dugan. And she was trembling.

She walked Carlo at gunpoint to the rear of the Impala. In her left hand now was Renfroe's stun baton . . . the smaller Panther model, three hundred thousand volts, and that would be plenty. There were no cars coming from either direction, and beside the open trunk she told him to drop his gym bag on the ground and turn all his pockets inside out. He did.

"Okay," she said, "get into the trunk."

"What," he half-whispered, "or otherwise you'll kill me?" He turned to face her. "I don't think so."

His empty stare no longer frightened her. "Jail time's made you dumber than ever," she said, and swung the baton up and touched the tip to his belly. Contact was less than a second, but his body stiffened and his face contorted, and she wondered if he could stay on his feet.

He did, though, and it was quickly over. He was backed up to the open trunk . . . but still made no move to get in. She holstered her gun. "I just saved your life," she said, keeping the baton between them, "so you—"

He lunged and grabbed the baton—and made contact with its metal side strips. The charge he took this time was far worse. He froze up, then crumpled backward, and she shoved him into the trunk. It took him a few minutes to recover, and while he did she cuffed his wrists together.

With one hand on the trunk lid she said, "You think that was pain? Think about the fun those those two goons would have had. You'd have been *begging* them to kill you. But no, they'd have taken you to your uncle Polly . . . for worse. But me? I saved you, Carlo, and I even cuffed your hands in front of you, and not behind your—"

"Kiss my ass."

"Right," she said. "But no time to thank me now, because those two mopes might wise up pretty soon and come back looking for us."

54.

Polly's thugs weren't about to come back, of course. That wasn't in the script.

Kirsten drove east, through farmland and a couple of tiny towns, past I-57 and into Indiana. Then, at a crossroad in the middle of nowhere, she pulled into what was once a gas station but was now a burnt-out shell on an island of crumbling concrete. She opened the trunk, showed Carlo the baton, and told him to stay put . . . and to listen.

"Until I came along you were headed for your uncle Polly," she said. "He'd have tortured you for a while to see if you knew where your sister Debra is, and then he'd have killed you. Everyone knows this. And if *you* don't know it, you're out of your mind."

"Fuck you," was his whispered answer. His throat still bore the ugly scar from the County Jail incident.

"I'm giving you a chance to avoid Polly," she said, "and here's why. Your sister is holding my husband somewhere. She plans to kill him. I'm going to offer her your life for his. If she doesn't like the deal, you die."

"You won't kill me, bitch. You don't—"

"Kill you? Not me. I just take you back to Polly. Finishing that job on your throat is the least of what he'll do. Count on it."

That seemed to get through to him, but all he said was, "He'd kill you, too. For taking me."

"He'd do his best, maybe," she said. "But that won't help *you.* What you need to know is this: unless I get my husband back, I don't give a damn what happens to me." Her voice was trembling. "Do you understand that?"

He didn't answer, but it was true and she was sure he believed her.

"So here's the deal. If you and Debra cooperate, I give you to Debra and she gives my husband to me, and that's it. Otherwise, you go back to Polly. And meanwhile if you behave, I treat you decently. I'm not into pain. But if I need to, I *will* hurt you . . . whether it's with this baton or by putting a bullet into your one good leg. You got it?"

Again, no answer.

"Okay," she said, "that was fun. We'll chat again later. Oh, and I hope you have good bladder control."

The next time they stopped was at a rest stop along I-94, in Michigan. She parked at the far edge of the area designated for trucks and took the long walk to the restroom. She left Carlo in the trunk. He wasn't going to kick his way out—not with one false leg and little room to maneuver. Renfroe had made it impossible to open from the inside, and then—his own idea—had reinforced the wall between the trunk and the backseat, and added a bit of soundproofing. He'd let Kirsten lock him inside for a while, to prove he hadn't cut off the air supply.

She bought two Cokes and three sandwiches at the vending

machines, then went back and maneuvered the car so its rear end faced away from the parked trucks. It was damp and cool and getting dark, but not raining.

She ate a sandwich, then opened the trunk. "Hungry?" she said.

"Fuck yes." The first real answer he'd given so far. Progress.

"I'm going to let you out, and if you run I'll catch you." She held up the baton.

"How fast can I run with this damn thing?" He patted his cuffed hands on his thigh.

He was stiff and sore, and she wasn't about to remove the handcuffs, so it took him a while to get out and get half-standing, half-sitting against the edge of the open trunk. Eating with handcuffs proved awkward, and she had to alternate giving and taking back the Coke, then a sandwich, then the Coke. He downed both sandwiches—turkey and Swiss—and seemed to enjoy them, although she hadn't detected any flavor at all in the one she ate. They didn't talk. She kept the baton handy.

When he was finished she let him stand up and stretch a little before she ordered him back into the trunk. He started to get in, then looked back at her. "I gotta go to the bathroom."

She glanced around. They were quite isolated. "Hey, don't mind *me*."

"No, I mean . . . you know . . . I gotta take a dump."

"Get in," she said. "I've been thinking. Just hold it a while." He got in and she closed the trunk and drove out of the rest area.

There was highway construction going on everywhere along I-94, with lots of idle machinery and no workers around this late in the day. She'd do whatever she had to, but she didn't look forward to standing close by as he squatted behind a bulldozer. She found a site with portable toilets and stopped and—thank God—

found one unlocked. She explained what he should do and then walked him to the toilet.

"Try anything," she said, waving the Panther baton at him, "and you'll spend the entire rest of our time together lying in your own filth."

He went inside and stuck his hands back out and she removed the cuffs and shut the door. When he came out again she didn't put the cuffs back on him, but—baton in hand—walked him to the car. He got into the trunk without her saying anything, and she still didn't cuff him. She sensed he was getting resigned to having to cooperate. Maybe hard time had done that to him. Or maybe hour after hour spent in the fetal position. And maybe the baton and the Colt .380 helped a little.

She closed the lid and drove on.

Nine hours after she had taken Carlo from Polly's goons, Kirsten stopped at a small, nearly deserted motel outside Saginaw, Michigan, and rented the end unit. She'd thought a lot about how to deal with Carlo overnight. She took her backpack and his gym bag inside. In his bag was the wallet she'd taken from him—with fifty dollars in it—a change of clothes, and a few toilet articles, including a disposable razor which she tossed up onto the roof of the one-story motel. She checked the bathroom to be sure there was no hair dryer or coffeepot, or any other potential weapon, then left the bags in the room and drove to a gas station and then to a KFC.

Back at the motel she parked down at their end with the rear of the car facing away from the row of units. She cuffed him again and got him out of the trunk. Inside the room he headed straight for the bathroom, turned, and held his hands out toward her.

"Uh-uh," she said. "Go figure it out."

When he came out she sat him at the little table. She left the TV off and neither of them spoke while she ate salad and he—with his hands still cuffed—ate chicken nuggets and french fries. When they finished she said, "Do you know where we are?"

He didn't answer.

"Right," she said, "who cares? We're only killing time until your sister calls. So get used to fast food and living in the trunk." She gathered up the remains of their meals and threw them out. "Maybe you're wondering how you can get away. You being big and strong and all that. But why? Even if you made it—and you won't—where would you go? You have no money, nowhere to hide from your uncle. The only reason he didn't go after you again, after that night in County Jail, was because it looked like you stopped talking to the feds. And some day you *might* lead him to Debra." She paused. "Do you know where she is?"

"Hell no. Why would I give a shit?"

"Because she loves you?"

"Fuck that. She's . . . you know . . . weird about stuff."

"Oh? I hadn't noticed." She wondered, though, whether his time away from Debra had made him wake up to how weird she really was. "Anyway, I guarantee you that Polly will track you down. He'll find out first if you know where she is, and then he'll kill you like a dog. You and Debra killed his only brother—his twin, for God's sake. You think he'll ever let that go? Debra knows how to hide. You don't."

"When you run out of bullshit," he rasped, "I wanna watch TV."

He settled on a rerun of *Everybody Loves Raymond* and watched it with his usual blank expression, but surprised her with a chuckle now and then. She sat across the room, her eyes on him and her mind racing. On Saturday morning Debra had said she'd call back in a few days. This was Monday night, and the call might come any time now.

However Carlo felt about Debra after being beyond her influence for so long, Kirsten was counting on Debra still caring about him. A lot. When she'd last seen them together the sexual tension was humming like current through high-voltage wires. Made all the more weird by Debra's maternal smothering of Carlo, her domination over him. He was a bit slow; Debra was the real crazy. Kirsten shuddered at the memory.

After back-to-back episodes of *Raymond,* Carlo wanted to watch something else, but she took him out and put him in the trunk. There were a few more cars in the motel lot, but none down near them. The night was cool, somewhere in the fifties. She went and got all the pillows and blankets from the bed, and set them on the pavement and opened the trunk.

"Here." She gave him the pillows. "Arrange yourself." He did the best he could, with his hands cuffed; and she helped the best *she* could, holding the baton. Then she covered him with the blankets. "You forgot to say 'thank you,'" she said, and closed the trunk.

She relocated the Impala, this time backing it into the slot right in front of the room. Inside she turned off the lights and dragged a chair over to the open door. She wrapped herself up in the bedsheets, and a spare blanket from the closet, and sat down. She'd be almost as uncomfortable as Carlo, but able to see anyone who wandered too close . . . and to hear Carlo if he raised a fuss.

She was way too keyed up to sleep.

55.

Kirsten had no recollection of how they got there, but she and Carlo and Polly Morelli were all in a room together. Carlo was tied to a chair, screaming and crying. Kirsten jolted him with the stun baton, over and over, laughing the whole time. Polly was laughing, too, and threatening to shoot her if she stopped. And behind it all her cell phone rang and rang.

She woke up with a start and turned on the light. Just past midnight. She fumbled with the phone and finally answered it.

"It's me," Dugan said. "I'm okay. Don't worry about me and don't do anything—" He stopped.

"Where are you?" He didn't answer. "Where *are* you, Dugan?"

"He doesn't know." It was the same woman. "And anyway, he's back in his box now."

"I know who you are, dammit."

"You know nothing. You—"

"I have Carlo," Kirsten said.

"What?"

"Your brother. I have him."

"He doesn't even get—" She stopped, but too late. "What are you talking about? What brother?"

"He got out two days early. I have him." By now she was at the car. "You can talk to him." She opened the trunk and Carlo blinked up at her. "It's Debra," she said. "Talk to her." Baton in hand, she held the phone to his ear.

He just stared at her, eyes wide,

"Tell her it's *you*, God damn it."

"It's me," he said, "Carlo." He listened, then spoke again in that same harsh whisper. "No, dammit, it *is*." He looked at Kirsten. "It's my fucking voice. She can't tell for sure if it's me."

Kirsten spoke into the phone. "It's him, all right. I'll have him tell you something only you and he could possibly know." She put the phone back to his ear with her left hand, with the stun baton in her right. "Go on!"

He seemed to be thinking. Then he grinned—not a pleasant sight—and said, "Remember my twelfth birthday? That old mattress in the attic?" He stopped and listened, and the grin disappeared. "Hey, it's not *my* fault. It was Uncle Polly's guys." Still the hoarse whisper, but whining now, too, like a small boy. "She tricked them. I *tried* to tell them, but they were too stupid to—" He stopped. "God damn it," he said, "you should be happy. Polly's fucking out of his mind. They told me he'd fucking cut my other leg off. He's gonna *kill* me, for chrissake, and all you do is blame me, like you always do, for every—"

He didn't finish, because Kirsten took the phone away and quietly closed the trunk lid.

"He's back in *his* box now," she said. "Anyway, he got out a couple of days early and I stole him away from Polly. Polly's mad as hell about it. But . . . hey . . . I thought you'd be pleased."

"You fucking—"

"Carlo says he can't wait to see you and . . . oh, just a minute." She paused, then went for it. "He says he wants you to know . . . he loves you."

It was the right thing to say. She knew that, first by the silence that followed, and then by the sound of Debra's voice when she finally answered. "If you hurt him," she said, "this fucking husband of yours will—"

"Call me again in twenty-four hours. Don't fail. Carlo is fine . . . until then. If you don't call, or if I don't get Dugan back healthy, I *will* hurt Carlo. And then I'll deliver him back to Polly."

"You—"

Kirsten switched off her phone. Her hands were shaking, but there'd be no more talk. Not for twenty-four hours.

She spent the rest of the night in the chair by the open door, nodding off from time to time, but never really sleeping.

In the morning the sun was shining, the temperature in the low sixties. She checked her voice mail and there'd been two calls, but each time the only thing recorded was a hang-up. She turned the phone off again, knowing it would infuriate Debra to have to follow orders. She uncuffed Carlo and got him out of the trunk and to the bathroom. He was so stiff he could hardly walk. He needed a shower, too, but she didn't mention that.

When he came out she put him back in the trunk and cuffed him again. She wanted her own shower, but instead she went to the motel office and signed up for another night.

She drove to a McDonald's for take-out breakfasts and a Saginaw newspaper, and from there to a mall. Neither the biggest store, a Target, nor anything else was open yet, and the huge parking lot was empty. She went to the far end and ate, and then removed the cuffs and let Carlo out so he could sit on the concrete curb and eat his breakfast. Then she took him for a walk along the edge of the lot, maybe fifty yards and back.

When she told him to get into the trunk he balked. "I don't fucking have to do—"

She touched the baton to him. She hated doing that, but it was effective. When he recovered he got inside and she cuffed him again. She slammed the trunk lid and turned away, and warm food rose up in her throat without warning and she vomited her entire breakfast out onto the pavement.

According to the paper there were no clouds or rain in the forecast and they were in a full moon cycle, which meant there'd be several bright nights in a row. Both she and Debra were using cell phones, and neither knew where the other was calling from. Kirsten, though, knew where Debra lived.

She found the house again easily.

She approached from the west, so the house was on her left, on the north side of the gravel road. Everything looked about the same, with the chain still blocking entrance to the driveway. But now there was a full-size van—a Ford, she thought, maybe ten years old—parked in the backyard facing away from the house, as though backed up to the rear stoop or to the sloping cellar doors.

She was wearing a White Sox cap and as she got closer she pulled the bill low over her forehead and leaned away, as though playing with the radio. She was going forty-five or so, and she didn't slow down. There were so few cars on this road, Debra might be especially suspicious of one that went by too fast or too slow. As she drove past the house heading toward the river, she glanced back and from that angle could see into the three-sided shed out near the evergreen trees. It wasn't a shed for tractors or farm implements. It was a hangar, and sitting inside was a small airplane, the kind she thought might be used for crop dusting.

She kept going east, up the slight rise and then down the steeper slope to the river and across the bridge. Where the road ended with a T at the crossroad, she turned north. From her canvass of the scattered homes in the vicinity a week ago, she remembered driving past a deserted farm with a FOR SALE sign. Today she made a few wrong turns, but eventually found the place again. The only structures still standing were the house itself, its paint worn away and its windows broken out, and half of a barn. Even the Realtor's sign looked old and ready to fall down.

She turned up a driveway being taken over by weeds, parked near the house, and got out of the car. She could hear Carlo calling to her from the trunk, but ignored him and retrieved a gun case from the floor of the back seat and opened it. The shotgun was a pump-action Remington 12-gauge short-barrel, with a Browning recoil suppressor custom-built into the stock and a tube magazine that held five shells. She had three additional five-packs, twenty shells in all, packed with double-O buckshot, standard police issue. Way too many, she hoped, even figuring the few she'd expend now in practice.

Twenty minutes later Kirsten was backing out onto the road again, the Remington unloaded and stowed in its case in the back seat. Until that day she hadn't fired a 12-gauge since she was a cop, and then only during training sessions at the range. Now, despite the recoil supressor, her shoulder was sore, but she'd learned one important thing. Using that double-O buckshot, with nine .32-

caliber pellets in each shell, from fifty yards away she *was* able to hit the side of a barn.

That would have to be good enough. The hard part now would be the wait, and putting up with Carlo for ten or twelve hours.

56.

The hours passed and the only surprise was that at about four o'clock, after taking a shower, Kirsten fell into a dead sleep on the bed in the motel room. She woke up in a panic, afraid she'd slept through the night. But it was only ten-fifteen and she was thankful, both for the rest and for the passage of time. Carlo, locked in the trunk the whole time, had wet his pants and wasn't happy at all. She managed to get him to the bathroom in time to avoid a more major embarrasment, and then kept him quiet with Pepsi and cheeseburgers.

As predicted, the night was cool and cloudless, bright with moonlight and not a whisper of wind. Kirsten made her approach to Debra's from the east this time, driving with the lights off. Just across the river where the land sloped up she drove to the top of the rise and stopped beside the road, in the shadow of the trees. Ahead, on the right side of the road and less than a half mile away across the flat farmland, the house and its outbuildings were clearly visible.

It was eleven-thirty, and no way could Debra be expecting her. She got out of the car and looked through the binoculars. Light shone behind the curtain at one window, but she saw no movement other than thin white smoke rising from the chimney. She went back and opened the trunk.

"You get the picture," she said. "If she cares about you she gives my husband to me and I give you to her and that's it." She'd given up all thought of capturing Debra by then, and didn't give a damn about Polly Morelli's threats. "We go our separate ways."

"And I'm back with my fucked-up sister," Carlo rasped.

"Look, I got you three hundred miles away from a man who'd love to watch you die a painful death. No one says you have to *stay* with Debra. She's not your damn *mother*, for God's sake." She thought he was listening for once. "But tonight, you're all hers."

"I'm hers until the goddamn cops come charging up and I'm in the shithouse again—for helping her kidnap your husband or some shit."

She stared at him. "First, if I had cops waiting, wouldn't they know you're not in on any kidnapping? Second, have you *seen* any cops? You know better than anyone how she is. She gets a hint of a cop, and Dugan's dead. My way, I get him and I'm outta here. And she gets you and she'll be gone, too. In a hurry. She's got way more than kidnapping on her plate."

"Way more what? What's she—"

"I'll testify you had no choice but to go with her tonight. But *after* tonight, Carlo, get away from her. Or she'll buy you a return ticket to Pontiac . . . maybe death row." She closed the trunk and adjusted the straps of her Kevlar vest. She had more to worry about than Carlo's future.

Kirsten waited in the car near the river, perspiring, shivering, scarcely able to breathe. No vehicles passed by in either direction.

At midnight she put on her headset and switched the cell phone back on. Five minutes later it rang and she answered it.

"Are you in Chicago?" Debra asked. "Where are you?"

"Are you ready to trade?"

"Dammit, where *are* you? Tell me, and I'll name the place and the—"

"Why not *your* house?" Kirsten said. "Why not now?"

"What?"

"Ready or not," she said, then started the car and turned on the headlights. "Stay on the phone."

She pressed hard on the accelerator and pushed the Impala as fast as she could—gravel flying, rear end fishtailing—and in seconds she skidded to a stop just past the house. She pulled forward another ten feet, to get beyond the driveway, too, then angled the car diagonally across the road to position the driver's side away from the house. She cut the lights and left the motor running. Her face and neck were damp with perspiration, and she lowered her window.

"Surprise!" she said into the phone.

No response.

She leaned across and studied the dark house through the passenger window. The building faced south, and the moon was in the southern sky, so there was plenty of light to see that the door was closed and there was no movement at any of the front windows, first or second floor. And none in any of the windows on the west side of the house, either, as far as she could tell from her angle.

She got out, climbed into the back seat, crawled across, and pushed open the passenger side rear door, for quick entry by Dugan . . . if and when things got that far. Then she backed out on the driver's side again, and took the loaded shotgun from the floor and leaned it against the driver's door. Crouching by the rear tire, keeping as much of the car as possible between her and the house, she reached and unlocked the trunk and raised the lid.

"Get out," she said, waving the stun baton, and Carlo—his hands cuffed in front of him—struggled out. She grabbed his arm and pulled him with her until they both had the car between them and the house. She was by the rear door on the driver's side, looking across the roof. Carlo was to her right, by the trunk, so that Debra could easily see him.

Using the headset freed up both of Kirsten's hands, and now she had the Colt .380 in one and the stun baton in the other. "Don't try anything, or I'll drop you where you stand," she told him, knowing Debra would hear, too.

A few seconds passed and finally the front door swung inward and Debra stepped into view.

"Let's get on with it," Kirsten said, fighting the obvious tremor she couldn't keep out of her voice. "Bring Dugan out."

"And then what?" Over the phone Debra's voice sounded firm and strong, which made Kirsten angry—at herself as well as at Debra.

"Then you send my husband toward me on the drive, and I send Carlo toward you. They meet halfway and Dugan keeps coming and gets in my car. You try anything . . . *anything* . . . and I drop Carlo in his tracks." She paused. "That's the deal."

"How do I know there aren't fifty police cars hiding by the river?"

"Because I say there aren't. Bring Dugan out, *now,* or I take Carlo back . . . to see how long he can stand up under Polly's—"

"Debra!" It was a croaking rasp, Carlo's version of yelling. He leaned toward Kirsten and the phone. "For chrissake, don't let her take me to Polly." And now he was whining again. "There's no fucking cops anywhere around. Please!"

Long seconds went by, and then Debra said, "I need time to get him out of . . . to get him up." She went back inside.

Kirsten waited, wondering. Maybe as much as sixty seconds went by, but then Debra appeared again in the doorway, this time with a rifle in her hand. Kirsten raised the Colt and pointed it at Carlo's head, and Debra stepped back out of sight.

"There'll be another day," Debra said on the phone, and when Kirsten didn't answer, she added, "Maybe sooner than you think."

And then Dugan stepped out onto the stoop.

"Dugan!" Kirsten cried, ignoring the phone. "It's me!"

He waved his upper body from side to side, but didn't answer. He wore a light-colored shirt and dark trousers, and what looked like duct tape covered his mouth and chin and was wrapped around to the back of his neck. His arms were behind his back, and he twisted around so she could see that his wrists were cuffed.

"Take the cuffs off him," Kirsten said.

"Not until you take the cuffs off Carlo."

Kirsten didn't want to do that, and didn't want to spend time arguing. "Forget it," she said. "Let's go."

Dugan stepped forward, walking carefully on bare feet, teetering from side to side as though barely able to keep his balance. She knew how hard it was for Carlo to walk when he first crawled out of the trunk, and Debra had spoken of Dugan being "back in his box." But he seemed so unsteady, so stiff. Worse than Carlo. She wondered if it was an act, to make Debra think he was worse off than he was. But why? Did he have a plan?

He stopped and shook his head and waved his torso from side to side again, clearly anxious to tell her something. Maybe just how happy he was to see her.

"Don't think about anything," she called. "Don't *do* anything. Just get to the car."

Stepping forward again, he stumbled and almost fell, then

303

managed to regain his balance. He stood still at the top of the steps and at first she thought he was worried about making it down. But he looked back behind him and Kirsten could tell Debra had told him to stop.

"Let Carlo go." Debra's voice came softly through the headphones.

"Only when Dugan is down the steps and starts down the drive do I let Carlo go," Kirsten said, speaking into the phone, but for Carlo to hear, too. "While Carlo goes up the drive and into the house, Dugan comes down and into the car. Then we're gone, and you're out to your plane and you're gone. And it's over."

"For now," Debra said.

"For now, yes. I'll have my gun trained on Carlo and I don't care about you. If you try anything or fire any shot, I will drop him. I will not miss." She waited, but there was no response, and she said, "That's it then. No more talk." She tore off the headset and tossed it, and the baton, through the open window into the car.

She watched Dugan make his way cautiously down the steps. Surprise was on her side, leaving Debra little time to ponder alternatives. If she tried anything before her brother made it to safety, it would almost certainly be to take out Kirsten first. The house was a good forty or fifty yards away, but Debra had a rifle, and maybe a scope.

When Dugan reached the driveway she sent Carlo on his way, then moved to the front of the car. She crouched beside the front tire and peeked across the hood. She wanted Debra to believe she really would shoot Carlo if Debra fired and didn't take her out with one shot. But she didn't care if Carlo lived or died. She wanted only to get Dugan out alive.

Both men moved forward with stiff, halting steps, Carlo in the center of the crushed stone drive and Dugan in the grass along the edge. Gripping her pistol with two hands, Kirsten kept her eyes moving across the entire front of the house. The door was still open, but there was no sign of Debra, and—

There! A lift of the corner of a curtain at one of the windows. An *upstairs* window . . . and the fabric didn't fall back into place. Keeping her eye on the window, but not lifting her head to give away that she'd seen, she stayed in her crouch, shifting from side to side to present a moving target, keeping the .380 aimed at Carlo without really looking at him.

The two men drew close to each other at the halfway point, Carlo limping noticeably now, and Dugan taking short, quick steps like a man walking on hot coals. They passed each other with barely a glance, and kept going in their opposite directions.

Finally, when Dugan was maybe ten yards from the car, Kirsten stood up and sidestepped quickly to the driver's door, and as she did a shot rang out and metal hit the car . . . somewhere . . . and she grabbed the shotgun. "Run, Dugan! Run!" she screamed, and heard two more rifle shots.

She fired at the upstairs window with the shotgun as Dugan, hands behind him, stumbled down the drive. She fired again, using the roof of the car to steady her aim with the Remington, and with her second shot the glass in the upstairs window shattered. She pumped and added another blast at the same spot, and Dugan hurtled headfirst into the back seat.

She tossed the shotgun into the car and was behind the wheel and pulling away, with the Impala fishtailing again on the gravel. More shots rang out, and at least two of them hit the car and the rear window exploded, and she kept going.

———

When the odometer hit three-tenths of a mile Kirsten stopped and twisted around in her seat. "Are you all right?" she asked. "Can you breathe okay?"

He nodded vigorously and she got out of the car. She didn't know the range of the rifle, but couldn't believe Debra would be accurate from that far. Besides, by now she expected Debra and Carlo to be already out the back door and headed for the plane. Looking back at the house with the binoculars, though, she didn't see them. Suddenly she heard a thudding sound beside her. Dugan had shifted around and was pounding his bare feet on the inside of the rear window. And, to her horror, smearing blood on the window as he did.

"Okay, okay," she said, and yanked open the door. Grabbing his ankles, she checked the soles of his feet. They were scraped and bloody from running on the coarse grass and sharp stones, but there were other wounds, too. Older wounds. Large blisters she could tell were from burns, some of them puffy and some broken open and raw, and oozing blood-tinged pus.

"And here I was," she said, forcing a laugh to keep from crying, "thinking you should get an Oscar for some phony 'I can hardly walk' routine, when—"

She shut up because he was obviously trying to tell her something, and couldn't. She reached for the duct tape, but he twisted around and obviously wanted the handcuffs removed first. She dug the tiny key out of her jacket pocket. As soon as she got one cuff unlocked Dugan pulled away and started clawing at the tape. There was layer after layer and she tried to help, but then her cell phone rang. She reached over into the front seat and grabbed the phone and answered it.

"Kirsten?" A man's voice. "Kirsten? Please . . . keep going. Don't worry about—" Then nothing.

306

She opened her mouth and finally drew enough breath to say, "Michael? Is that you?"

Michael didn't answer, but Debra did. "Now it's *your* turn," she said. "Aren't surprises fun?"

57.

That's what I've been trying to tell you," Dugan said, finally getting the tape away from his mouth. "That crazy woman has—"
Kirsten waved him quiet and listened to Debra rant on about priests who ruin the lives of helpless little children. "Take your husband and go," she said. "Some day I'll be back for you. But meanwhile this one? This priest Father Nolan? He will pay a just and painful price for his evil."

"Do you even know what he did?" Kirsten was out of the car now, standing in the road. "It had nothing to do with a little—"

"So . . . is he worth saving? Then save him."

"What?"

"I'll trade his life for yours. Come back now—at once—and we'll do it. Meanwhile, any sign of police and I will slice this one to ribbons . . . with my last breath if it comes to that. I'm watching you. Come back now. Otherwise, I will take him and—"

Kirsten terminated the call and reached into the front seat for the Remington.

"What are you doing?" Dugan said.

"Stay with the car." She reloaded the shotgun. "I'm going back."

"You can't do that, dammit. Call the cops."

"She'll kill him if they come. And anyway, if we wait for them she'll be gone. She has a plane."

"And she has a rifle," he said. "You won't get halfway there."

"I can't leave him. Think about your feet. Think about what she *would* have done to you if she hadn't needed you to get to me."

"No, *you* think," he said. "She's going to kill Michael whatever you do. And if you go back, she'll kill you, too. You can't save Michael, but you can save yourself . . . and me."

"I have to try," she said. "I can't just—"

"You *can*. But you won't. So I'm coming with. But first call the—"

"No."

"But you—" He looked past her, out the windshield. "What's that?"

She turned and saw headlights coming toward them from the west. It was someone in a hurry and the lights bounced and swerved back and forth wildly. She stood in the road, arms out wide, waving the shotgun.

The car skidded to a stop less than five yards from her. She stepped to her right, out of the blinding headlights, and saw then that it was a Jeep. "Get out!" the driver yelled. It was Cuffs. "I said *out*, dammit."

The man who climbed out of the passenger seat was George Kleeman, the postmaster. Kirsten stepped closer. "Cuffs, how did—"

"Where's Dugan?" Cuffs said. She was on the driver's side of the Jeep and he pulled forward and stopped right beside her. He wore the same fedora and black raincoat, and despite the night air and the open vehicle, his face was shiny with sweat. "Where *is* he?"

"He's right there, in the car. But Debra Morelli's up at that house." She turned and pointed with the shotgun. "She got Michael somehow, and—"

"I know what happened. I got word this evening, in Cleveland." His voice was strangely flat, but too loud at the same time. "I called you five times over the last three or four hours. Kept getting voice mail."

"That's because I—"

"Gimme that!" Before she could react he snatched the shotgun out of her hand.

"Cuffs! What are you—"

"Fuck it. Get outta my way." Cuffs almost always seemed mean and angry, but now he was a volcano, shuddering and about to blow. He checked the Remington's magazine for shells. "Call the fucking cops if you want. But that bitch killed my guy to get to your uncle, and now she's mine. You stay here."

"No!" She moved to climb up into the Jeep behind him. "I'm going—"

"*Move!*" He shoved her away and slipped the clutch, and the Jeep roared off toward the farmhouse.

Kleeman grabbed her arm as she started back to the Impala. "Gives me five hundred cash to show him where you are," he said. "I knew you found this place, 'cause I drove out that day and saw you. Hah! You see my red pickup? I was—"

"Shut up!" She yanked her arm away. "Dugan!" She tossed the phone to him in the backseat. "Call nine-one-one!" She reached in across the steering wheel and snatched the ignition key and dropped it in her pocket. "You wait here." No way he could follow her on those bloody feet, and if Debra took her out, the cops would be there before Debra could get to him. She hoped.

With her pistol in her hand, she broke into a run. Cuffs had already gotten to the house. He'd seen the chain, because he was stopped at the driveway and out of the Jeep, obviously looking for a good place to take it across the ditch.

As she ran, she screamed, "Cuffs, look!"

He looked up, first at her and then toward where she was pointing. Silhouetted in the bright moonlight, three figures were headed across the yard away from the house, toward the shed out back by the evergreen trees. One of them, Debra, had a small duffel bag in one hand and the rifle in the other. Carlo walked in front of her, limping. The handcuffs were off him and he was dragging a smaller man—it had to be Michael—by the arm. Michael stumbled and fell to his knees. Carlo looked at Debra, then grabbed Michael and hoisted him up and over his shoulder, and kept going.

Kirsten stopped running long enough to draw breath and yell. "She has an airplane, Cuffs. She'll get away!" Then she ran again.

To her surprise, instead of jumping across the ditch and running after Debra, Cuffs got back in the Jeep. He tore off eastward, then suddenly swerved off the road and tried to take the ditch at a diagonal.

The shed with the plane was far behind the house, maybe a hundred yards from the road, so it made sense to use the Jeep to get there . . . if he got it across the ditch. But he didn't. Kirsten stopped running and stood, horrified, as his left front wheel dropped down and caught. The rear end rose into the air, and the vehicle flipped, rear over front. Cuffs was thrown out of the open vehicle and went tumbling like a doll into the field. The Jeep landed upside down, wheels spinning. Cuffs didn't get up.

311

Kirsten ran again, leaving the road to cut across the field toward the plane. She jumped and made it easily over the ditch, but her foot landed in a little hole in the ground. Her ankle twisted the wrong way, hard. She went sprawling face-first into the dirt, and the gun flew out of her hand.

When she got to her feet her ankle hurt terribly, but she couldn't stop now. She used up valuable seconds scrambing around for her weapon, found it, and took off again. By the time she got close to the house Debra and Carlo and Michael were all out of sight.

She kept going until finally she could see into the shed, still fifty yards off. She saw only Debra, her rifle in her hand and obviously about to climb up and into the plane. Kirsten stopped and raised the Colt with two hands and fired, once.

She was too far away, though, and the shot did nothing but alert Debra, who turned and raised the rifle and fired back. Kirsten dove to the ground and rolled, then got up and ran—as well as she *could* run with that grinding, screaming pain in her ankle. She made it to the shade trees near the house, then suddenly heard two shotgun blasts.

She crouched behind a large oak, peered around, and saw Cuffs, in the field east of the house, heading toward the shed. He was crabwalking on one leg and one arm, dragging one useless leg with him. He tripped and fell to the ground, got himself into a sitting position, and fired again. Two more shots, but so clearly wild that he might as well have been shooting at the full moon.

She turned back toward the shed and saw Debra again, now aiming her rifle at Cuffs. Debra fired once, then again, and Cuffs gave a roar like an angry lion, and fell backward into the dirt.

Kirsten yelled, too, and fired off another useless pistol round, and Debra swung around to face her. Kirsten, screaming now from anger and from the fearful pain shooting through her ankle, ran in a crouch, zigzagging, stumbling, and tripping her way across the uneven ground. But always toward Debra. Firing an occasional round, not stopping to take better aim, not wanting to make a better target.

Even when she saw Debra fall backward, hard, against the wall of the shed, and the rifle fly out of her hand, Kirsten kept going. Then she saw Debra slide down into a sitting position, and suddenly realized she was standing still, aiming at Debra from ten feet away, squeezing off round after round . . . except that her gun was long empty.

Debra wasn't dead. She sat there moaning and rocking forward and then back against the wall, her hand pressed to her left shoulder, blood oozing out between her fingers. Kirsten picked up the rifle and flipped it, end over end, as far as she could out into the field. Her whole leg throbbed now, keeping time with the beat of her heart, as she turned to go do what she could for Cuffs.

"Hold it!" It was Carlo. "Drop the fucking gun," he said, "or—"

"Jesus," Debra yelled, "her gun's empty, you idiot." Kirsten turned to see Carlo standing by Debra. He had a pistol in his hand, a nine millimeter. "Shoot her," Debra said. "Just shoot her. Do as I say, dammit."

"I don't know." Carlo shook his head. "I just got out, and I don't wanna go back again." So he *had* been paying attention to her, Kirsten thought. But he kept the pistol pointed at her.

She let her own gun fall to the ground and raised her hands. "You're right, Carlo," she said. "She'll buy you a return ticket to—"

"You told me that already," he rasped. "So shut up."

"That's a good boy," Debra said. "You get me up into this fucking plane before the cops get here and I can fly it into Canada, to a place I know. But first you have to shoot her and—"

"You shut up, too," he said. "I'm trying to fucking *think* here."

"Carlo!" Debra's voice was harsh and Carlo jumped as though

she'd slapped him. "Don't *ever* talk to me like that. Now you stand up straight." He did, as though yanked up by a chain, and pulled his shoulders back. "That's a good boy." Debra spoke soothingly now, a mother to her son. "Look, Carlo honey, you don't *have* to think. I'm the one who thinks." She struggled to her feet, using the wall as support. "I'm the one who takes care of you. I'm the one who *loves* you. Now . . . do what I say . . . and shoot that fucking bitch."

"Yeah," he said, "but I don't wanna go back—"

"But nothing!" Her face was strained and flushed. "*Listen* to me. Shoot her!" A mother enraged now. "*Shoot,* you stupid little shit. Do as I say, right now, or *else.*"

And Carlo turned . . . and shot his sister, twice, in the face. He stood there a moment, staring down at the gun in his hand, then heaved it out into the darkness.

When Kirsten got to Cuffs he was on his back, his left leg twisted out at a grotesque, sickening angle. She crouched down and reached to close his raincoat to keep him warm, and discovered blood soaking through the left side of his sweatshirt. He was staring up at the sky, eyes wide open . . . but he was breathing, although in harsh, rapid gasps.

She heard sirens in the distance, and then heard her name being called. She looked around and saw Dugan maybe seventy-five yards away, hobbling toward her, with George Kleeman helping him. She waved, to show that she was okay, and Dugan stopped immediately and sat down right where he was. She was sweating and felt very cold, and was afraid she'd pass out from the throbbing pain in her ankle and leg. So she sat down, too, in the dirt beside Cuffs.

"You'll be okay," she told him. "The paramedics are coming.

Can you hear the sirens?" He gave one barely perceptible nod, and tears filled her eyes. "Thank you, Cuffs," she said. "Thanks for coming to help us."

His eyes widened even farther at that, and he was trying to say something. She leaned close to his mouth to hear him. ". . . can skip the bullshit," he was saying. "She's mine, dammit."

58.

Dugan's feet were healing "remarkably well" according to the doctor, and although Kirsten's ankle required surgery to set it properly, she was up and around right away on crutches. So they were both able to go and help with the arrangements a few days later when Cuffs was airlifted from the hospital in Saginaw, Michigan, to one in Chicago.

Kirsten would never forget the looks on the faces of the hospital staff when Cuffs left. "An *interesting* patient," one of the nurses said. But clearly, even sedated and bedridden, he was nobody's favorite.

Michael told Kirsten he'd missed several weeks of AA meetings before falling off the wagon that night in the janitor's room, and he realized how much he still depended on those meetings. Then, shaken by the deaths of Habi and Anthony Ernest, he felt guilty and more frightened than ever. He developed a craving for alcohol stronger than he'd felt in years, and insisted on going to his meeting that Monday night. One of Cuffs's hand-picked men drove, saw him to the door, and said he'd be waiting just outside.

But Debra obviously knew about the AA meetings, too, and when Michael came out it was Debra who met him. She bound and gagged him and laid him in her van beside the coffinlike box she was keeping Dugan in. She drove all night to her place in Michigan, obviously thinking she'd set up an encounter with Kirsten on her own terms. Cuffs's man was found in the morning, dead of a single gunshot wound to the head.

Of course, Michael blamed himself for that death, too. Cuffs, though, once he'd gotten off the heavy meds and was somewhat lucid, brushed Michael's guilt aside. He said it was clearly "*my man's screwup*." He insisted it was never the fault of the "protectee," who was assumed from the start to be "a dumb shit who doesn't know his or her ass from a crack in the plaster." Kirsten appreciated the gender-inclusive language, but thought Cuffs seemed more upset about it being *his* man who made the mistake than about the man's being dead.

Regarding Debra's death, Carlo had a lawyer and was keeping his mouth shut. Kirsten kept her own version of that particular part a little vague and, it appearing that Debra had been the crazed priest killer, no charges were contemplated. And Polly Morelli? Though deprived of his chance at Debra, he seemed satisfied with the outcome and granted amnesty to Kirsten and—so far at least—to Carlo, too. Kirsten had a feeling, though, that her name had been added to Polly's Rolodex.

What with doctors and hospitals and police and FBI agents, she and Dugan had little time to think, let alone communicate. She finally let him talk her into going to Bermuda, thinking they'd lie on the beach and she'd tell him about Florida. But a tropical storm kept hanging around out there and finally, the day before they were scheduled to leave, they had to cancel.

"Good," Kirsten said, "because I have a new client who—"

"Nope," Dugan said, "Mollie set up a substitute trip."

So now they were on a plane—in first class, since how often did they go anywhere?—to Charlotte, North Carolina. From there they'd drive to Asheville and this resort hotel Dugan knew about, with a great pool. The flight attendant confiscated their unfinished martinis because they were about to take off. "Not bad, huh?" Dugan said. "I just wish it was a longer flight, because—"

"I have something to tell you," Kirsten said. They were in the last row of first class, and the seats right in front of them were empty. No one would hear. "It's important and it can't wait, because I'm scared."

"Sure," he said. "Go ahead." As though he hadn't really heard her.

"I should have told you long ago. When I think how close we are, and yet there's this one thing I haven't shared with you and . . . I don't know . . ."

"Yeah, well, whatever." The plane roared down the runway. He settled into the comfortable seat, leaned his head back, closed his eyes. "Go ahead," he said. "Shoot."

"Dammit, Dugan, if you fall asleep I will kill you. And after that, I'll divorce you. And . . . and I'm starting to cry."

Which didn't exactly make sense, but Dugan seemed finally to get the picture, and he sat up and listened. And she told him about Florida.

"Well," he said, when she finished. "Jesus."

By then they were well on their way to Charlotte, and Kirsten

318

felt short of breath. She busied herself with folding over the corners of the little napkin that had come with her drink. "Tell me," she said, "what are you thinking right now?"

"Thinking? Well . . . three things, actually. One, I love you. Two . . ." He paused, then said, "Two, I always knew you'd tell me, sooner or later."

"You mean you *knew*? How could you have possibly known?"

"Well, I didn't know what it *was*, but I knew there was *something*. You'd start . . . and then never finish. Now I know how dumb I was not to have *made* you finish. Because obviously not telling just made it get bigger and more important than it was." He stopped. "I mean, it was a big deal, you know, and I'm not trying to downplay it, but—"

"It's *still* a big deal," she said. "The doctor's not sure, but it *could* have something to do with why we're not getting pregnant."

"Maybe." He nodded. "Or it could be my sperm count is low. Which is, of course, completely beyond possibility."

"Right," she said. "Completely. So what's number three?"

"Three? Oh . . . well, that goes back to when Michael admitted what he did. We were both disgusted and angry, but I never understood why you made such a big deal specifically about his never *telling* you about it."

"That's because you didn't know how I'd been taken advantage of by that creep in Florida. It just seemed so dishonest of Michael to hide from me the fact that he'd done something similar, to another young girl."

"Right, I get it now. But . . . what *you* hid from *me*—running off and getting involved, the pregnancy, the abortion—it was all . . . well . . . at least you had the excuse of being young and stupid. Or . . . I mean . . . naïve. And you weren't able to tell me for all these years? So how the hell could Michael—a priest, for

319

God's sake—how could he tell you about the much more shameful thing *he* did? Ever."

"I guess . . . guess you're right. He and I aren't so different, really." She nodded, and felt a little shift in her mind, or her heart . . . or somewhere. "I can forgive him for not telling me." She closed her eyes, then opened them. "And as for what he *did*? No one could ever excuse it, but when you think about it, he'd been locked away in the seminary half his life. He must have been as immature as I was—even if he was older. And he was drinking, too, and got in way over his head. It was terribly wrong, but I think I can forgive him even that. Or *almost*. More than before, anyway."

"Uh-huh." Dugan seemed unimpressed.

"I *will* forgive him," she said, "because I *want* to. I want my uncle back."

"Yeah? Well, not me," Dugan said. "But that's okay, too. It'll have to be." He pushed the button above his head. "And hey . . . maybe someday I'll be able to tell you my own secret . . . the sordid details about how Debra got close enough to kidnap me."

"What? What are you—"

"Maybe *some*day, when I'm ready." He grinned. "But for now, I'm having another martini."

"You do that," she said. "Maybe it'll boost your sperm count."